THE CHALK GIANTS

KEITH ROBERTS

THE CHALK GIANTS

KEITH ROBERTS

A BERKLEY MEDALLION BOOK
published by
BERKLEY PUBLISHING CORPORATION

For Michael Moorcock

Wallace, Aitken & Sheil, Inc.
118 East 61st Street
New York, N.Y. 10021

SBN 425-03115-2

*BERKLEY MEDALLION BOOKS are published by
Berkley Publishing Corporation
200 Madison Avenue
New York, N.Y. 10016*

BERKLEY MEDALLION BOOK ® TM 757,375

Printed in the United States of America

Berkley Medallion Edition, MAY, 1976

*Foweles in the frith,
the fishes in the flod—
And I mon wax wod.
Much sorw I walke with
for best of bon and blod.*

Anon., thirteenth century

Contents

ONE

Monkey and Pru and Sal

To Monkey, the movement of the sun across the sky always seemed essentially a sideways matter. It was this innate feeling—a thing of the blood rather than the intellect—that helped him in his first uncertain attempts at map reading. For years, the maps he owned had been meaningless to him. He would draw them from the wooden pocket in which they were kept, steadying himself against the lurching movements of Truck, and fold and unfold them, admiring the rich light blue of their edges, the patches of green and brown overlaid with delicate networks of marks and lines. And he would blink and frown, grappling with something more nebulous than memory.

The sea gave him his first real clue; the great blue presence of it, looming and dazzling between the shoulders of watching hills. How Truck, in its erratic career, came to be in sight of the water will never be known; but Monkey crowed with delight, extending blackish, sticky fingers to the brightness. Then he fell wholly quiet.

He remained quiet for a day, a night and part of another day. All that time, Truck veered and rattled along within sight of the vastness. Then a dead tree, sprawling grotesquely across the road, caused Pru and Sal to swerve aside. They fled, backs humped, from the clutching, bleached branches; and Monkey lay frowning, thoughtfully oblivious, sucking at his fingers. In time, he began to doze. He dreamed of formless shapes that hovered aggravatingly just beyond reach. When he opened his eyes again, Truck was passing along a narrow sunken lane. Walls of reddish-brown rock jerked past on either side, hung here and there with the translucent green leaves of ferns. Above, the foliage of over-arching trees shone golden in sunlight.

Monkey, still bemused, lay seeing the green and brown and blue; and suddenly it was as if a great idea, already formed somewhere in his brain, pushed itself forward into consciousness. He stopped his thumb-sucking, drew out once more the precious, grubby sheets; and the truth burst on him. He bawled his loudest, bringing Truck to a precipitate halt; sat up crowing and dribbling, a map clutched destructively in one great fist. He waved his arms, startling Pru and Sal from their immemorial indifference; and Truck turned, jerkily obedient, under control at last.

Monkey, his mind buzzing with new ideas, stopped Truck when the blueness was once more in sight. He sat a long time frowning, screwing his eyes against the miles-long dazzle; then finally, unsurely, he waved to the right. Though 'right' at that time was a concept beyond his grasp; rather, he turned his destiny five-fingerward. To his left, or three-fingerward, lay the water; in his hand, still tightly and juicily gripped, was the map. His intention was as irrevocable as it was strange. He would follow, or cause Truck to follow, the edge of the sea.

Through the day, and on into the night, Pru and Sal kept up a steady pace. For a time, Monkey lay restless; finally their steady pounding soothed him to sleep. Dawn light roused him, streaming over the high canvas flap of Truck. He sat up, mind instantly full of his great design. The spyholes of Truck, ahead and to either side, afforded too narrow a field of view. He stood precariously to his full height, hands gripping the edge of Truck's bleached hood; and crowed once more, with wonder and delight, at what he saw.

He was parked on the crest of a great sweep of down-

2

land. Ahead the road stretched away, its surface cracked and broken, bristling with weeds. Across it lay the angular shadow of Truck, topped by the small protuberance that was Monkey's head. Beyond, and far into the distance, the land seemed to swell, ridge after ridge pausing and gathering itself to swoop saw-edged to the vagueness of the sea. Below him, a great distance away, Monkey saw the curving line of an immense offshore beach. Waves creamed and rushed against it; above it were hovering scraps of birds, each as white as the foam. The noise of the water came to him dimly, like the breathing of a giant.

He collapsed abruptly, huddled back to the darkness and protective warmth of Truck. Later, gaining courage, he traced with one finger the little green line that was an image of the mightiness. He sat proudly then, chin on fist, the master of all he surveyed.

At midday the great beach still stretched ahead. Behind the long ridge of pebbles, lagoons lay ruffled and as blue as the sky, dotted with the bobbing pinpoints of birds. The lagoons too Monkey traced on the map, and hugged himself with an uncommunicable excitement.

His good mood was tempered in the days that followed. Always, relentlessly, he urged Truck on toward the sunset; always, at dawn, he stared anxiously ahead, expecting to see the narrowing of the land, the blue glint of sea five-fingerward. But the land went on endlessly, leaping and rolling; and his faith was sorely tested. To Monkey, the notion of scale was as yet as hard to grasp as the notion of God. He became aware, for the first time, of the frustration of helplessness. His thought, lightning-swift, outran the stolid jogging of Pru and Sal. Sometimes he urged his companions on with high, cracked shouts; but they ignored him, keeping up their one stubborn pace.

It was a dull, drizzling morning when Monkey reached the end of the world. The sea, grey as the sky, was fretted with long white ridges; a droning wind blew from it, driving spray like hail against the impervious hood of Truck. Monkey, woken from a grumbling doze, sat up

3

blearily, crawled to the forward spyhole and yelped with triumph. The land on which Truck stood ran, narrowing at last, into the ocean; the water had swung round five-fingerward, barring further progress. Monkey crowed and howled, bobbing till Truck shook on its tall springs; for after all, the great idea was true. He had understood a Mystery.

North, or headwards, was a concept already relegated to the state of things known. Headwards Truck turned, then five-fingerward toward the sun and three-fingerward again. During his first great journey the notion of contour had also come to Monkey; he studied his maps, fitting each painstakingly to the next, and in the depth of winter was undismayed to see, rising ahead, the outlines of hills greater and more terrible than any he had known. Pru and Sal stopped at the sight, clucking and stamping in alarm; but he made no further move to urge them forward. For a time Truck wandered as it had always wandered, aimlessly; and Monkey was content. Snow came, and the long howling of the wind. In time the snow passed. The sky grew blue again, buds showed green against the stark twigs of trees. Then the maps were once more produced; and once more, Truck went a-voyaging.

In this way Monkey came to understand the land in which he lived. The concept of 'island', though suggested by the maps, was more difficult to grasp. The many sheets, placed edge to edge, alarmed with their suggestion of headward immensity. At first, Monkey's brain tended to spin; with time, he grew more assured. He kept tallies of his journeys now, scratching the days carefully on the greasy wooden sides of Truck. Soon he found his head could tell him, nearly without thought, the time of travel between any two points on his maps. Also the drawings themselves grew other marks, made by Monkey with the yellow drawing-stick that was his greatest treasure. He sketched where wild wheat grew, and where the land was good for hunting; and Pru and Sal, though they betrayed no outward gratitude, became sleek and well-filled. The larder of Truck was stocked to capacity; and Monkey, as is the way with men, looked about him for fresh worlds to conquer.

The adventure on which he decided almost proved his undoing. He turned Truck headwards, or north, resolved to travel as far as possible in this as yet unexplored direction; though he no longer harboured illusions as to the magnitude of the journey. Pru and Sal clopped steadily, day after day, indifferent as ever; and day after day Monkey squatted on his little rubbery heels, staring through the forward spyhole in breathless expectation of wonders. The tally lines grew again, wobbling across the dark wooden sides of Truck; hills appeared obediently to either hand, each in its allotted place. Monkey knew them now at a glance, reading their brown thumbprints on his maps. For a time, all went smoothly enough; then difficulties started to arise.

The first had to do with certain areas on the maps where the roads ran together in ever-thickening jumbles. Monkey steered for one of these, curious to see what such oddness could portend; but a whole day from his destination Pru and Sal stopped abruptly, stamping and shivering, giving vent to little hard anxiety-cries. Monkey, irritated, urged them forward; but his howls and bangings went unheeded. Pru and Sal danced with distress, shaking their heads and snorting; then, abruptly, they bolted. Truck, turned willy-nilly, jolted and crashed while Monkey clung on grimly, rolling from side to side in a confusion of legs and arms and maps. Dusk was falling before the wild flight eased; the tallies were ruined, and Monkey himself was lost.

He lay a day or more in a dull stupor of rage before he again took heart. As ever, the sidewaysness of the sun encouraged him; he spread the maps out once more, while Truck ambled slowly between rolling, gently-wooded hills. In time a higher hill, rearing dark against the sunset, gave him a reference. His good humour returned; for Pru and Sal jogged submissively, and the tallies were not wholly lost. The sideways or three-fingerward projection to which he had been subjected during their flight counted for little; he marked the map, using his drawing-stick, and turned Truck again on to its proper heading.

Twice more, the odd confluences were avoided by Pru and Sal; these times Monkey, prepared for their defection, found it easier to redirect their course. Whatever lay at the mysterious junctures must, it seemed, be avoided; for the present, he bowed to the inevitable.

For five more days the journey proceeded smoothly; then came the greatest shock of all. Far too soon—barely a half of the tally was complete—Monkey found the way impassably barred. Ahead, and to either side, stretched the sea.

The shock to his overstrained nerves was considerable. For a time, stupidly, he urged Truck forward, as if refusing to acknowledge the impossibility; the water was hissing round the axles, and Pru and Sal were keening with dismay, before he came to his senses. He sat a whole half day, glaring and fretting, staring at the map and back to the great blue barrier. Then he turned Truck three-fingerward. Two days passed before the sea once more swung round to bar his path; the proper sea this time, in its designated place. Monkey turned back, every hour adding to his alarm. The green and brown, green and brown of the map went on; yet still the lying, deceitful land shelved to the water, vanished beneath the waves. The tally grew again, senseless now and wild. Monkey howled and sobbed, picking his nose with rage; but the salty goodies brought no comfort. He threshed impotently, till the springs of Truck groaned and creaked and Pru and Sal stooped clucking, voices harsh with concern. But Monkey was unconsolable. His bright new world was shattered.

He felt himself losing control. His hands and limbs, wobbly at the best, refused to obey him. His nights were haunted; he wetted himself uncontrollably, till Truck exuded a rich sharp stink and half a whole map was spoiled. Madness, had it intervened, would have been a merciful release; but he was saved, finally, by a curious sight.

For a day or more the ground had been steadily rising; now, just after dawn, Monkey saw ahead of him the crest of a mighty cliff. The land, no longer gentle, broke away in a great crashing tumble of boulders and clay round which the sea frothed and seethed, flinging streamers of foam high in the air. Monkey huddled back, waving Truck on, anxious to be gone from the place; but at the height of the rise he began to thump and squeal. Pru and Sal stopped indifferently, their hair whipping round their heads, their curved, hard fingers hooked across the handle of Truck. The wind seethed in the grass; clouds sailed the early, intense sky; but Monkey had eyes for nothing but the Road.

It had been a great road, the widest and finest he had seen. It came lancing out of distance, its twin broad ribbons dark blue and cracked and proud. It soared to the edge of the cliff; and at the edge, on the very lip, it stopped.

Monkey raised himself, cautiously; then banged the side of Truck, ordering it forward. Pru and Sal moved slowly, unwilling now, straining back from the lip of the cliff; but Monkey's fear was forgotten. He stared, seeing how the road ended terrifyingly in a sudden, jagged edge. Below, white birds rode the updraught, tiny as scraps of paper. The sea crashed and boiled; and Monkey, screwing his eyes, saw what in his misery had eluded him. Far across the water, dim with distance but unmistakable, the brown and green, brown and green started again, marching out of sight.

He fell back; and relief was like a balm. Once more, he had understood; and the second Mystery was stranger than the first. The land had been changed after the maps were made.

The maps lived to the right of Truck, in their shallow compartment. Each part of Truck, each fragment of the tiny inner space, was apportioned with equal care. To Monkey's left was the area designated, in later times at least, Garage Accessories. The Accessories themselves didn't amount to much. There was a sleekly polished red oil can; beside it, tucked in tightly to prevent unpleasing rattles, the piece of rag with which Monkey furbished the metal, keeping it bright. Next to the oil can lived a tin of thick brown grease, with which Monkey anointed the axles of Truck whenever the elements conspired to draw from them high-pitched, irritating squeaks. Other Accessories were even less prepossessing. There was the galvanised nail with which Monkey prised up the lid of the tin (seconded lately for the important function of journeymarking) a small rusty spanner which fitted nothing about Truck but which Monkey kept anyhow, and an even more curious fetish; a little yellow wheel, made of some substance that flexed slightly in the fingers and was pleasant to hold and suck. Like the spanner, it served no discernible function; but Monkey was equally loth to throw it away. 'You can never tell,' he would bawl sometimes at the unresponding heads of Pru and Sal, 'when it might Come In.'

At Monkey's feet a locker closed by a rusty metal hasp constituted the Larder. Here he kept the flat grey wheatcakes that sustained him, and his bottles and jars of brook water. Other chunks of rag, stuffed carefully into the spaces between the containers, checked the clinking that would otherwise have spoiled his rest. Next to Larder, a corner compartment was crammed with spare rag, blankets and a blackened lace pillowslip. It also housed a broken piece of mirror, carefully wrapped and tucked away. Once, Monkey had gashed himself badly on its edge; now it was never used.

To either side of his head as he lay were the Tool Chest and the Library. The Tool Chest contained an auger, a small pointed saw, three empty cardboard tubes and a drum of stout green twine. The Library was full to overflowing, so full its lid could scarcely be forced down.

Sometimes Monkey would take the topmost books out, lie idly turning the pages, marvelling at the endless repetition of delicate black marks. The marks meant nothing to him; but the books had always been there, and so were accepted and respected. Like Truck, they were a part of his life.

Between its several compartments Truck was fretted by a variety of holes, all seemingly inherent to the structure. The spyholes, covered when not in use by sliding flaps of leather, afforded Monkey sideways and frontal vision. Beneath him, concealed by a hinged wooden trap, was the Potty Hole; to either side smaller apertures, or Crumb Holes, enabled him occasionally to clean the littered interior of Truck. He would spend an hour or more carefully scraping together the mess of wheatcake crumbs, twigs and blanket fluff, pushing the fragments one by one through the holes. The activity had enlivened many a grey, otherwise unedifying afternoon; it cheered him, giving him a sense of purpose.

Pru and Sal formed the other major components of Monkey's mobile world. How they had come to him, or he to them, he was unsure. Certainly there had been a time—he remembered it now and then in vague, dreamlike snatches—when there had been no Pru and Sal. And also, he was nearly certain, no Truck. He remembered firelight and warmth, and lying on a bed not enclosed by tall wooden sides. He remembered hands that touched, a voice that crooned and cried. Also he remembered a bleak time of wailing and distress. The figures loomed round him, dim and massive as trees; there were other deeper voices, harder hands. One such pair of hands, surely, had placed him for the first time inside Truck. He remembered words, though they made little sense.

'Lie there, Monkey. You're with me now. Poor bloody little Monkey. You're with me . . .'

He didn't like the dream to come too often. It woke him alone in Truck, miserable and cold, crying for the hands and voices that had gone.

Maybe Pru and Sal had stolen him, as he lay supine in

his bright new Truck. No one else would ever know; and they, perhaps, no longer remembered or cared. They too had become a part of his life. Always, as he lay brooding or contentedly dozing, their shoulders and heads were visible, outlined darkly against the sky. Their brown thin hands were clamped, eternally it seemed, round the wide handle of Truck; their feet thumped and pattered down the years.

In appearance, Pru and Sal were not unalike. Their hair, long, frayed and bleached by the sun, hung stiffly from their small rounded skulls. Their skin, tanned by the outside wind, had assumed the colour of old well-seasoned wood. Their eyes were small, slitlike and blank; their faces, untroubled by thought, ageless and smooth. Their fingers, over the years, had grown curved and stiff; good for killing, useless for the more delicate manipulations at which Monkey excelled. They dressed alike, in thick kilts of an indeterminate hue; and their voices, when they troubled to use them, were also alike, as harsh and croaking as the voices of birds.

For Monkey, secure in his endlessly roving home, the seasons passed pleasantly enough. Pru and Sal, in their motiveless fashion, tended him well. On rainy days, and in the dark cold time of winter, they drew across the open hood of Truck a tall flap of stiff grey canvas. Then Monkey would crawl invisibly in the warm dark, sucking and chuckling, groping among the crumbs of Larder, tinkling his jars of ice-cold chill, while the feet of Pru and Sal thudded out their comfort on paths and roads unseen. These, perhaps, were the best times of all; when snow whirled dark against the leaden strip of sky, and ice beaded the high hood of Truck and wolves called lost and dim.

Sometimes the snowflakes whirled right into Truck, tiny unmelting stars from outer air; and fires would leap, in clearings and unknown caves. In the mornings Pru and Sal must smash and crash at the ice of brooks while the wind whistled thin in thin dead grass.

Though springtimes too were good. The breeze stirred gentle and mild, rich with new scents; the sky brightened, filling with the songs of birds. Pru and Sal, clucking and mumbling, would draw back the canvas cover, allowing the cheesey air to whistle cheerfully from Truck; and Monkey would sit up, chuckling, feeling the new warmth on his great blotched hairless face. Summers he would lie naked, rubbing pleasure from his mounded belly while the warm rain fell, sizzling on his heated flesh. At night the stars hung lustrous and low, and trees were silent mounds of velvet cloth.

But the map reading changed, for all time, Monkey's life. The great adventure ended, it seemed a hollowness formed in his mind. Truly, he was satisfied with his conquered Island; and not unmoved by his discovery of its truncated state. New sights and sounds presented themselves each day; a waterfall, a forest, a bird, a lake. But novelty itself can pall. Monkey, mumbling and frowning, hankering for he knew not what, began, irritably, the formal tidying of Truck. Each object he came to—so known, once loved—seemed now merely to increase his frustration. His wheel, his drawing-stick, his spanner, lay discarded. The axles of Truck set up an intermittent squeal, but Monkey merely sneered. He tidied Larder and Blanket Store, dipped desultorily into Garage Accessories. Nothing pleased him. Finally, he turned to Library.

Almost at once he discovered a curious thing. The locker was deeper than it had always appeared. The blockage was caused by books that had swelled with damp, jamming their covers firmly against the outer wooden skin of Truck. Monkey puffed and heaved, straining unaccustomed muscles. Finally the hindrances came clear. He emptied the compartment to its bottom, sat back surrounded by books he had never seen. He opened one at random and instantly frowned, feeling a flicker of excitement for the first time in weeks.

The book was unlike the others in one major respect. Monkey huddled nearer the light, crowing and drooling, turning the pages with care. Some were glued irretrievably by damp; on others he saw, beside the squiggling marks, certain drawings. They were detailed and complex, many

11

of them in colour; he had no difficulty in recognising flowers and trees. Monkey, who had invented drawing, felt momentarily abashed; but the rise of a new idea soon drove self-awareness from him. He stared from the drawings to the little marks, and back. He tilted his head, first to one side then to the other. He laid the book down, picked it up, opened it again. Later he sat for an hour or more peering over the side of Truck, seeing the stony ground jog and jerk beneath. In time he made himself quite giddy. He closed his eyes, opened his mouth, laid his gums to the hard wood edge. Small shocks from the wheels and springs were transmitted to his skull.

From all this pondering, one idea emerged. He opened the new book once more, studied the flowers and trees. After a while he spread a second beside it. He discerned, now, certain similarities in the little black marks. Some of them, he saw, rose above their fellows, like tall bushes among lesser. Something in his brain said 'head' to that, or 'north'. It was the first key to a brand new Mystery. Illiterate, Monkey had divined which way up one holds the printed page.

For a season, and another, and part of a third, Truck squeaked and rumbled aimlessly while Monkey lay absorbed. The whole equipage might have become irretrievably lost had not the sinews of Pru and Sal remembered what their scorched brains were unable to retain. They followed, faithfully, their course of previous years. They harvested wheat, pounded and husked the grain, baked the flat hard cakes; they hunted rabbits and deer, ate and drank and slept. They came finally to the New Sea again, and the broken road; and there, triumphantly, Monkey added his own gull-cryings to the wheeling birds. The words floated down, vaunting and clear, to lose themselves in the roar and surge of the water.

'Even so our houses and ourselves and children have lost, or do not learn for want of time, the sciences that should become our country . . .'

How the wonder had come about will never be wholly

12

explained. It was an achievement comparable to the first use of fire, the invention of the wheel; but of this Monkey remained unaware. Certainly, the concept of a map aided his first steps to literacy. That the books in his keeping were maps of a curious sort was never in question; though what such charts expressed he was wholly unable to define. He was conscious of an entity, or body of awareness; something that though vastly significant was yet too shadowy for the mind wholly to grasp. He grappled with it nonetheless while his bones—the bones of genius— divined the inner mysteries of noun, adjective and verb. It was slow work, slow work indeed; 'tree', for instance, was simple enough, but 'oak', 'ash' and 'hawthorn' baffled him for months. 'Green tree' was likewise a concept fraught with difficulty, though he mastered it finally, adding to it the red, blue and violet trees of his mind. The noises he made, first fitting breath to cyphers, were less comprehensible than the utterings of Pru and Sal. It was patience that was needed; patience and dogged, endless work.

Truck rolled on, while Monkey bleated and yelped. Seasons, hours, moods, all now brought forth their observation. To Pru, sucking at a scab on her leg, he confided his opinion that 'lilies that fester smell far worse than weeds'. Sal, seen piddling into a deep green brook, provoked an equally solemn thought. 'In such a time as this,' mused Monkey, 'it is not meet that every nice offence should bear his comment.' Staring into a leafy sunset reminded him of the lowing herd, while a sight of the sea brought forth memories of Coastwise Lights. 'We warn the crawling cargo tanks of Bremen, Leith and Hull,' he expounded gravely. Yet for all his learning he remained centrally baffled; for despite Kipling he saw no ships, despite Shakespeare he met with no great Kings. In the beginning, God might very well have created the heavens and the earth; but God, it seemed, was no longer an active agent. No spirits sat on thistle tops, in flat defiance of Tennyson; and though Keats's nightingales still sang,

13

indubitably Ruth no longer walked.

Monkey found himself sinking once more into despondency. The books he owned he had read, from cover to cover; yet understanding seemed as far away as ever. Pru and Sal jogged as they had always jogged; the sun rose and set, rain came and wind, mists and snow. The sea creamed and boomed; but Monkey's mind was as rock-girt as the coasts. Nowhere, in any book, had he come upon a description remotely resembling Truck, or himself, or Pru and Sal; while all those things on which books most loved to dwell—armies and Legions, painters and poets, Queens and Kings—seemed lost for ever. 'Left not a rack behind,' muttered Monkey balefully. He lay sucking his wheel and brooding. Somewhere, it seemed, some great clue had evaded him. The books showed a world unreachable, but sweetly to be desired. As the maps had showed a world, incomprehensible at first, that now lay all about him.

He frowned, wondering. Then for the first time in many months he pulled the maps from their compartment. He unfolded them, tracing the confluences of roads, the strange knots he had never been permitted to explore. Their meaning was plain enough now. They were of course towns; their very names lay clear to read. He sat puzzling, and was struck by a wholly new thought. What if all the wonderful things of which he had read—the ships and Kings, the castles and palaces and people—still existed? What if, all this time, they had been waiting for him in the never-visited towns? He lay sleepless well into the night, turning over the brilliant, unsettling idea. Everywhere, glowing prospects opened; and when he finally dozed, he was visited by a splendid dream. He seemed to stand outside himself, and outside Truck; and Truck was bowling, unaided, along a great broad highway. To either side, half lost in a golden haze, reared towers and steeples; and everywhere, as Truck moved, there seemed to rise a great and rolling shout. It was as if all the people in the word—the glittering, wondrous people of the books—had come together to greet him; and there were hands and eyes, cheering and laughter, voices and the warmth he had so seldom known.

He sat up, peering from the confines of Truck. Dawn was grey in the sky; overhead, a solitary bird piped. Monkey's whoop of triumph sent it scuttling from its branch. 'Away toward Salisbury!' he cried to the sleeping land. 'While we reason here a Royal battle might be won and lost . . .'

The intention, once formed, was irrevocable; but at first the practical difficulties seemed impossible to overcome. For all their stolid obedience, on one point Pru and Sal stood firm; neither threats nor cajolery would get them near a town. Monkey tried the experiment several times more, always with the same result. As Truck neared each objective they would move slower and slower, keening and wailing in distress; and finally they would balk completely, or bolt like startled deer. Eventually, Monkey was forced to accept the obvious. Whatever was done must be done by his own efforts.

For several days more he lay frowning, puzzling at the problem. Finally a decision was reached, and he started work.

What he contemplated—a modification to the fabric of Truck itself—seemed at first like sacrilege. Eventually he overcame his qualms. Certain measurements, made for the most part secretly after dark, confirmed the practicability of his scheme. He worked carefully with his drawing-stick, scribing two broad circles on the sides of Truck. When the work was marked out, the auger came into play. With it he bored carefully through the planking on the circumference of one of the circles. When half a dozen holes had joined he was able to insert the tip of the little saw. The job was slow and tedious; more difficult, he imagined, than learning to read. His hands, unused to such exercise, grew blisters that cracked and spread; he bore the pain, keeping on stubbornly with his task. Finally he was successful. A circle of wood dropped clear; beyond, an inch or so away, revolved the battered, rusty rim of one of Truck's wheels.

He stared awhile, fascinated by the unusual sight; then

set to, puffing, on the other side. The second job was finished quicker than the first; the wood here was partly rotten, aiding the saw. The new holes let in a remarkable amount of draught and dampness; but Monkey was content. It was a small enough price to pay.

The next phase of the plan was more difficult still. Wheedling, coaxing, using all his skill, he persuaded Pru and Sal nearer and nearer to the town of his choice. He had selected it mainly for the flatness of the surrounding ground; that he deemed a vital factor in eventual success. The last stage of the approach was the most delicate of all. Pru and Sal were stamping and trembling; the slightest mismanagement could have sent them wheeling back the way they had come, and all the valuable ground gained would have been lost. When it was obvious they would go no farther Monkey allowed them to camp, in a spinney adjoining the road. He lay quietly but with thudding heart, waiting for night and the start of his greatest adventure.

The vigil seemed endless; but finally the light faded from the sky. Another hour and the moon rose, brightening the land again. Very cautiously, Monkey sat up. The springs and axles of Truck, well greased the day before, betrayed him by no creak. He inched forward, a fraction at a time. His height when fully erect was little more than a yard; but his arms were of unnatural length. Squatting in Truck, well forward of the hood, he could easily reach through the new holes he had made, grip the wheel rims with his great scabbed hands.

He pushed, tentatively. To his delight Truck moved a yard or more. Pru and Sal lay still, mouths stertorously open. Another shove, and Truck had glided the whole distance from the little camp site to the road. Monkey, without a backward glance, set himself to steer his clumsy vehicle toward the distant town.

An hour later he was panting and running with sweat, while every muscle in his body seemed on fire. His hands were raw and bleeding from contact with the rusty rims; he had been obliged to stop, and bind his palms with rag. But progress had been made. Crawling to the spyhole—the rearward spyhole now, for Truck was technically moving in reverse—he saw the copse where Pru and Sal still lay as nothing more than a dim smudge on the horizon. Ahead, close now, lay the focus of his dreams.

By dawn, Truck was bowling merrily if jerkily along a smooth, paved road. To either side, dusty and grey, rose the remnants of buildings, their roofs and wall-tops bitten and nubbled away. Grass sprouted and bushes, here and there stunted, unhealthy-looking trees. The sight both appalled and fascinated Monkey. He thrust at the wheel-rims, harder than before, staring round anxiously for signs of life; but a total hush lay over all the acres on acres of ruin. Apart from the trundling of Truck's wheels, there was no sound; even the wind seemed stilled, and no birds sang.

The sunrise proved Monkey's undoing. His eyes, weak at the best of times, were dazzled by the pouring light; he failed to observe and heed the steepening gradient ahead. Truck moved easily, without apparent effort, steadily increasing its pace. By the time understanding came it was too late. Monkey wailed despairingly, clutching at the wheelrims; but the flying iron tore the rags away, ploughed up the skin on his palms in thick white flakes. He shrieked, snatching his hands away; and instantly Truck was out of control. The rumbling of the wheels rose to a roar; Monkey, howling with pain and fright, felt himself banged and slewed before, with a heart-arresting jolt, Truck stopped dead. Monkey was propelled, catapult-fashion, in an arc. The blurred road rose to meet him; there was a crash, and the unexpected return of night.

He woke, blearily, a considerable time later. For a while, understanding was withheld; then realisation came, and with it a blind terror. The sun beat down on the hot white road; behind him, seeming a great distance away, Truck was upended in a heap of rubble like a little foundered ship.

The panic got Monkey to his feet. He tottered, wildly,

17

the first three steps of his life, stumbled and fell. He crawled the rest of the way, grazing his knees on the unfriendly surface of the road; but when at last he clutched the tall spokes of a wheel with his lacerated hands, some measure of sanity returned. A wave of giddiness came and passed. Monkey lay panting, staring round him at the awesome desolation.

From his low viewpoint little was visible but the bases of ruined walls. He raised his head, squinting. It seemed taller ruins reared in the distance. He thought he caught the glint of sunlight on high, bleached stone; but his head was spinning again, and with his streaming eyes he could not be sure. He lay still, gathering strength; then, with a great effort, pulled himself to his feet.

Truck seemed to be undamaged, though the crash had mortally disarranged the lockers and their contents. Books and blankets sprawled everywhere inside, mixed and confused with the remnants of Larder. Monkey, scrabbling, managed to retrieve a few scraps of rag, and an unbroken bottle of water. He plumped back, gasping, in the shade. Unscrewing the cap of the bottle hurt his hands again; but the liquid, though lukewarm, restored his senses a little. The rag he bound, as tightly as he was able, round his palms. He rested an hour or more; then, painfully but with dogged determination, he drew himself to his hands and knees. He began to crawl slowly away from Truck, into the ruined town.

Some hours later, an observer stationed beside the broken road would have witnessed a curious sight. The night was black as pitch, neither moon nor stars visible; but despite the overcast the road was by no means dark. It was lit, in places quite brightly, by a wavering bluish glow that seemed to proceed from the ruined shells of building themselves. By its aid, a small wooden truck was jerking itself slowly along. Its method of propulsion was curious. From a hole at the rear of the vehicle protruded two long, smooth poles. Each in turn, to the accompaniment of

18

grunts and labouring gasps, groped for the cracked surface, found a purchase and heaved. Truck, under the influence of this novel motivation, lurched and veered. Sometimes, as if its occupant were very, very tired, it rested for long periods motionless; but always the upward movement was resumed. In time, the slope eased; and there could have been heard, rising from the ungainly little vehicle, a cracked but triumphant refrain.

> 'Silent the river, flowing for ever,
> 'Sing my brothers, yo heave ho . . .'

Pru and Sal were waiting beneath the fringe of trees.

For a while, as Truck laboured toward them, they stood poised as if for flight. The hailing of Monkey, and his shouted exhortations, steadied them. His face, blackened and terribly peeling, loomed moon-like above a mound of tattered, browning paper; his arms terminated in dark red balls of rag; but it was Monkey, still indubitably and defiantly Monkey, who greeted them.

They ran to Truck with hard, gabbling cries, seized their long-accustomed handle and fled. Their feet galumphed, up hill and down dale, away from the sinister, shining town; and as they ran Monkey, his brain burning with strangest visions, regaled them with news of the world.

'Subscribers' dialled trunk calls are recorded at the exchange on the same meters used for local calls,' he carolled. 'These meters are extremely reliable, *and are regularly tested*.' He flung down the pamphlet, grabbed another. His eyes swam; fierce shooting pains stabbed suddenly through his head. 'How to take care of Your New House,' he shouted. 'Taps and Ball Valves, Gulleys and Gutters. Paths and Settlement Cracks . . .' Pru and Sal shrieked back; but Monkey's voice boomed triumphantly, overriding them. 'What is Shrinkage?' he cried cunningly. 'Is an Imperfection a Defect?'

Truck heeled, struck a stone and righted. Monkey leafed at the jizzing papers. 'These are your Service

Authorities,' he intoned. 'Rating Authority, Water Supply Authority, Gas Board, Electricity Board!' He snatched up another paper from his hoard. 'I never wanted to be a Star,' he bellowed. Then, turning two pages at once, 'Separates that Add Up in your Wardrobe . . .'

Truck slowed at last, in the sun and shadow of a dappled wood where a grassy road ran between grassy banks.

Monkey wasn't feeling too good any more. He gulped and blinked, fighting the rise of a sudden swelling pain. 'Goodbye,' he said sadly, to the Bikini Girl of Nineteen-Seventy-Five. Next year will be Cover Up Year . . .' The pain centred itself into an acute epiglottal knot; and Monkey burped. The burp was red and bright, and ran across his chin. He groaned, and brought up his wind again. The second belch was worse than the first. He splashed the wetness with his hands, and started to shriek.

The attention of Pru and Sal was riveted. They stooped, staring and mumbling. Their hands, iron-hard and hooked, scrabbled concernedly; and the cheeks of Monkey fell wholly from his face, lay on the pillows bright as flower petals!

A mask, whether it be of blood or another substance, is a form that depersonalises. Now, new triggers operated within the curious brains of Pru and Sal. The red thing that writhed and mewed was no longer Monkey, but a stranger that had taken Monkey's place. They seized it at once, shrieking with rage, and hurled it to the ground. Still it cried and wailed, its fear-smell triggering in turn desire to kill. Pru and Sal stamped and leaped, keening, their unused grass-dry bosoms joggling beneath their shifts. In time the sounds stopped, and what was on the path lay still. They gripped then the handles of the empty Truck and fled, backs humping, knees jerking regular as pistons. When they had gone, the lane was quiet.

The day was warm, and still. Flies buzzed, steady and soothing, through the afternoon. Toward dusk a wild creature found, in the path, something to its liking. For a time it chewed and mumbled warily; then leaf shadows, moved by a rising wind, startled it away. It retired to its hole, under the roots of an elderly, spreading oak; there it cleaned its fur, washed its nose and paws, and died.

Clouds piled in the sky, amber-grey in the fading light. Overhead, the leaves of trees glowed pale against the thunderous masses of vapour. The first rainspots fell, heavy and solitary, banging down through the yielding leaves; and the storm broke, with a crashing peal. In time it passed, grumbling, to the east. It left behind it, in the cleansed lane, a great new smell of earth and wet green leaves.

TWO

The God House

I

If you had lain as Mata lay, stretched out on the wiry grass,
and pressed your ear to the ground, you would have heard,
a long way off, the measured thud and tramp of many feet.
If you had raised your head, as she now raised hers, you
would have caught, gusting on the sharp, uncertain breeze
of early spring, the heart-pounding thump and roll of
drums. Since dawn, the Great Procession had been winding its slow way from the sea; now, it was almost here.

She sat up quickly, pushing the tangled black hair from
her eyes; a dark-eyed, brown-skinned girl of maybe thir-
teen summers. Her one garment, of soft doeskin, left her
legs and arms bare; her waist was circled by a leather
thong, on which it pleased her to carry a little dagger in a
painted wooden sheath. Round her neck she wore an
amulet of glinting black and red stones; for Mata was the
daughter of a chief.

The valley above which she lay opened its green length
to the distant sea. Behind her, crowning the nearer height,
was a village of thatched mud huts, surrounded by a
palisade of sharply pointed timbers. In front, rearing
sharp-etched against the sky, was the Sacred Mound to
which the Procession must come. Here the Giants had
lived, in times beyond the memory of men; and here they

had once reared a mighty Hall. The top of the Mound was circled still by nubs and fingers of stone, half buried by the bushes and rank grasses that had seeded themselves over the years; but now none but the village priests dare venture to the crest. The Giants had been all-powerful; their ghosts too were terrible, and much to be feared. Once, as a tiny child, Mata had ventured to climb the steep side of the Mound toward where Cha'Acta the Chief Priest tethered his fortune in goats; but the seething of the wind in the long yellow grass, the bushes that seemed to catch at her with twiggy fingers, the spikes and masses of high grey stone half-glimpsed beyond the summit, had sent her scuttling in terror. She had kept her own counsel, which was maybe just as well; and since that day had never ventured near the forbidden crest.

The sound of drumming came sudden and loud. The head of the Procession was nearing the great chalk cleft; any moment now it would be in sight. Mata frowned back at the village, pulling her lip with her teeth. The other children, placed under her care, had been left to fend for themselves in the smoke and ashes of the family hut; chief's daughter or not, she would certainly be beaten if she was discovered here.

Nearby a tousled stand of bramble and old gorse offered concealment. She wriggled to it, lay couched in its yielding dampness; felt her eyes drawn back, unwillingly, to the Sacred mound.

At its highest point, sharp and clear in the noon light, stretched the long hogsback of the God House; reed-thatched, its walls blank and staring white, its one low doorway watching like a distant dark eye. Round it, the fingers of old stone clustered thickly. Above it, set atop the gable ends, reared fantastic shapes of rushwork; the Field Spirits, set to guard the house of the Lord from harm. Mata shivered, half with apprehension, half with some less readily identifiable emotion, and turned her gaze back across the grass.

Her heart leaped painfully, settled to a steady pounding.

In that moment of time the Procession had come into sight, debouching from the pass between the hills. She saw the yellow antennae and waving whips of the Corn Ghosts, most feared of all spirits; behind them the bright, rich robes of the exorcising priests, Cha'Acta among them in his green, fantastic mask. Behind again came cymbal-men and drummers, Hornmen capering in their motley; and after them the great mass of the people, chanting and stamping, looking like a brown-black, many-legged snake. She bestowed on them no more than a passing glance; her whole attention was concentrated on the head of the column.

She wriggled forward once more, forgetful of discovery. She could see Choele distinctly now. How slender she looked, how white her body shone against the grass! How stiffly she walked! Her hair, long and flowing, golden as Mata's was dark, had been wreathed with chaplets of leaves and early flowers; she held her head high, eyes blank and unseeing, lost already in contemplation of the Lord. Her arms were crossed stiffly, in front of her breasts; and from the crown of her head to the soles of her feet she alone was bare. Quite, quite bare.

The whole Procession was closer now. The Corn Ghosts ran, skirmishing to either side, leaping fantastically, lashing with their whips at the bushes and old dead grass; the animal dancers pranced, white antlers gleaming in the sunlight. Mata edged back in sudden panic to the shelter of the bushes, saw between the stems how Choele, deaf and unseeing, still unerringly led the throng. Her figure, strutting and pale, vanished between the bushes and low trees that fringed the base of the Sacred Mound. The people tumbled after, exuberantly; the drums pounded ever more loudly; then suddenly a hush, chilling and complete, fell across the grass. Mata, screwing her eyes, saw the tiny figure of her friend pause on the causeway that led to the Mound. For a moment it seemed Choele turned, looking back and down; then she stepped resolutely on, vanished from sight between the first of the rearing stones.

24

Already people were breaking away, streaming back gabbling up the hill. Mata rose unwillingly. Her father would be hungry; like the rest of the village, he had been fasting since dawn. She remembered the neglected bowls of broth, steaming on their trivets over the hut fire, and quickened her pace. At the stockade gates she paused. Below her, folk toiled up the slope; others still stood in a ragged black crescent, staring up at the Mound. The priests in their robes clustered the causeway, tiny and jewel-bright. From this height the God House with its long humped grey-green roof showed clear; Mata, shielding her eyes with her hand, saw a tiny figure pause before the doorway of the shrine. A moment it waited; then slipped inside, silent and quick as a moth, and was lost to sight. A heartbeat later she heard the rolling cry go up from all the people.

Once again, the God Bride had entered the presence of her Lord.

Mata ran for her hut, legs pounding, not feeling the hardness of the packed earth street beneath her feet. The fire was low; she blew and panted, feeding the embers with dried grass and bunches of sticks, and for the moment heat and exertion drove from her the thought of what she had seen.

The drums began again, late in the night. Great fires burned in the square before the Council Lodge; youths and men, fiercely masked and painted, ran torches in hand in and out the shadows of the huts; girls swayed in the shuffling, sleep-inducing rhythm of a dance. On the stockade walls and watchtowers more torches burned, their light orange and flickering. Old men and crones hobbled between the huts, fetching and carrying, broaching cask after cask of the dark corn beer. The other children were sleeping already, despite the din; only Mata lay wide-eyed and watchful, staring through the open doorway of the hut, seeing and not seeing the leaping grotesque shadows rise and fall.

Every year, since the hills themselves were young and the Giants walked the land, her folk had celebrated in this fashion the return of spring. They waited, fearfully, for the hooting winter winds to cease to blow, for the snow to melt, for the earth to show in patches and wet brown skeins beneath the withered grass. Little by little, as the year progressed, the sun gained in strength; little by little vigour flooded back into trees and fields, buds split showing tiny, vivid-green mouths. Till finally—and only Cha'Acta and his helpers could say exactly when—the long fight was over, the Corn Lord, greatest of the Gods, reborn in manhood and loveliness. Then the hill folk gave thanks to the Being who was both grain and sunlight, who had come to live among them one more season. A Bride was chosen for him, to live with him in the God House as long as he desired; and the Great Procession formed, milling round the God Tents on the distant shore.

Choele had been a season older than Mata, and her special friend. Her limbs were straight and fine as peeled rods of willow, her hair a light cloud yellow as the sun. To the younger girl she had confided her certainty, over half a year before, that she would be the next spring's chosen Bride.

Mata had shrugged, tossing her own dark mane. It was not good to speak lightly of any God; but especially the great Corn Lord, whose eyes see the movements of beetles and mice, whose ears catch the whisper of every stem of grass. But Choele had persisted. 'See, Mata; come and sit with me in the shade, and I will show you how I know.'

Mata stared away sullenly for a while, setting her mouth and frowning; but finally curiosity overcame her. She wriggled beside the other girl, lay sleepily smelling the sweet smell of long grass in the sun. The goats they had been set to watch browsed steadily, shaking their heads, staring with their yellow eyes, bumping and clonking their clumsy wooden bells.

Mata said, 'It is not wise to say such things, Choele, even to me. Perhaps the God will hear, and punish you.'

Choele laughed. She said, 'He will not punish me.' She

had unfastened the thongs that held the top of her dress; she lay smiling secretly, pushing the thin material forward and back. 'See, Mata, how I have grown,' she said. 'Put your fingers here, and feel me. I am nearly a woman.'

Mata said coldly, 'I do not choose to,' She rolled on her back, feeling the sun hot against her closed lids; but Choele persisted till she opened her eyes and saw the nearness of her breasts, how full and round they had become. She stroked the nipples idly, marvelling secretly at their firmness; then Choele showed her another thing, and though she played in the dark till she was wet with sweat she couldn't make her body do it too. So she cried at last, bitterly, because Choele had spoken the truth; soon she would be gone from her, and there was no other she chose to make a friend. For a year, each Bride lived with the God; but none of them had ever spoken of the Mystery, and all afterwards avoided their former friends, walking alone for the most part with their eyes downcast.

But next day Choele was kinder. 'This will not be true of us,' she said. 'For a time I shall live in the God House, certainly; but afterwards we will be friends again, Mata, and I will tell you how it is when you are loved by a God. Now come into the bushes, and let us play; for I am a woman now, and know more ways than before to make you happy.'

The drums were still beating; but the fires, that had flickered so high, were burning low. The Corn Ghosts were dead, driven by Cha'Acta's magic from the fields; their old dry husks, empty as the shells of lobsters, had already been ritually burned. In the winter to come the old women, who had seen many Corn Processions pass, would plait new figures; for next year, too, the God would need a Bride.

Mata gulped, and swallowed back another thought half-formed.

She slipped from the hut, moving quietly so as not to disturb the little ones. From the Council Lodge, set square facing the end of the one street of the village, sounds of revelry still rose; for the moment, she was safe. She shadowed between the huts, heading away from where the fires still pulsed and flickered. By the stockade, the outer air struck chill. She climbed the rough wooden steps to a guard tower. As she had expected, the high platform was deserted. She stood shivering a little, staring down into the night.

The moon was sinking to the rim of hills. Below, far off and tiny at her feet, the Sacred Mound was bathed in a silvery glow. Across its summit, black and hulking, lay the God House. It was still, and seemingly deserted; but Mata knew this was not so.

She tried to force her mind out from her body, send it soaring like the spirit of Cha'Acta. She heard a hunting owl call to its mate; and it seemed she flew with the flying bird, silently, across the moonwashed gulf of space. Then it was as if for an instant her spirit joined with Choele, lying waiting silent on the great brushwood bed. She heard a mouse run and scuttle on the floor, thought it was the scratching of the God; and giddiness came on her so that she staggered, clutching the wood of the watchtower for support. Then, just as swiftly it seemed, she was back in her body; and fear of the God was on her so that she shook more violently than before. She pulled her cloak closer round her throat, staring about her guiltily; but none had seen, for there were none to watch. She huddled a long time, unwilling to leave her vantage point, while the fires in the street burned to embers and the moon sank beneath a waiting hill. Its shadow raced forward, swift and engulfing, half-seen; and the God House was gone, plunged in the blackest dark.

She licked her mouth and turned away, groping with her bare feet for the edges of the wooden steps.

The God, as ever, was pleased with his Bride. Cha'Acta announced it, before all the people; and once more the horns blew, the drums thundered, the vats of corn beer were broached and drained. Every day now the sun gained visibly in strength, the hours of daylight lengthened. A burgeoning tide of green swept across the land, across the forest tops in the valleys, across the little patchwork fields where the corn pushed sappy spears up from the ground. The time of breeding came and passed; the coracles ventured farther from the coasts, bringing back snapping harvests of sea things, lobsters and crabs. The villagers, from headman and priests to the lowest chopper of wood, grew sleek and contented. High summer came, with its long blue days and drowsy heat; and only Mata mourned. Sometimes, as she lay watching her father's goats, she wove chaplets of roses for her hair; sometimes she joined in the children's play and laughter; but always her thoughts slid back to the great house on the hill, to Choele and her Lord.

In the mornings she woke now before it was light, with the first sweet piping of the birds. Always, the Sacred Mound drew her irresistibly. She would sit and brood, in some hollow of the grassy hill, watching down at the long roof of the God House, still in the new, pearly light; or she would run alone and unseen, down to the brook that meandered softly below the Mound. Trees arched over it, cutting back the light, their roots gripping the high banks to either side; between them the water ran clear and bright and cold. Her ankles as she walked stirred greyish silt that drifted with the current like little puffs of smoke. The coldness touched first calves and knees, then thighs; then as she dipped and shuddered, all of her. Sometimes she would look up, unwilling, to the high shoulder of the hill, and see the nubs and spikes of stone watching down, run scurrying to drag her clothes on wet and sticking. Then she would bolt from the secret place to the high yellow slope of hill below the village; only there dare she turn, stare down panting at the Mound and the God House, rendered tiny by distance and safe as children's toys. And once, on the high hill, a whisper of cool wind reached to her, touched her hot forehead and passed on into distance, to far fields and the homes of other men. She sat down then, unsteadily; for it

29

seemed to her the God had indeed passed, laughing and glad, to play like a child among the distant hills. A gladness filled her too so that she rose, stretching out her arms; for the Lord speaks only to his chosen. She turned, excited, for the village, bubbling inside with still-unadmitted thoughts.

Later, she was vouchsafed more convincing proof.

Toward the end of summer she was set to gathering reeds; the village folk used them in great quantities for thatching both their own homes and the God House. The sacred hut, alone of all buildings, was refurbished every year. For its great span, only the finest and longest reeds would serve; so Mata in her searching wandered farther and farther afield, hoping secretly her harvest would adorn the home of the God, and that he would know and be pleased. The afternoon was hot and still; an intense, blue and gold day, smelling of Time and burning leaves. She worked knee-deep for the most part, shut away among the great tall pithy stems, hacking with a keen, sickle-bladed knife, throwing the reeds down in bundles on the bank for the carts to pick them up. In time the endless, luminous-green vistas, the feathery grass-heads arching above her, worked in her a curious mood. She seemed poised on the edge of some critical experience; almost it was as if some Presence, vast yet nearly tangible, pervaded the hot, unaware afternoon. The reed stems rubbed and chafed, sibilantly, water gurgled and splashed where she stepped. She found herself pausing unconsciously, the knife blade poised, waiting for she knew not what. Unconsciously too, later with a strange rapture, she pressed deeper into the marsh. Its water, tart and stinking, cooled her legs; its mud soothed her ankles. The mud itself felt warm and smooth; she drove with her toes, feeling them slide between slimy textures of root, willing herself to sink. Soon she had to tuck her skirt higher round her thighs; finally, impulsively, she drew it to her waist. She fell prey to the oddest, half-pleasurable sensations; and still the magic grass called and whispered, still she seemed drawn forward.

She heard the wind blow, a great rushing rustle all about; but her vision was narrowed to the brown and yellow stems before her eyes. Her free hand now was beneath the water; and it seemed in her delirium a great truth came to her. The grasses, in their green thousands, were the body of the Corn Lord; and his body, mystically, the grasses. She cried out; then her own body seemed to open and she knew the Magic Thing had happened at last. She pressed the reed stems madly, awkward with the knife, sucking with her mouth; and life ended, in a wonderful soaring flight.

The world blinked back. She opened her mouth to gasp, and water rushed in. She threshed and fought, fear of the deep mud blinding reason. Dimly, she felt pain; then she had dropped the knife she carried and the bank was close. She reeled and staggered, clawed to it, rolled over and lay still.

The sun was low before she opened her eyes. She lay a moment unaware; then memory returned. She half sat up, pushing with her elbows against a weight of sickness. Somewhere, there were voices. She saw a waggon moving along the river bank. It came slowly, one man leading the ox, a second stooping to fling reed bundles on to the already towering pile.

Her chest felt sore and sharp. She stared down, frowning. Her dress was stuck to her, glued with dark red; the rest of her was muddy still, and bare.

The waggoners had seen her. It seemed they stood staring a great while; then they stepped forward carefully, placing each foot in line. One of them said in a low voice, 'It's the headman's child. She who was sent to cut the reeds.'

She laughed at them then, or showed her teeth. She said, 'I harvested more than reeds. The God came to me, and was very passionate.' She fell back heavy-eyed, watching them approach. They fiddled awkwardly with her dress, giving her more pain. At last the fabric jerked clear; and the villagers huddled back frowning. Across her chest ran deep, curving gashes; the marks the Corn Lord gave her, with his nails.

The wounds healed quickly; but the dullness of spirit induced by the God's visit took longer to disperse. For many days Mata lay in the family hut, unmoving, drinking and eating very little; while all the village it seemed came to peck and cluck outside, stare curiously round the door-posts into the dark interior. Meanwhile prodigies and wonders were constantly reported. Magan, Mata's father, saw with his own eyes a great cloud form above the God House, a cloud that took the baleful shape of a claw; the marshes glowed at night with curious light, sighings and rushings in the air spoke of the passage of monsters.

Finally, Cha'Acta came. He arrived in considerable state, three of his priests in attendance; he wore his official robes, blazoned with the green spear of the Corn Lord, and Mata as she saw him stoop beneath the lintel huddled to the farthest corner of the bracken bed. Never before had Cha'Acta acknowledged her directly; now he seemed terrible, and very tall.

Lamps were brought, the other children banished; and the High Priest began his examination. The wounds were subjected to the closest scrutiny; then Mata told her tale again and again, eyes huge in the lamplight, voice faltering and lisping. The thin face of Cha'Acta remained impassive; the dark, grave eyes watched down as she talked. But none could say, when he rose to take his leave, what decision he had come to, or what his thoughts had been. Later though he caused gifts to be sent to the hut; fresh milk and eggs and fruit, a tunic to replace the one the God had soiled. All knew, perhaps, what the portent meant; only Mata, it seemed, could not believe. She lay far into the night, eyes staring unseeing in the dark, clutching the soft fabric to her chest; but as yet her mind refused to make the words.

Autumn was past by the time her strength returned; the

harvest gathered, the animals driven into their stockades. Round the village the fields and sweeping downs lay brown and dry, swept by a chilling wind. Eyes followed her as she moved through the village street, cloak gripped round her against the cold. She flushed with awareness; but held her head high and proud, looking neither to left nor right. She climbed to the stockade walk, stared down at the God House on the Mound. Cloud scud moved overhead; the pass between the hills lay desolate and bleak, grey with the coming winter.

Usually the God House was empty well before this time, its doors once more agape, its walls ritually breached. But Cha'Acta remained silent, and Choele was not seen. The village muttered curiously; till finally word came that the Corn Lord had once more left his valley home. The men of the village scurried on to the Mound, fearful and slinking, dragging after them the long grey bundles of thatch. Through the shortest days they worked, renewing the great roof and its framing of timber and poles. The walls of the God House were patched and rewhitened, its floors pounded and swept ready for the coming spring. Mata, who now did little of the housework, watched all from the rampart of the little town. She saw the Field Spirits carried down the street, hoisted distantly to their places; two days later, she saw Choele walking alone through the village.

She ran to her gladly; but a dozen paces away she faltered. For her friend's face was white and old, the eyes she raised toward her dark-ringed and dead. And Mata knew with certainty that despite the promise of Choele the Mystery had come between them, as blank and impenetrable as a wall.

She ran, dismayed, to her father's hut. An hour or more she lay on her pallet, squeezing the hot tears; then she rose, wiped her face and fell to with the household chores. A decision had formed in her, cold and irrevocable; and at last the forbidden thoughts were freely admitted. Next year, Mata herself would be the Corn Queen. Afterwards, when she too knew the Mystery, she would go to Choele; and all between them would be as it had been before.

Mata was often seen about the village in the brightening days that followed. She took to placing herself, consciously or unconsciously, in Cha'Acta's path. Always she moved with becoming modesty; but her downcast eyes missed nothing. Sometimes, wrapped in talk or bent upon his own affairs, the Chief Priest seemed not to notice her; at others he turned, watching her as she moved on her errands, and Mata felt the keen, impenetrable stare burn on her neck and back.

Her father finally sent for her late one night. He sat in some state in the Council Lodge, a pitcher of corn beer at his elbow. Cha'Acta was also present, and the elders and priests. Mata stood head bowed in the smoky light of torches while her father spoke, sadly it seemed, saying the impossible words; and later, when she left, there was no sensation of the earth beneath her feet. Already it seemed she was set apart from normal things, the chosen of the Lord.

She lay sleepless till dawn, watching the embers glowing on their shelf of clay, listening to the breathing of her sisters and her mother's rattling snore. A score of times, when she thought of what would come, her heart leaped and thudded, trying it seemed to break clear of her body. At length the longed-for dawn broke dim and grey; she rose and dressed, went to seek a hut at the far end of the village. In it lived Meril, the old woman who instructed the God Brides and for many years had preserved their Mysteries.

Mata stayed a month with the crone, learning many things that were new and by no means wholly pleasant. Choele, it was true, had often taken her to the hills for purposes not dissimilar. But Choele's fingers were brown, and sweet as honey; Meril's were old and horny, sour-smelling. They left her feeling unclean. Mata shuddered and stiffened, sweating; but she endured, for Choele's sake and the sake of the God.

Cha'Acta she now seldom saw. There was still much to be done; grain to be prepared for sowing, beer to be brewed, pens and stockades repaired, the God Tents and all the paraphernalia of the Great Procession made ready once more. In most, if not in all, these things the Chief Priest took an interest. Meanwhile, the buds swelled perceptibly. Rain fell, waking new grass; and finally came a time of clear, bright sun. The skies dappled over with puffy, fast-moving white clouds; the wind came gusting and warm, lifting trails of dust from hill-tops and the sloping fields, and Mata knew her waiting was all but ended.

Then came tragedy, stark and unexpected. Choele was missed from the village. For some days uneasy bands of men desultorily searched the hills and surrounding ground; then one morning an oldster came gabbling and puffing up the hill, shouting his incoherent tidings to the sleepy guards on the gate. In the brook that ran below the Mound, the grey, cold brook where Mata once had bathed, floated a sodden bundle of cloth and hair; all that was left of the Corn Lord's Bride.

The omen threw the village into a ferment. Drums beat before the Council Lodge, where Cha'Acta and his priests prayed and sacrificed to avert the undoubted wrath of the God. Men rose fearfully, watching up at the clear skies; but strangely the weather remained fine, the land continued to smile. So that by the week of the Great Procession the death was all but forgotten; only Mata felt within her a little hollow space, that now would never be filled.

She already knew her duties, and the many ways existing to please a God. What remained after Meril's rough instruction had been imparted by Cha'Acta in his harsh, monotonous voice. For two days before the great event she fasted, drinking nothing but the clearest spring water, purging her body of all dross. On the day before the ceremony she made her formal goodbyes to her family. A waggon was waiting, decked and beribboned, drawn by the white oxen of Cha'Acta; she mounted it, stood stiffly staring ahead while the equipage jolted out through the broad gates of the stockade. The guards raised their spears, clashed a salute; then the village was falling away behind, the wheels jerking and bumping over the rough turf of the hill.

Every year, so ran the litany, the God came from the south, drawn by prayers across the endless blue sea. The little camp the priests had set up by the shore already bustled with activity. Hide tents had been pitched; over the biggest, on a little staff, hung the long green Sign of the God. Here Mata would lie the night. Some distance away the nodding insignia of the Chief Priest marked where Cha'Acta would rest on this most important eve; beside his quarters, waggons unloaded more bundles of hides, the poles and withies on which they would be stretched. Other baggage was stacked or strewn around; Mata saw the motley of the Hornmen, the antlers and hide masks, by them the green lobster-shells that in the morning would become the Corn Ghosts, and shivered with a medley of emotions.

Difficult now to retain even the memory of Choele. Her tent was ready for her, its lamps lit, the grass inside strewn with precious water bought at great expense from the traders who sometimes passed along the coast. She was bathed, and bathed again; then lay an hour, patiently, while the fluffy down her body had begun to grow was scraped from her with sharpened shells. Her breast-buds were stained with bright dye, her hair combed and stroked and combed again; and finally, she was left to sleep.

She slept soundly, curiously enough, tired out by the time of fasting and preparation; it was a shock to feel her shoulder shaken by old Meril. A cloak was held out to her; she crept from the tent, into the first glow of dawn. The sea lay cold and flat; a droning wind blew from it bringing with it the harsh, strange smell of salt.

The God Tents were triangular and black, built not of hides but of thick, impermeable felt. The flap of the nearest was raised for her; she crept inside, shivering, already knowing what she would find.

On the ground inside the little booth had been placed a great copper bowl. In it, charcoal smouldered and the magic seeds of plants. The little space was thick already with an acrid, pungent-smelling smoke; she coughed, catching her breath, leaned her head over the bowl as she had been taught. Instantly she heard the sighing as the bellows, worked from outside by an attendant priest, forced air over the burning mass, bringing it to a glow.

The smoke scorched her lungs; she retched and would have vomited had her stomach not been empty. She inhaled dutifully, closing her streaming eyes; and in time it seemed the fumes grew less sharp. Then strange things began to happen. Her body, she was sure, had floated free of contact with the earth; she groped awkwardly, pawing the hard ground for reassurance. Then the bowl and its contents seemed to expand till she felt she was falling headlong and at great speed toward an entire world on fire. The inside of the booth, small enough for her to span, likewise enlarged itself to a soundless black void, infinite as the night sky. In it, sparks and flashes burned; there were stars and moons and suns, comets and golden fruit, God-figures that passed as fleeting as they were vast. She opened her eyes, screwed them closed once more; the forms still swam, in the darkness behind the lids.

Lastly it seemed that Mata herself had grown to immense stature; she felt she might grasp with her arms the headlands that closed the bay, stoop to catch up the running figures of men like ants or grains of sand. She rose slowly, swaying, knowing she was ready.

Outside the tent the light had grown. She felt, dimly, the presence of the people; heard the shout as the cloak, unwanted now, was drawn from her. Muffled fingers touched her, plaiting the green wreaths in her hair; and already she was moving away, angling with difficulty her mile-long legs and arms, stepping up the rocky path from the bay. Behind her the Procession jostled into order; cymbals crashed, horns shouted, the drums took up their insistent thudding. Her ears registered the sounds; but disconnectedly, in flashes and fragments, mixed with a roaring like the voice of the sea.

The wind blew, steady and not-cold, pressing to her tautened body close as a glove; while from her great height she saw, with wonderful acuteness, the tiniest details of the land across which she passed. Pebbles and grass-blades, wet with sea-damp, jerked beneath her bright as jewels. She sensed, in her exalted awareness, the rising of mighty truths lost as soon as formed, truths that her body nonetheless understood so that it laughed as it moved, exulting; while stepping so far above the ground a part of her mind marvelled that she did not fall.

The Corn Ghosts skipped, lashing with their whips, chasing their half-terrified victims from the path. The priests chanted; Cha'Acta, eyes implacable behind his bright green mask, blessed the land, casting spoonfuls of grain to either side. The sun, breaking through the high veils of mist, threw the long shadow of Mata forward across the grass. She glanced down, along the length of her immense body to the far-off, forgotten white tips of her feet. The vision was disturbing; she raised her eyes again, rested them on the distant line of the horizon.

Already—it seemed impossible—she saw before her the high pass in the hills. On the right was the village with its stockade; to her left, close and looming, the Sacred Mound and the waiting house of the God. She could feel now, faintly, the textures of grass and earth beneath her feet; but the intense clarity of sight remained, she saw tiny flowers budding in the grass and insects, sticks and bracken and dead straw. The way steepened, beside the Brook of Choele; she pressed on, hurrying the last few yards. And here was the causeway, built of ancient stone; beyond, the Sacred Mound, empty and desolate and vast.

Never before had she been so high. Subtly she had expected grass and bushes, the very stones, to be changed here somehow, so close to the home of the God; but even to her exalted sense they seemed the same. At the causeway end she remembered to turn, showing herself again to the people. She heard them cry, felt their stares against her like a prickling wind; then she was alone, threading her way between the spires of stone.

She climbed now in earnest, using her hands to steady herself. She rounded a lichened buttress, trudged across an open space where dead grass tangles stroked her thighs; and the God House was ahead, awesome and close. She faltered then, hands to her throat; and memory flooded her dulled brain, she wished herself for one heart-stopping moment back at her father's hearth, smutty and unknown, and all she had done, undone. Then the time was passed; she paused once more to wave, heard the scattered shouts from the hill and stepped inside, to darkness and quiet.

The quietness, at first, oppressed her worst; a singing silence, heightened by the rushing of the blood in her ears. She stood still, clutching her shoulders, trying to draw herself into a tiny compass. The long house was empty, and quite bare. The floor, swept of all but the tiniest grains of dirt, gleamed a dull grey-brown; the walls rose, rough and cobbled, to shoulder height; the long gable stretched away above, thatch-poles showing equidistant and pale. Between them the reeds lay even and close, filling the place with the scent of grass and ponds.

She walked forward, slowly, still with her arms crossed in front of her. As her eyes became used to the gloom she saw that what she had taken to be the end wall was in fact an open wattle screen, pierced by a narrow entrance. She stepped through it. Beyond, an arm's span away, was a second screen, also pierced. The entrances she saw were staggered, blocking from sight the great outer door. Beyond the second screen was a chamber, small, square and dark. She saw a couch of thick-piled bracken; beside it a water jar and dipper, standing on the smooth, beaten floor.

And that was all.

Her legs shook suddenly. She unwound the garlands from her hair, clumsily, tossed them down unnoticed. She knelt by the pitcher, dipped water. It was clear, sweet and very cold. She drank deeply, slaking herself; then rolled on her back on the bracken bed. She was conscious, now, of a rising weariness; she let her limbs subside, luxuriously, her eyes drift closed. In time the singing in her ears faded to quiet.

She woke in darkness. The little chamber itself was pitchy black; she turned her head, slowly, saw the intervals of the wattle screens lit by a silver-grey glow. For a time, she was confused again; then she realised the hours she must have slept. The cold, metallic light was the moon.

The effects of the seed-smoke had wholly left her now. She shivered, wanting a coverlet; but there was nothing in the hut. Then she remembered she was not there to sleep.

She swallowed. Something had roused her, surely. She listened, concentrating her whole awareness. The wind soughed across the Mound, stirring the grass and bushes. A timber creaked, somewhere in the great hut. Her heart leaped, it seemed into her throat; but nothing further came. The God House was as silent as before.

She frowned, brooding. Were all the tales, the stories, false? Her training, thorough as it had been, stopped short of this. What if no God ever really came, to live in the house on the hill? Or what if—terrible thought—the Corn Lord had rejected her? What if he had already come, in the darkness and quiet, found her unpleasing as a Bride and passed on? Then he would leave the valley for ever; and the corn shoots would rot in the ground, the people starve. She would be stoned, disgraced . . . She clenched her fists, feeling her eyes begin to sting. The disgrace would be the least of her pain.

She made herself be still again. He would come in his own time and fashion; for who, after all, could command a God? Once, already, he had visited her in the reeds; what more did she need, in proof? It had been a mark of favour such as no other, in her memory, had received. He would come; because he always came, and because he had chosen her.

The thought brought fresh fears in its train. What would he be like, when he came? Perhaps he would be burning hot, or terrible to look on. Perhaps his eyes would be like the eyes of a beast . . . She willed her mind to stop making such thoughts. It was hard, this time of waiting. She wished for the magic smoke again and the strength it gave, the great thoughts that in the morning had seemed so clear. In time she slipped, unwillingly, into a doze.

The moon was higher, when she woke again; and this time, she knew without doubt, she had been roused by something more corporeal than the wind. She lay still, trembling, straining her ears. Almost she cried out; but the thought of her voice echoing through the dimness of the hut choked the sound in her throat. Then she heard them; the stealthy, padding footfalls, coming down the moon-shot dark toward her.

She rolled over, scrabbling at the bracken. Her vision swam and sparked. A blur of movement, sensed more than seen; and a figure stepped into the chamber. She stayed crouched and still, glaring up. The moon, touching the wattle screens, gave a dim, diffused light. For her eyes, tuned to blackness, it was enough; she could see, now, every terrible detail.

The creature before her was naked, seeming taller than a man. Round calves and thighs ran delicate, scrolling lineworks of tattoo; above the thighs the manhood swung, a great, thrusting, forward-jutting column. More tattoos marked the breasts; while in one hand the figure gripped a Staff of Power, topped by the Sign of the Corn Lord. Its head alone was invisible, covered by a great fantastic mask; black in this light but green she knew, green as the sprouting grain. She did scream then, high and shrill; and the creature growled impatiently. 'Be quiet, little fool,' it said. 'The God is here.'

The form was Godlike; but the voice, though muffled by the mask, she knew too well. It was the voice of Cha'Acta.

Her limbs, that had been stiff with fear, were loosened. She scuttled for the doorway, ducking, fending off the clutching arms; but the High Priest caught her by the hair, flung her heavily back to the couch. She lay panting, tried to roll aside. He stooped above her; the mask caught her a bruising blow on the cheek. She scrabbled, biting and scratching; and the thing fell clear, showed her Cha'Acta's contorted face. She flung herself at him then, beating and pummelling with her fists; but her wrists were caught, blows rained on her body. She curled whimpering, wrapped round a bright ball of pain; she was lifted, thrown down and lifted again. Lights spun before her eyes, like the magic lights of the seed-smoke. When the beating was over she could no longer see; and her mouth felt loose and stinging. She lay dully, unable to resist, feeling the great weight of Cha'Acta press across her. After that the dream or nightmare was repeated many times, till the middle of her body felt one great burning pain; but toward dawn, the High Priest let her be.

II

She moved slowly, in the cold grey light, hanging her draggled hair. Rolled over, groped with her heels for the hard earth floor. The movement caused giddiness, and a vast sickness; she hung her head again and tried to vomit, but nothing came.

In time the sickness passed a little. She opened her eyes blearily, stared down. Her body, that had been smoothly white, was ugly now with bruises, marked with dried blood. She panted, holding her hands out in front of her face. They were dark-striped too.

She set her teeth, edged to her knees beside the pitcher. The water, splashed over shoulders and head, brought a little more awareness. She worked clumsily, rubbing herself clean. Lastly she drank, swilling the metallic taste from her mouth.

Lying across the bed was a tunic of fine bleached linen, decorated on the breast with the motif of the God. She stared at it for a while then stood, worked it painfully over her head. She peered out between the wattle screens. The dawn light showed her a huddled shape by the outer door. She began to creep toward it, an inch at a time, setting her feet down noiselessly.

Some sixth sense roused Cha'Acta. He sat up, holding out an arm; and the great mask of the God crashed against his skull. He groaned, gripping his hands round the ankles of the Bride. Mata struck again, frenzied, bringing the mask down from a height. The eyes of Cha'Acta rolled upward, disclosing the whites. The High Priest arched his body, breath whistling through his nose; but his fingers still held firm. The third blow opened the skin of his scalp in a white half moon that flooded instantly with red. He fell back, head against the pale rough wall; and Mata ran.

Fear lent her speed. Only at the bottom of the Mound she paused, doubled up, hands gripping beneath her kilt. The spasm ebbed; she stared up fearfully, certain she had been seen. But the village and the high rough slope of grass lay deserted.

She set off again, walking and running by turns, rubbing to ease the stitched cramps in her side. For a time she followed, more or less blindly, the path of the Great Procession. Once out of sight of the pass and the Sacred Mound, instinct made her turn aside. In the low ground between hills and sea, an arm of forest thrust black and ragged in the early light. Here her people never ventured; for the forest was the haunt of wolves and bears, wildcats and savage ghosts, and shunned by all right-minded dwellers on the chalk. By mid-morning she was deep among the trees, safe for the time from observation.

Her fasting, and the terror of the night, were rapidly taking their toll. She fell often, stumbling over creepers and unseen snags. Each time it was longer before she rose. She stopped at last, staring round her fearfully. About her the trees had grown higher; their vast shapes, black and looming, cut back all but a glimmer of light. Between the gnarled trunks the ground was rough and broken, carpeted with old briars; branches and twigs hung motionless, and there were no sounds of birds.

She rubbed a hand across her wet face, staggered on again. Her blindness led her finally to the head of a little bluff. She saw it too late; the rank grass slope, sheen of water and mud ten feet below. She landed heavily, with a thudding splash. The soft ground saved her at least from broken bones; she crawled a yard, then two, lay thinking she would never rise again.

The wind blew then, stirring at last the tops of the trees, whispering in the tangled undergrowth.

She lifted her head, frowning, trying to force her mind to work. The breeze came again; and she seemed to see, with great clearness, the yellow slopes of the hills she had left forever.

She raised herself, moaning. Here, between the trees where nothing came but Devils, no God would ever search to find her bones. Her limbs jerked puppet-fashion, outside her control; tears squeezed from her eyes; but her mouth moved, whispering a prayer. To the Corn Lord, the Green One, the Waker of the Grain.

The way lay across a shallow marsh, its surface streaked with bands of brownish scum. She crossed it, floundering. The sun was higher now; her mind recorded, dully, the impact of heat on back and arms. On the far bank she rested again, thrust half from sight beneath a tangle of lapping briars. Beyond, the ground sloped smoothly upward; and it seemed her Lord called from ahead, ever more strong and clear. She toiled forward, sensing the thinning of the trees. She broke at last from a fringe of bracken, stumbled and dropped dazedly to her knees.

Ahead of her, bright in sunlight, stretched a long, smooth ridge of chalk. Across it, curving close to the forest edge before swinging to climb to the crest, ran a rutted track; and crowning the ridge at its farthest end was a village, fenced about by watchtowers and a stockade. In such a place she had been born, and reared; but this was not her home. She had never seen it before.

She lay a while where she had fallen, face against the soft, short turf. She was roused by a jangling of harness, the trundle of wheels. She sat up, thankfully. Along the track, jogging gravely, moved a bulky two-wheeled cart, loaded high with faggots. Its driver reined at sight of her; and she forced her bruised lips to make words. 'Bring me to your headman,' she said. 'And my God will reward you, granting you great happiness.'

The driver stepped forward cautiously, bent over her. She twisted her face up, trying to smile; and for the first time, saw his eyes.

Gohm, the woodman, had never been too strong in the head; he bit at a broken nail, frowning, puzzling his sluggish wits. 'Who are you?' he said slowly, in his thick voice. 'Some forest spirit, fallen from a tree?' He turned her over, roughly; then snatched at the top of the filthy tunic. The fabric gave; he stared at what he saw, and began to giggle. 'No spirit,' he said. 'Or if you are, you have no power here.' He drove two calloused fingers beneath her kilt; then, because she screamed so, kicked her in the mouth. After this he did several more things before tossing her into the cart, covering her roughly with bundles from the load. 'Now certainly,' he said, 'the Gods have smiled on Gohm.' He shook the reins; the cart lurched, trundling on up the steep rise toward the village.

At the far end of the muddy street the woodman reined. 'Woman,' he bellowed, 'see what the Gods have sent. A slave to scour your pots and blow the fire; and better still for me.'

The woman who peered from the low doorway of the hut was as grey and lined, as thin and lizard-quick as he was bear-like and slow. 'What are you babbling about, you old fool?' she grumbled, scrambling on to the rear step of the cart. She pushed the faggots aside; then stayed stock still, eyes widening, hand pressed across her mouth. Gohm too was arrested, his wandering attention riveted for once; for the bag of bones and blood with which he had cumbered his life still owned two white and blazing eyes, fixed on him now in a stare terrible in its intensity. 'This is your evil day, Gohm Woodchopper,' it whispered. 'Those fingers, first to defile, hew no more sticks; no water will they draw for you, not if you lie dying.'

With that the shape collapsed abruptly, lying still as death; and the woman reached thin fingers to the mud-stained cloth of the tunic, traced there beneath the dirt the Mark of the Lord.

To Mata existence was a dull and speechless void, shot through with flashes that were greater pains. She was lodged in a fresh-swept hut, and women appointed to wash and heal her body, minister to her needs; but of this she was unaware, and remained unaware for many days to come. Meanwhile the Fate called down on Gohm worked itself out swiftly enough. A bare week later, while cutting wood at the forest edge, he gashed two fingers deeply with his hook. The wounds, instead of closing, widened, yellowed and began to stink; while the pain from them grew so great it drove him wild. One day he took an axe and, going behind the hut, struck the agonised members from him; but the wild surgery did little to improve his condition. He took to wandering by himself, grey-faced and mumbling, and it was no surprise when his body was brought in from the trees. The corpse was much disfigured, torn as if by bears, and the face quite eaten away. This happened within a month of Mata leaving the wood; and the village that sheltered her grew silent and fearful. Men crept to the hut where she lay, avoiding its shadow, to leave rich gifts; so that when she finally woke it was to considerable estate.

The news at first meant little to her. She lay in the hut, surrounded by her women, eating little, watching the sailing clouds in the sky, the rich waving green of trees. Summer had come once more; the Corn Lord, though thwarted of his Bride, had yet fulfilled his promise. She frowned at the thought, revolving many things; then rose and sought an audience with the headman.

He received her in the Council Hut; very similar it was to the Lodge in which her father had once sat. Beside him stood his Chief Priest; and at him Mata stared comfort-lessly a great while. Finally she turned, tossing her head. 'Chief,' she said, 'what do you wish of me?'

The headman spread his hands, looking alarmed. The tale of Gohm had not been lost on him; this pale-faced, brilliant-eyed child made him uneasy in his chair of office. 'Our wish,' he said humbly enough, 'the wish of all my people, is that you stay here with us and let us honour you. Also if you will speak well for us to your Lord, our crops will grow straight and tall.'

The Chief Priest had begun to fidget; Mata turned back to him her disquieting stare. 'This is good to hear,' she said carefully, 'and pleasing to the God. But I have heard of other towns where though fine words are spoken they are not supported by deeds.'

The headman burst into voluble protests, and Mata was pleased to see that sweat had formed on his forehead. 'Look, then, that it be so,' she said. 'For my Lord loves me well, and invests much strength in me. My touch brings death and worse; or pleasure, and great joy to men.' She stretched her hand out, and was secretly amused to see the other draw back. 'Now this is the wish of the God,' she said. 'You shall build, on the hill beside the town, a great house. Its length shall be thirty paces, measured by a tall, strong man, its breadth five and a span . . .' She went on, as well as her memory served, to give a description of the God House of Cha'Acta. 'Here I shall live with my Lord,' she said, 'and such women as I choose to gather and instruct.' She glanced sidelong at the growing darkness of the Chief Priest's face, and spoke again rapidly. 'Here also,' she said, 'your holy Priest shall come, and many good things will happen to him. Also he must bless the work, and oversee each stage of building; for he is loved by the God, and a great man in your land.' She dropped to one knee before the priest, and saw his expression change from hatred to wondering suspicion.

So a new God House was built; and there Mata lived, in some luxury. She took as bedmate a slim brown child,

Alissa; her she taught carefully, instructing her in Mysteries and the pleasuring of Gods and others. There also, when the mood was on her, she summoned Cha'Ilgo, the Chief Priest; and made herself, with time, most pleasing to him.

They were good days, in the Long House on the crest of the hill; but all summers reach their end. The leaves of the forest were changing to red and gold when Mata once more called the priest and headman to her. 'Now I must leave you,' she said without preamble. 'For last night my God came to me in the dark, while all the village slept. His hair was yellow as the sun, brushing the rafters where he stood beside my bed; his flesh was green as rushes or the sprouting corn, his member greater than a bull and wonderful to see. He told me many Mysteries, not least this; that out of love for you I must leave Alissa, who is dear to me as life, to be your new Corn Queen. In this way you will be happy, when I am gone; the barley will spring and you will have your fill of beer, cheese and all good things.'

They heard her words with mixed emotions. Cha'Ilgo at least had come to regard her presence highly; yet it was not without relief he saw her litter pass, for the last time, the armed gates of the town. She had come friendless and alone; she left in mighty state, Hornmen and fluters before her and a company of spears. Her kilt was white as snow; necklaces of pebbles and amber adorned her throat, round her slim ankles were rings of bright black stone. Behind her swayed other litters with her treasures and going-gifts; seed grain and weapons, jars of honey and beer, moneysticks of fine grey iron. Behind again came trudging sheep and oxen, and a great concourse of villagers.

Cha'Acta was warned of her approach by the horns and thudding drums. He came to the village gates to see for himself, while Mata's folk lined the stockade walks with their spears, biting their beards uncertainly. It was Magan the headman who first recognised his daughter; he rushed to greet her rejoicing, amazed at her return from the dead. The gates were swung wide, the company tramped through; and there was a time of great rejoicing. For the Corn Bride was reborn; the Gods could smile again on the village in the steep chalk pass.

For a time Cha'Acta and his priests held aloof, huddling in the Council Lodge talking and conspiring; till black looks from the villagers, and a plainer hint from Magan, forced the issue. The High Priest entered the hut where Mata was lodged suspiciously enough, leaving a handful of armed followers at the door; but she ran to him with cries of joy. She brought him beer, serving him with her own hands; afterwards she knelt before him, begging his forgiveness and calling him her Lord. 'My eyes were blinded, till I could not see the truth,' she said. 'I saw Cha'Acta, but could not see the God; though he blazed from him most splendidly.' She poured more beer, and more, till his eyes became less narrow, and he unbent toward her fractionally. Across his brow ran a deep diagonal scar, the mark she had given him with the mask; she touched it, tenderly, and smiled. 'For this I was punished, and justly so,' she said. She showed him the white half-moon on her chin, where Gohm's boot had torn the lip away, the crossing wheals on legs and thighs from her wild flight through the wood. 'Also,' she said, lifting her kilt still further, 'see how I have grown, Cha'Acta my priest. Now the God has ordered that I return, to love you better than before.' Then despite himself the manhood in Cha'Acta rose, so that he took her several times that very night, finding her sweet beyond all normal experience. 'The God first entered me when I worked at cutting his reeds,' she said later. 'Now he comes to me again, in you. Let it be so forever, Lord.'

The trees blazed, slowly shed their leaves. For a time the air remained warm; but when the first frosts lay on the ground, whitening the long slopes of the fields, news came that disturbed the new-found tranquillity of the tribe. Strangers appeared in the valley, refugees from the unknown lands that stretched beyond the Great Heath. They brought with them wild tales of a new people, a race of warriors who lived not by the peaceful tilling of the soil but by plunder, by fire and the sword. Some said they came from the Middle Sea, some from Hell itself, braving the roughest seas in their fast, long ships. Each warrior, it seemed, was a King in his own right, claiming kinship with certain Gods; wild Gods, rough and bloody and dark, whose very names sent thrills of fear through the storytellers as they uttered them. There were tales of whole villages destroyed, populations wiped out; for the invaders preyed on the land like an insect swarm, leaving it bare and ruined behind them. The elders shook their heads over the stories. Nothing like them had ever come their way; but there seemed little to be done, and with the first real snow the trickle of refugees stopped. For a time, nothing more was heard.

Mata paid little attention to the tales. Her power with the people had increased; for her wanderings had taught her very well how to win respect. Always now she was at Cha'Acta's side; and always behind her stood the great Corn Lord, warming her with his presence. Children and babes in arms were brought to her; for it was believed magic dwelt in her touch, the young ones she blessed would grow up healthy and strong. Yet always she was careful to defer to Cha'Acta, so that Chief Priest had little cause for complaint. Each night he came to her in the God House; for the child who had once proved such an able pupil was now a willing mistress. So much was she to his liking that when the seed time was nearly due again and the ploughs went out to scratch the thin-soiled fields, the question of a new Bride for the God had not been raised.

It was Cha'Acta who broached the matter, late one night. The sea mist lay cold and clammy on the hill, eclipsing the torches on the village watchtowers, swirling round the fire that burned in the great hut. Mata heard him for a while; then rose impatiently, flicking a heavy shawl across her shoulders, and walked to the hut door. She stood staring into the void, feeling the cold move on stomach and thighs. After a while she spoke.

'Where will the God find a Bride to equal what he loses?' she asked amusedly. 'Can another do the Magic Thing, that pleases Cha'Acta so much? Will another be loving, and as warm? Will the barley spring better for her than me?'

The High Priest waited, brooding; for he knew her power. Also, he was loth to lose her. He made no answer; and she turned back, walked swaying toward him, her eyes dark and huge. 'Also,' she said, 'what would become of me? Would I be found too one day face down in a pool, with the brook fish nibbling me?'

He stirred impatiently. 'Let us have no more of this,' he said. 'For all your beauty you are still a child, Mata. You do not understand all Mysteries.'

She felt the God inside her, giving her strength. She kicked the fire barefooted, sending up a shower of sparks. 'This I understand,' she said. 'That there are Mysteries best not told, Cha'Acta priest; or spears would be raised, and sacred blood would surely make them unclean.'

Cha'Acta rose, eyes smouldering with rage. He moved toward her, lifting his hands; but she stood her ground, flung the shawl back and laughed. 'Look, Cha'Acta,' she said. 'Look before you strike, and see the Magic Thing.'

He stared for a time wild-eyed. So easy now to strangle her and cut, show what was left for the work of some wild beast . . . Sweat stood on his forehead; then he fell back, rocking and groaning. 'Do not taunt me, Mata,' he said hoarsely. 'I mean no harm to you.'

His chance was gone; and they both knew it. She stood a moment longer, smiling down; then dropped to her knees beside him. He gripped her, gasping; and she was very loving to him. They lay all night, in the close light of the fire, and Mata gave him no rest; till toward dawn he slept like one of the dead. She roused him in due course, feeding him broth and beer; afterwards she dressed, came and sat obediently at his feet. 'My Lord,' she said, 'tell me now of these thoughts that I am to go, and another take my place.'

He shook his head, eyes hooded. 'No one will take your

51

place, Mata,' he said. 'You know that well enough.'

She pursued him, gently. 'But, Lord, the people will wish it.'

He said, 'The people can be swayed.'

'I would not bring grief to my Lord Cha'Acta.'

He said hopelessly, 'You can persuade them, Mata. If no other.'

She stared up under her brows, eyes luminous. 'Then do you give me leave?'

He banged his fists on his knees, pressed them to his forehead. 'Do what you will,' he said. 'Take what you wish, speak as the Lord moves you; but for my sake, stay his Bride.'

She sat back, clapping her hands delightedly. 'Then let Cha'Acta too swear his constancy,' she said. 'By the great God, who stands at his shoulder as he stands at mine. For I have seen him many times, my Lord; his prick is long as a rush bundle, and as hard and green.'

He groaned again at that; for she had a way of rousing him with words even when her body was quiet. 'I swear,' he said finally. 'In the God's own house, where he must surely hear.'

So a pact was made between them; and Cha'Acta found he could not break the invisible bonds with which she had tied him.

By early summer, the people had begun to murmur openly; for the planted corn was springing and still no Procession had been called, no new Bride chosen for the God. Mata herself stilled them, speaking from the step of the Council Lodge; an unheard-of thing for a girl or woman to do. 'Now I tell you,' she said, 'the Procession will take place, as always before. Also the God, speaking through Cha'Acta, has let his choice be known. It is this; that I, and no other, will lead his priests, his Bride of a second summer.'

There were shocked mutterings at that, and some fists were shaken. She quelled the disturbance, instantly. 'Listen to me again,' she said. She raised her voice above the rest. 'In another place, a man once lifted his hand to me; the flesh dropped very quickly from his bones. My Lord, who is swift to bless, is swifter yet to punish; for his voice is the rolling thunder of heaven, his anger the lightning that splits the stoutest trees.'

The villagers still growled uncertainly. Men stared at each other, gripping the handles of their daggers and pulling at their beards.

'Now hear another thing,' said Mata. She spoke more quietly; by degrees, the crowd stilled again. 'Your grain will sprout higher and stronger than before,' she said. 'Your animals will thrive, and you will prosper. No evil shall come in all the season, while I rule the God's House. And if I lie, I tell you this; you may fling me from the Mound, and break my bones.' She said no more but turned away, pushing impatiently through the crowd. It parted for her, wonderingly; and no man raised his voice when she had gone.

Her words had been bold; but when Cha'Acta taxed her with them she merely smiled. 'The God spoke truth to me,' she said serenely. 'As you will see.'

The summer was such as the valley had never known. The grain stood taller than the oldest villager could remember, waving and golden and rich. No wind or rain came to spoil the harvest, so that the storage pits were filled to their brims and more had to be dug, lined with wickerwork and clay. The cattle and sheep grew fat on the valley pastures, the harvest celebrations were the finest ever known; and after that all made way for Mata as she walked, stepping respectfully clear of her shadow.

To Cha'Acta also it seemed she was possessed. She had taken to sniffing the magic seeds again; she used them constantly, claiming they gave her clearer sight. Often, now, she had visions of the God. Also he came to her more frequently; and once took her in full sight of all the people, so that she lay arching her back and crying out, and spittle bearded her chin. At that even the Chief Priest fled from her, in more than religious awe.

Then more signs of the raiders began to appear.

Once again, bands of wanderers started filtering through the valley. All were ragged; many bore gaping wounds. The villagers fed them from their own supplies, turning troubled eyes toward the north. Some nights now the horizon glowed an angry red, as if whole towns were burning far across the Plain. Once a party under Magan ventured in that direction, several days' journey; they came back telling of scorched fields, blackened ruins where once had stood peaceful huts. At this Cha'Acta sat in council with the priests and elders of the tribe; a long and solemn council that went on a whole day and night. Mata attended for a time; but the smoke that filled the big Lodge annoyed her, stinging her eyes, while the babble of so many voices confused her brain. She ran away to her own great house on the Mound, lay all night dreaming and watching up at the stars. At dawn she sniffed the Magic Smoke again; and a vision came to her so splendid she ran crying to the village while the sun still stood red on the hills, throwing her long flapping shadow across the grass. The news she told sent men scurrying, uncertainly at first and then more eagerly, toward the Sacred Mound. Today, she proclaimed, the God held open house; and the people trooped after her, not without superstitious shudderings. Cha'Acta, emerging with his followers, found the watch-towers empty, the street deserted save for the witless and the very old; while the crest of the Sacred Mound was black with folk. There was nothing left him but to follow, raging.

The people had gathered in a great half-moon on that side of the Mound that faced the village; the space before the God House was filled by them. Mata herself stood facing them, outlined sharply against the brilliant sky. Beneath her heels, a sheer stone face plunged to the yellow cliff of grass; beyond, tiny and far-off, rose the russet heads of the trees that lined the brook.

Cha'Acta, panting up the last incline at the head of his troupe, was in time to catch her final words.

'And so by this means we shall be saved; for none will dare raise a hand against us, while the God himself watches from the hill and his limbs are scoured and bright. It will be a work like no other in the world. By its aid, and my Lord's protection, you will become famous, and wealthier than before; for men of other tribes will surely journey many days to see.'

Cha'Acta had heard more than enough. He marched to the centre of the circle below the wall, holding up his arms for quiet. In his robes of office, blazoned with the Mark of the God, he made an impressive figure. The hubbub that had risen was stilled; Mata alone remained smiling, hands on her hips. She watched indifferently from her wall, the black, long hair flicking across her face.

'Come down from there,' said the Chief Priest sharply. 'And hear me, all you people. This is an evil thing that you have done.'

The villagers buzzed angrily; and he turned, pointing, the sleeve of his robe flapping in the wind. 'This is no time for toys,' he said. 'To the north, not five days' journey away, are many warriors; more warriors than you or I, any of us, have ever seen. Where they come from, no man can tell; but they bring with them death and fire, and that you know full well, as well as I. Now for a night and a day we have sat in the Council Lodge, debating many things, always with the safety of the people in our hearts. For a time, we were unsure; then there came among us a certain God, who was green and tall . . .'

'That is surely strange,' piped up an old, grizzled-bearded man. 'For the God was with his Bride, with Mata here. From her own lips we heard it.'

Cha'Acta had never in his life been contradicted by a commoner; his brow flushed with rage, for a moment he considered striking the other to the ground. He swallowed, and forced himself to remain calm. 'I am the High Priest of the God,' he said coldly. 'You forget your station; thank the God that in his mercy he lets you keep your tongue.' He raised his arms again. 'I am your Priest,' he said.

55

'Have I not counselled you wisely, and brought you to prosperity? Is this not true?'

A roar cut him short. Voices shouted, above the din.

'Mata . . . Mata led us . . .'

Cha'Acta felt sweat running beneath his robes. The mob surged forward; he checked it, imperiously. 'Hear me,' he said. 'Hear me, for your lives. The people from the north have told us, and some of you have seen, that a stockade is no defence against these warriors. For they press so thick against it, cutting and stabbing with their swords, that the stoutest fence is finally thrown down. Now what we must do is this. We must ring the village, on its weakest side, with a great bank and ditch. The chalk we shall pile high, so it is steep and slippery to climb; and in the ditch, planted close together, we shall set forests of pointed stakes. The stockade we shall line with our best slingers and archers, and hold the enemy away until he tires. This the God revealed to me; and this we must do at once.'

'And this the God revealed to me,' shouted Mata. She stooped and snatched up something that lay at her feet, held it out for all to see; a goat hide, cured to suppleness, bearing in great black charcoal strokes the figure of a man. The club he carried he brandished fiercely over his head; his eyes glared; his great member rose proudly, thrusting up before his chest. 'See the God's own shape,' said Mata. 'For so he appeared to me not two hours since, as I sat here on the grass. While you and your greybeards, Cha'Acta, wagged your silly heads in the Council Lodge and talked long, stupid words.'

At that the blood seemed to flow from Cha'Acta's face and arms, leaving him icy cold. 'Mata Godbride,' he said, 'you lie . . .'

Mata's eyes were sparkling at last, brilliant with hate. 'And you lie, holy priest,' she shouted. 'Before the people, and in sight of the God.' She danced on the wall, wrenching at the neck of her tunic. 'In the reedbed, before he took me to wife, the Corn Lord put his Mark on me,' she said. 'This is a great Mystery; greater than Cha'Acta's . . .'

The crowd bellowed; and the Chief Priest, face blazing white to the lips, called hoarsely. 'Mata, as you love me . . .'

'As I love you?' she squalled. 'For this I have waited, Cha'Acta, many moons, and suffered your weight on me . . .' She flung out an accusing arm. 'Cha'Acta Priest,' she shouted, 'took me against my will, forcing me in the Sacred House there when I was promised to the God. And Cha'Acta took the Bride Choele, killing her afterwards to seal her tongue—'

Cha'Acta waited for no more. He ran with surprising speed across the grass, up the swell of ground to the wall. In his hand gleamed a short, curved knife. Mata didn't move; she stood contemptuously, feet spread on the wall, hair flogging her bare white shoulders. Ten paces he was from her, five, three; and something flickered in the high, warm light. Few saw the flight of the spear; but all heard the thud as it struck home, full between the High Priest's shoulder-blades.

Cha'Acta had gained the base of the wall. He stood quite still for a moment, eyes wide, ashen face turned towards the girl. One hand was to his chest; across the fingers, where the iron tip of the weapon pierced the flesh, ran a thin, bright trickle of blood. He raised the knife, uncertainly; then his legs lost their strength. His body toppled, crashing through the bushes below the wall; then it was bounding, faster and faster, down the sheer slope of grass. The onlookers, rushing forward, saw it strike the base of the Mound, fly loose-limbed into the air. A stout tree shook to its top, a splash arose; then he was gone, and the stream was rolling him away.

For a moment longer the crowd stared, pale-faced and shocked, edging back from where Magan stood wide-eyed, glaring at the fingers that had made the cast. Then Mata raised her arms.

'Build the God . . . !'

The shout spread, on the instant; she was seized and swung from hand to hand, carried by the surging, rejoicing mob down the long slope of the Mound.

Through the rest of the day the villagers scurried across the face of the great hill, roping out a grid pattern two hundred paces deep, nearly a hundred and fifty broad. At nightfall, fires sprang up at a score of points around it. The work went on far into the hours of darkness; women and children toiled forward and back across the slope, bringing fuel for the beacons. At first light Mata, who had not slept, began her part. Men followed her, wonderingly. She carried the tiny drawing of the thing to be; over it, they saw, she had inscribed a network of the same fine crossing lines. She worked methodically, with many pauses and checks, pressing lines of white pegs into the ground; by midday nearly half the Giant was visible, and work had started on the cutting of the head. Men tore at the turf with hatchets and antler pricks; others shuffled forward and back up the hill, doubled over by the weight of baskets of chalk rubble that were tipped out of sight among the bushes of the Mound. In the village hearths burned low, babies cried unfed; while lines of women, both old and young, scurried across the hill, wearing a maze of new tracks in the grass, bringing platters of fish and meat to the workers, and jugs of milk and beer. At nightfall Mata left her marking-out to supervise the digging at the shoulders. The trenches, she proclaimed, were everywhere too narrow; she ordered them widened to the span of a tall man's arm, and deepened by a foot or more. Fresh shifts of workers scurried to the task; and by the second dawn the head and shoulders were complete.

With the dawn came a little group of strangers. They stood far off below the Sacred Mound, well out of the longest bowshot, and stared up at the hill. Magan marked them worriedly, shading his eyes with his hand. They were too distant for details to be clear; but their clothes seemed not to be the clothes of chalk dwellers, and on their heads he caught the gleam of iron. Also he saw that each had come on horseback, a nearly unheard-of thing; he could make out the animals grazing, farther down the slope. A party was detached to investigate; but long before they came within hail the strangers wheeled their mounts and trotted away.

Mata, dark lines of tiredness under her eyes, still scurried from point to point, directing every detail of the work; and slowly, sparkling-white, the Giant grew. The arms developed hands, the hands burst into fingers; then the great club came into being, vaunting across the grass. But by midday the valley floor was once more a-straggle with refugees. They shuffled past in groups, staring in wonderment at the toiling villagers; and one of them called up. 'What are you doing, fools who live on the chalk?' he said. 'Do you think the Horse Warriors will be frightened of your little picture? Will they run with hands above their heads, crying "Oh"?'

Magan, poised on a slight eminence with the spears of his bodyguard clustered round him, answered loftily enough. 'Get to the sea, old man, and do not trouble us with chatter. This is God's work, and a magic thing.' But even as he spoke the headman lifted his eyes worriedly, scanning the vacant outlines of the hills.

By the third evening, the trickle of refugees had once more thinned; but fires burned close, reflecting angrily from the clouds. Also, carried on the wind, came the dull throb of drums; and for the first time folk paused uneasily in their work, stared questioningly at each other. Then it was that Magan sought out his daughter; but she brushed him away. 'Be silent, Father,' she said. 'You have already killed a Chief Priest; hold your peace, or perhaps the God will kill you too.'

By the fourth dawn the Giant's great prick lay proud and gleaming across the hill, and the diggers were working on his feet and calves. The drums had beat throughout the night; now they fell ominously quiet. One scout, posted by Magan a mile or more out on the heath, returned swearing he had seen the glint of armoured marching men; the others never came back at all.

Then Magan frowned, seeing where faith had led them; but there was no time left for further reflection. From over the skyline beyond the Sacred Mound galloped a column of riders. They came with terrifying speed, fanning out across the turf, banners and standards fluttering; from them as they swept closer rose a harsh, many-throated roar.

Magan, shouting despairingly for his spears, ran down the hillside, whirling his own sword above his head. Everywhere men flung down their mattocks, grabbed for weapons. A line formed, packed and jostling. It checked the charge; though the weight and pace of the riders tore great gaps in the villagers' ranks. The warriors, fighting well, re-formed; and a desperate retreat began, up across the sloping grass to the stockade gates. Behind the fight women and old folk scurried across the hill, flinging their baskets of rubble aside as they ran. Mata, hacking wildly at the turf, glared up to find herself nearly alone. The Giant was all but complete, part of one foot only remaining to be worked; but her voice, shrill as a bird, went for the moment unheeded.

Magan, fighting his hardest, heard behind him a fresh sound of disaster. He glanced back, appalled; and a groan burst from him. Over the stockade black smoke climbed into the sky, fringed at its base with leaping tongues of flame; on the ramparts tiny figures swayed, locked in deadly combat. The attack had been two-pronged after all; the second column of raiders, approaching unseen, had already taken the all-but-deserted village, and fired the huts.

Hope had gone; now only one thing remained. The headman raised his voice in a great shout.

'The Giant . . . Fight to the Giant, and stand . . .'

The lines reeled, locked and breathless; a battling half-moon formed, withdrawing step by step across the grass. Against it the raiders charged again and again, with reckless skill. Everywhere men had fallen, lay tumbled in ungainly heaps, half-seen through the drifting smoke. Magan opened his mouth to shout again; and a lance, wickedly barbed, took him in the throat, stood out crimsoned a foot beyond his head.

Behind the fighting men, almost between the legs of the horses, a frenzied little group still hacked at the turf. Sweat ran, blinding, into Mata's eyes; her hair hung across her face; and arbitrarily it seemed, two trenches met. The God was finished.

She turned, yelling defiance, sent the mattock spinning at the face of a mounted man. She ran upward, diagonally across the hill. Her hair flew round her; her breasts, uncovered, swung and jolted from her dress. The grass, close before her eyes, raced and jerked; but the frenzy in her brain blinded her to all else. Level with the Giant's head she turned, squalling with triumph, staring down at the great thing Cha'Acta hadn't lived to see; and the line below her broke, the last men of the village went over in a writhing heap.

Something hummed past her, and again. She ran once more, doubling like a hare; for only her own folk used the sling. Beside her a woman staggered in mid-stride, twisting to show her shattered forehead. Mata glared up, at the stockade and watchtower; and there was the dark blur of a descending missile. For a moment, while sense remained, she wondered how the sky could have made a fist, hit her so terribly in the mouth; then her legs buckled, she rolled back with the slope. She fetched up, finally, in the Giant's heel; behind her on the grass stretched wavering spots of red.

He came floating at last from agony and dark, brighter and more lovely than she had seen him before. He stooped above her, frowning, his great gold eyes compassionate. Shudders shook her, racking her ruined body. It seemed she raised her arms; and his entering was first the greatest pain she had known, and afterward the greatest peace. She sighed, yielding; and the Corn Lord took her up, flew with her to a far place of delight.

The invaders were well pleased. The storage pits of the village, undamaged by the flames, had yielded grain for an

61

entire season; the valley was sheltered, opening to the south; and in all the land there were no enemies left. Their chieftains strutted, jangling the trinkets they had stolen from the dead; while those who took other pleasures from the wreckage on the hill found many of the bodies still warm.

THREE

The Beautiful One

For weeks now the heat had not abated. Day after day the hard sky pressed on the rounded chalk hills; the leaves of trees hung listless and dry, the growing grain yellowed, rivers and ruins shimmered with mirage. The nights were scarcely cooler. Men tossed and grumbled in the stockaded towns, dogs ran snapping and foam-flecked. At such times tempers are short; and the temper of the Horse Warriors was at its best an unsure thing.

Toward the end of one such baking day a column of waggons and riders rumbled steadily between hills of smooth brown grass. At the head of the cavalcade rode a troop of Warriors, their skins tawny, their beards and flowing hair dark. They carried bows and spears; and each man wore a skullcap of burnished steel. Behind them jolted an ornate siege engine, the tip of its throwing arm carved in the likeness of a great horse's head. More Warriors brought up the rear, driving a little rabble of wailing women. Clouds had thickened steadily through the day, trapping the heat even closer to the earth. Thunder boomed and grumbled overhead; from time to time men glanced up uneasily, or back to the skyline where showed the palisade and ruined watchtowers of a village. Flames licked them, bright in the gloom; a cloud of velvet smoke hung and stooped, drifting slowly to the south.

Behind the tailboard of the last waggon staggered half a dozen men. They were naked, or nearly so, and streaked with dust and blood. Their wrists were bound; ropes of plaited hide passed round their necks, tethering them to the vehicle. Two more wretches had given up the unequal struggle; the bodies towed limply, jolting over the ridges and boulders of the track.

Shouts from ahead brought the column to a halt. The pale dust swirled, settling on men and horses; the prisoners dropped to their knees, groaning and fumbling at the nooses. A group of men cantered down the line of waggons, reined. They were richly dressed in trews and tunics of figured silk; and each wore a mask of woven grass, fringed with heads of green barley. Their leader carried a gilded Staff of Power; on his chest, proudly blazoned, was the great spear of the Corn Lord.

He nodded now gravely to the Horseman at his side. 'You have done well,' he said. 'The spoil of the first waggon, the grain and unbleached cloth, is forfeit to my God. Also one in ten of the draught animals, and what sheep and goats you drive in from the hills.' He held his palms up, fingers spread. 'The rest the God returns to you, to do with as you choose. This the Reborn ordered me to say; will it be pleasing to you?'

The other showed his teeth. 'Cha'Ensil,' he said, 'it will be as your Mistress desires. The Horse Warriors too know how to be generous.'

But the other had stiffened, eyes glittering through the mask. He said, 'What have we here?'

The Horseman shrugged. 'Prisoners, for the sacrifice,' he said. He glanced at the lowering sky. 'Our God becomes impatient when the nights are sultry,' he said. 'Have you not heard his hooves among the clouds?'

'I heard the Corn Lord chuckle in his sleep,' said the priest crushingly. He pointed with the Staff. 'Show this one to me,' he said. 'Lift his face.'

The Warrior grunted, waving an arm. A man dismounted, walked to the prisoner. He twined his fingers in the matted hair, yanked. The priest drew his breath; then reached slowly to unlatch the mask. 'Closer,' he said. 'Bring him here.'

The victim was dragged forward. Cha'Ensil stared; then leaned to place strong fingers beneath the other's jaw. The cheekbones were high and delicately shaped, the nose tip-tilted and short. The green-grey eyes, glazed now with pain, were fringed with black. Blood had dried on muzzle and throat; the parted lips showed even white teeth.

A wait, while the oxen belched and grumbled, the horses jangled their bits. Then the priest turned. 'He is little more than a child,' he said. 'He will not be pleasing to your God.' He reached again to jerk at the leather noose. 'The Corn Lord claims him,' he said, 'Put him in the waggon.'

The Horseman glared, hand on his sword hilt, face flushed with anger; and Cha'Ensil raised the glittering staff level with his eyes. 'This is the God's will,' he said. 'A little price to pay, for many blessings.'

Another wait, while the other pulled at his beard. The priest he would have defied readily enough; but behind him stood One whose displeasure was not lightly to be incurred. The thunder grumbled again; and he shrugged and turned his horse. 'Take him,' he said sardonically, 'since your God gains such pleasure from striplings. The rest will serve our needs.'

The priest stared after him, with no friendly expression; then turned, gesturing once more with the Staff. A knife flashed, severing the noose. Released, the prisoner stood swaying; he was bundled forward with scant ceremony, slung into the leading cart. The tail-gate was latched shut; and Cha'Ensil rose in his stirrups, with a long yell. Whips cracked; the waggon turned jerkily from the line of march, lumbering to the south.

In the last of the light the vehicle and its escort reached a pass set between high chalk hills. The cloud-wrack, trailing skirts of mist, alternately hid and revealed the bulging slopes, crossed with sheep tracks, set with clumps of

65

darker scrub. On the nearer crest, smears and nubbles of black showed the remnants of a village. On the flanks below sprawled a great chalk figure, while foursquare in the pass rose a steep and grassy mound. Across its summit, revealed by flickerings from above, curved a long ridge of roof; round it, among spikes and nodules of stone, straggled a mass of secondary building, pale plastered walls, gables of green-grey thatch. There was a stockade, topped with disembowelling spikes; and a gateway fronted by a deep ditch and flanked by vast drums of stone, themselves leaning till the arrow slits that once had faced the valley stared sightless at the green jungle below. Between them the party cantered, with a final jangle and clash. Torches were called for and a litter, the gates re-manned; and Cha'Ensil moved upward across the sloping lower ward. The rising wind fluttered at his cloak, whipping the pine-knots into streaming beards of flame.

The little chamber was windowless and hot, hazed with a blue smoke heavy with the scent of poppies. Torchlight gleamed on white walls and close grey thatch, flickered on the Chief Priest's face as he stood expressionlessly, staring down. Finally he nodded. 'This is well,' he said. 'Prepare him. Clean the dirt away.'

A rustling of skirts, whisper of feet on the bare earth floor; clink of a costly copper bowl. The limbs of the sleeping boy were sponged, his chest and belly washed with scented water. Lastly the stained cloth-scrap was cut away.

The priest drew breath between his teeth. 'His hands and feet,' he said. 'Neglect no skill.'

The nails of the sleeper were cleaned with pointed sticks, the hair scraped from beneath his arms. His head was raised, his hair rinsed, combed with bone combs and rinsed again. Thunder grumbled close above the roof; and Cha'Ensil whitened his knuckles on his Staff. 'Prepare his face,' he said. 'Use all your art.'

Stoppers were withdrawn from jars of faceted crystal;

the women, working delicately, heightened the eyelids with a ghosting of dark green, shaped the full brows to a gentler curve. The lashes, already lustrous, were blackened with a tiny brush. The sleeper sighed, and smiled.

'Now,' said Cha'Ensil. 'Those parts that make him like a God.'

The nipples of the boy were stained with a bright dye; and the priest himself laid fingers to the groin, pressing and kneading till the member rose and firmed. Belly and thighs were brushed with a fine red powder; and Cha'Ensil stepped back. 'Put the big necklet on him,' he said. 'And circlets for his arms.'

The dreamer was set upright, a cloak of fine wool hung from his shoulders. The women waited, expectantly; and Cha'Ensil once more gripped the boy's chin, turned the face till the brilliant drugged eyes stared into his own. 'You were dead,' he muttered, 'and you were raised. Blood ran from you; it was staunched. Mud dirtied you; it was washed away. Now you go as a God. Go by the Staff and Spear; and the God's strength be with you.' He turned away, abruptly. 'Take him to the Long House,' he said. 'Leave him in the place appointed, and return to me. We must pray.'

The rumbling intensified, till it seemed boulders and great stones were rolled crashing through the sky. Lightning, flickering from cloud to cloud, showed the heads of grasses in restless motion, discovered hills and trees in washes of broad grey light. The light blazed far across the sea, flecking the restless plain of water; then the night was split.

With the breaking of the storm came rain. It fell not as rain customarily falls, but in sheets and solid bars; so that men in far-off villages, woken by the roaring on their roofs, saw what seemed silver spears driven into the earth. The parched dust leaped and quivered. Rivulets foamed, on the eroded flanks of hills; twigs and green leaves were beaten from the taller trees. In the chalk pass, the brook that circled the base of the Mound raced in its deep bed; but toward dawn the violence died away. A morning wind moved across the hills, searching and cold as a knife; it brought with it a great sweet smell of leaves and fresh-soaked earth.

At first light two figures picked their way across the Mound, moving between the fingers and bosses of stone. Both were cloaked, both masked. Once they turned, staring it seemed at the flanking slope, the ruins and the chalk colossus that glimmered in the grass; and the taller inclined his head. 'My Lady,' he said in a strong, musical voice, 'when have I injured you, or played you false? When have my words to you not become true?'

The woman's voice when she answered was sharper-edged. 'Cha'Ensil,' she said, 'we are both grown folk; grown older than our years perhaps in service of the God. So keep your tales for the little new priestesses; their lips are sweeter when they are afraid. Or tell them to the Horsemen, who are little children too. Perhaps there was a Great One in the land, long ago; but he left us, in a time best forgotten, and will scarcely return now. It isn't good to joke about such things; least of all to me.'

They had reached the portal of the great hut crowning the Mound. Above, green rush demons glared eyeless at the distant heath. To either side stood bundles of bound reeds, each taller than a man; the Signs of the God. The priest laid his hand to the nearer, smiling gravely. 'Lady,' he said, 'wise you are most certainly, and wiser in many things than any man. Yet I say this. The God has many forms, and lives to some extent in each of us. In most men he is hidden; but I have seen him shine most gloriously. Now I tell you I found him, lashed to a Horseman's waggon. I knew him by the blood he shed, before I saw his face; for all Gods bleed, as penance for their people. I raised him with these hands, and placed him where he waits. As you will see.'

She stared up at him. 'Once,' she said coldly, 'a child came here, hungering for just such a God. Now I tell you this, Cha'Ensil; I raised you, and what is raised can be thrown down again. If you jest with me, you have jested once too often.'

He spread his arms. 'Lady,' he said humbly, 'my hands are at your service, and my heart. If I must give my head, then give it I shall; and that right willingly.' He stooped, preceding her into the darkness of the hut.

She paused, as always, at sight of the remembered place. She saw the floor of swept and beaten earth, the gleam of roofpoles in the half dark; she smelled the great pond-smell of the thatch. At the wattle screens that closed off the end of the long chamber she stopped again, uncertan; and his hand touched her arm. 'Behold,' he said softly. 'See the God . . .'

The boy lay quiet on the bracken bed within, his breathing even and deep. A woollen shawl partly covered him; the priest lifted it aside, and heard her catch her breath. 'If I mistook,' he said, 'then blame the weakness of my eyes on gathering age.'

She took his wrist, not looking at him. 'Priest,' she said huskily, 'there is wisdom in you. Wisdom and great love, that chides me what I spoke.' She unfastened her cloak, laid it aside. 'I will wait with him,' she said, 'and be here when he wakes. Let no one else approach.' She sat quietly on the edge of the bed, her hands in her lap; and Cha'Ensil bowed, slipping silently from the chamber.

Beyond the fringe of trees the hillside sloped broad and brilliant in sunlight. Above the boy as he lay the grass heads arched and whispered, each freighted with its load of golden specks. Between the stems he could see the valley and the tree-grown river, the reed beds where dragonflies hawked through the still afternoons. Beyond the river the chalk hills rose again, distant and massive. On the skyline, just visible from where he lay, stood the stockade and watchtower of his village.

His jerkin was unlaced; he wriggled luxuriously, feeling the coolness of the grass stroke belly and chest. He pulled a stem, lay sucking and nibbling at the sweetness. He closed his eyes; the hum of midsummer faded and boomed close, heavy with the throb of distant tides. Below him the sheep grazed the slope like fat woollen maggots; and the ram moved restlessly, bonking his wooden bell, staring with his little yellow eyes.

The boy's own eyes jerked open, narrowed.

She climbed slowly, crossing the hillside below him, gripping tussocks of grass to steady herself on the steepening slope. Once she straightened, seeming to stare directly toward where he lay; and he frowned and glanced behind him, as if considering further retreat. She stood hands on hips, searching the face of the hill; then turned away, continuing the long climb to the crest. On the skyline she once more turned; a tall, brown-skinned girl, dark hair blowing across face and throat. Then she moved forward, and clumps of bushes hid her from his sight.

He groaned, as he had groaned before; a strange, husky noise, half between moan and whimper. His teeth pulled at his lip, distractedly; but already the blood was pounding in his ears. He glared, guilty, at the indifferently cropping sheep, back to the skyline; then rose abruptly, hurrying from the shelter of the trees. Below the crest he stooped, dropping to hands and knees. He wriggled the rest of the way, peered down. The grass of the hillside was lush and long, spangled with the brilliant cups of flowers. He glimpsed her briefly, a hundred paces off; ducked, waited, and scuttled in pursuit.

There was a dell to which she came, he knew it well enough; a private place, screened with tangled bushes, shaded by a massive pale-trunked beech. He reached it panting, crawled to where he could once more see.

She lay on her back beneath the tree, hands clasped behind her head, her legs pushed out straight. Her feet were bare, and grimy round the shins; her skirt was drawn up, showing her long brown thighs. He edged forward, parting the grasses, groaning again. A long time she lay, still as a sleeper; then she began. She sat up, passing her

70

hands across her breasts, squeezing them beneath her tunic. Then she pulled at its lacings; then shook her head till the hair cascaded across her face and rolled again and again, showing her belly, the great dark patch that meant now she was a woman.

His whole being seemed concentrated into his eyes; his eyes, and the burning tip of him that pressed the ground. He saw the shrine, unreachable; he saw her fingers go to it, and press; he saw her body arch, the vivid grass. Then sun and leaves rushed inward on him as a centre, the hillside flickered out; and he lay panting, fingers wet, hearing the echo of a cry that seemed as piercing as the long cry of a bird. After which he collected himself, ran with terror as he had run before, jerkin flapping, to the valley and trees and the safe, crunching sheep. Later he sobbed, for the empty nights and days. His neck burned, and his cheeks; he begged her forgiveness, she who could not hear, Dareen whose father was rich, owning fifty goats and twice that number of sheep; Dareen whose eyes he never more could meet, never, in the village street.

The dream disturbed him. He moved uneasily, wanting it to end; and in time it seemed his wish was answered. A fume of acrid smoke seared his lungs; voices babbled; hands were on him, pressing down. It seemed he had descended to one of the Hells, where all is din and lurid light. He fought against the hands, bearing up with all his strength; and a bowl was thrust before his face. In it coals burned; their fiery breath scorched his throat. He writhed again, trying to pull back his head; but his hair was caught. The coals loomed close then seemed to recede, till they looked like a whole town burning far off in the night. After which the hard floor no longer pressed his knees. It seemed he was a bird, flying effortlessly upward into regions of greater and greater light. Then he knew he was no bird, but a God. And Dareen came to him, after all the years; he sank into her, rejoicing at last, and was content.

He was conscious at first of cool air on his skin. He rolled

71

over, mumbling. The dream-time, though splendid, was
finished; soon he must rise and dress, start his morning
chores. The soup-pots must be skimmed, the fire stoked;
billets waited to be split, the two lean cows must be
milked. He wondered that he did not hear his father's
snores from the corner of the hut. A cock crowed, somewhere close; and he opened his eyes.

At first the dim shapes round him made no sense; then,
it seemed on the instant, all memory returned. He leaped,
trembling in every limb, to the farthest corner of the
bracken bed. The movement woke the woman lying at his
side.

Her body was brown; as brown as the remembered body
of Dareen, and crusted on arms and legs with bands of
gold. Save the rings she wore nothing but a mask of
kingfisher-blue, through which her dark eyes glittered
with terror in their gaze; but her voice when she spoke was
musical and soft. 'Don't be afraid,' she said. 'Don't be
afraid, my lord. No one will hurt you here.' She stretched
an arm to him; he shrank farther into the angle of the wall,
pushing shoulder-blades into the rough wattle at his back.
She chuckled at that and said again, 'My Lord . . .' She
pulled at the shawl he held gripped. He resisted, knuckles
whitening; and it seemed behind the mask she might have
smiled. 'Why,' she said, 'you are proud and shy, which is
as it should be. But the God has already entered you once,
and that most wonderfully.' She fell to stroking his calf
and thigh, moving her fingers in cool little sweeps; and
after a while the trembling of his body eased. 'Lie down,'
she said, 'and let me hold you; for you are very beautiful.'

Truly it seemed the effects of the Magic Smoke had not
yet left him; for despite his fear he felt his eyelids droop.
She drew his face to her breasts, crooning and rocking;
and lying with her was like lying with a great rustling bird.

The sun was high when next he opened his eyes, and the
chamber empty. He sat up seeing the light stream through
the chinks of the wattle screens. He rose shakily, staring

down at the gold that ringed his own body, the great pectoral on his breast. This last on impulse he slipped from his neck, holding the shining metal close up to his eyes. The face of a stranger or a girl watched back. He laid the thing aside, frowning deeply, walked a pace at a time to the hut door. He cringed back then, terror rising afresh; for he knew the manner of place to which he had come. After which he needed to piss; this he did, trembling, against the wattle wall. An earthenware water jug stood beside the bed; he drank deeply, slaking his thirst. Then he wrapped the shawl round him and sat head in hands on the edge of the bed, and tried to think what he could do.

She came to him at midday, bringing food and drink. She helped him dress, washing him with scented oil, tucking his glory into a cloth of soft white wool. Although he cringed at first her hands were gentle; so that he all but overcame his fear of her. The fruit and bread he ate hungrily enough; the drink he spat out, expecting the taste of beer, and she laughed and told him it was Midsea wine. His head spun again at that for none of the village had ever tasted such a thing, not even T'Sagro who was the father of Dareen and who owned fifty goats. He drank again, and the second sip was better; so that he drained the cup and poured himself more, after which his head spun as it had spun when he sniffed the Magic Smoke. Also the wine made him bolder so that he said, 'Why am I here?' These were the first words he had spoken.

She stared at him before she answered. Then she said, 'Because you are a God.' He frowned at this and asked, 'Why am I a God?' and she told him in terms of forthrightness the like of which he had not heard, least of all from a woman. Also she had a trick of speech that seemed to go into his body, hardening it and creating desire. When she had left him he lay on the bed and thought he would sleep; but her words returned to him till he pulled the cloth aside and stared down at himself wondering if he might be as beautiful as she had said. Then he remembered his father and sister and the manner of their deaths, and wept. Toward nightfall he sat at the hut door and saw far off below the great fall of the hill smoke rise from where perhaps the Horsemen burned another village that had refused its dues, and felt lonelier than ever in his life. Then tiredness came on him strongly so that he lay down once more and slept. She returned by moonlight, flitting like a moth; he woke to the cool length of her pressed at his side, her hands working at his cloth. He did as he had done in the dream, entering her strongly, making her cry out with pleasure; till she had taken his strength, and he slept like one of the dead.

Later, when she brought his food, he said to her, 'What are you called?' and she said in a low voice, 'The Reborn.' The fear returned at that; but night once more brought peace.

The days passed, merging each into the next; and though he dare not wander far from the hut he found himself anticipating her visits more keenly than before. Also no fear is wholly self-sustaining; he slept more soundly, colour returned to his cheeks. She brought him a polished shield, in which to see his reflection; he took to posing secretly before it, admiring the slender strength of his body, the savage painted eyes that stared back into his own. At such times he grew big with thinking of her, and fell to devising new means of pleasuring. Also he wondered greatly at her age; for at some times she seemed old as a hill or the great Gods of the chalk, at others as young and fragile as a child. He thought how easy it would be, one day, to pull the mask away; but always his hand was stayed. He talked now, when she came, with increasing freedom; till one day, greatly daring, he told her his wish that she could always be with him in the hut. She laughed at that, a low, rich sound of joy, and clapped her hands; after which she was constantly at his side, and a green-masked priest would, come or a girl to bring their food, scratch the doorpost and wait humbly in the sunlight. She talked at great length, of all manner of things, and he to her; he told her of his life, and how he had herded sheep, and how it was to live in a village and be a peasant's child.

She said, 'I know.' She was sitting in the hut door; it was evening, the grass and tumbled stones of the hill golden in the slanting light. Goats bleated, on the slopes of the great Mound; and the air was very still.

He laid his head in her lap; she stroked him awhile, then pulled back her hand. He sat up, meaning finally to speak of the mask; and she rose, stood arms folded staring out across the hill. After a while she spoke, back turned to him. 'Altrin,' she said, 'do you truly love me?'

He nodded, watching up at her and wondering.

'Then,' she said, 'I will tell you a story. Once there was a little girl; younger than your sister, when you loved her and used to stroke her hair. She was in love too, with a certain God. He came to her in the night, promising many things; so that in her foolishness she wanted to be his Bride.'

She half turned; he saw the long muscles of her neck move as she swallowed. 'She came to a certain House,' she said. 'She lay in that House, but there was no God. So she ran away. She became rich, and powerful. When she returned it was with gold and money-sticks, and soldiers of her own. Because of her wealth her people loved her; because of their love, she gave them a Sign.' She nodded at the flanking slope, the sprawling giant with his mighty prick. 'While the Sign lay on the hill, her people would be safe,' she said. 'This the God promised; yet he turned away his face. The Horse Warriors came; the people were killed, the village put to the fire. The servant of the God was killed, there on the hill.'

He stared, swallowing in his turn; and the hut seemed very still.

'I was that child,' she said. 'I am the Reborn.'

She stepped away from him. Her voice sounded distant, and very cold. 'I lay on the hill,' she said. 'The God took me, and was very wonderful. Later, when he grew tired, he returned me to life. It was night, and there were many dead. I was one of them; and yet I crawled away. I crawled for a night and part of a day. I did not know where I was, or what had happened to me. I could not see, and there were many flies. I lay by a stream, and drank its water. Later I ate berries and leaves. I did not know what had happened to me. One day I decided a thing. I crawled to the stream and looked in, over the bank. The sun was high, so I saw myself clearly.'

She shuddered, and her hand went to the mask. 'I knew then I must die again,' she said. 'I had a little knife; but I lacked the strength to put it into myself. I got into the water, thinking I would drown; but the pain of that was too great also. I lay a day and night trying to starve; then I thought my heart might stop for wishing it. But the God refused my life, holding me strongly to the earth. I ate berries and fruit; and my strength returned.'

The boy frowned, toying with a necklace she had given him; golden bees, joined by little blue beads. He reached forward, trying to trap her ankle; but she moved aside. 'Can you think what it was like?' she said bitterly. 'I had been beautiful; now the Gods had taken my face away.'

He flinched a little; then went back to playing with the necklace, frowning up under his brows.

'I thought then, how I could get revenge on men,' she said. 'For men it was who had brought me to this pass. Then one day the God came to me, stirring me just a little. I had forgotten my body, which was as beautiful as ever. Also I couldn't find it in me to hate Him, who is yet the mightiest of Men. I clapped my hands; and he sent another Sign. A fishing bird flew past, dropping a feather on the water. I took it in my hand, seeing how it shone. I knew I could be beautiful again.'

She twined her fingers, still staring at the great hill figure. 'I made a mask, of grasses the sun had dried,' she said, 'and a crown of flowers for my hair. I bathed myself in the stream, and washed my clothes. I walked to where there had been huts and fields; but they were burned. So I walked to where there were other towns that the Horsemen

76

had not destroyed. Near one of them I saw a girl-child herding geese. "Leave your flock," I said, "and come with me. I am the Reborn, and the God is at my side."

'Truly, he was with me; for she came. We lay together, and she pleasured me. Her fingers were shy, like flowers. In the morning she brought me food. I saw a young man sowing winter wheat. "I am the Reborn," I said. "Come with me, for the God is at my side."

'So we came to where a village had stood, in a chalk pass by the sea. The Horse Warriors burned it; but being simple folk they had not dared my Hall. Nearby they had camped; for as yet they built no towns. I went to them. Thunder followed me, and fire-drakes in the sky. "Put down your weapons," I said. "I am the Reborn, and the God is at my side." The gold they had stolen I took from them, and cloth from the Yellow Lands to dress my priests. So I came home; in a litter, as of old, with Hornmen before me and my own folk round about. Yet there were none to welcome me. Instead were many ghosts; Cha'Acta, whom I killed, and Magan, whom I killed, and many more. They would not let me be.

'The Horsemen came, asking what tribute the God desired. I made them fetch me skins of fishing birds. The sower of wheat came to me. I asked how he was called. "Ensil," he said, "if it please my Lady." "Then you are Cha'Ensil," I said, "and a mighty priest. Be faithful, and you shall be mightier."

'Yet my Hall was empty; he whom once I knew had fled. The wheat sprang green and tall; naught sprang from me but tears. The Horsemen brought me tribute; yet I grieved. Then one day Cha'Ensil came to me again. He told me how he had found the God. I did not believe. He brought me to his house; and there he lay, young and beautiful, with no cloth to cover him.' She turned suddenly with something like a sob, fell to her knees and pressed her face against his thighs. 'Never leave me,' she said. 'Never go away.'

He stroked her lustrous hair, frowning through the doorway of the hut, his eyes remote.

The long summer was passing; mornings were misty and blue, a cold chill crept into the God House of nights. Faggots were brought and stacked, a great fire lit on the hard earth floor of the hut. Some days now she would barely let him rise from the couch. Many times when he was tired she roused him, showing a Magic Thing her body could do; when all else failed there was the seed-smoke, and the yellow wine. She bathed him, stroking and combing his hair; wild it was and long, brushing his shoulders like silk. Finally these things palled. Winter was on the land; the fields lay sere and brown, cold winds droned through the God House finding every chink in the wattle walls. He brooded, shivering a little, beside the fire; and his decision was reached. Custom had taught him her ways; he broached the subject delicately, as befitted his station.

'Sometimes,' he said, 'as you will know better than I, even Gods desire to ride abroad and see something of the country they own. I have such a desire; perhaps the God you say is in me is making his wishes felt.'

She seemed well pleased. 'This is good,' she said. 'When the people see you they will be glad, knowing the God is with them. I will ride with you; we must speak to my priest.'

In the months that had passed he had rarely seen Cha'Ensil; now he was summoned in haste. He came in state, resplendent in his robes of patterned silk. With him he brought his women; but at that the Reborn demurred. 'I will prepare the God,' she said. 'I and no other; for his is no common beauty.'

His hands, which had been calloused, had softened from idleness. She pared and polished his nails, tinting his palms and feet with a dark red stain. His hair she bound with delicate silver leaves, and clothes were brought for him; a cloak of dazzling silk, a tunic with the Corn Lord's broidered Sign, boots of soft leather that cased him to the knee. Lastly she gave him a strong white mare, tribute from a chieftain of the Horse People. He sat the creature gingerly enough when the time came, being more used to plough-oxen; but she was docile, and his ineptness went unremarked.

So the party set out; Cha'Ensil with his priests and soldiers, his Horn and Cymbal men; the Beautiful One on his splendid mount; the Reborn and her favoured women in tinkling litters, borne on the backs of sturdy bearers and swaying with the God's gilded plumes. They crossed the Great Heath to the villages of the Plain, curved north and west nearly to the lands of the Marsh Folk, who pay no taxes and do strange things to please their Gods. Everywhere the Horsemen bent the knee, placing hands to their beards in awe; for the Corn Lord was a mighty spirit, his fame reached very far. For Altrin, each day brought further earnest of his strength; and Mata watched with pride to see the young Prince she had made dash happy as a puppy, circling to her call.

Chieftain after chieftain hastened with gifts; and the tribute from the grim towns of the Horsemen was richest of all. The treasure waggons towered toward the end, while behind them trotted a bleating flock of goats. The eyes of the Beautiful One grew narrow at that, his mind busy; till he summoned Cha'Ensil, more curtly perhaps than one should summon a Chief Priest, to demand an accounting of the God's dues.

Cha'Ensil frowned, holding up the notched sticks on which he carved his marks; but the Prince pushed them scornfully aside. 'Everywhere I see villages that are rich,' he said. 'Both our own folk's towns and those of the Horsemen. Yet we are poor, owning barely five hundred goats and scarce that number of sheep. The Corn Lord brings this prosperity; let his tallies be increased.'

Cha'Ensil set his lips into a line. 'That is for the Reborn to decide, my Lord,' he said gently. 'For she is your Mistress, as she is mine.'

But Altrin merely laughed, flinging the bone of a game bird into the fire round which they were camped. 'Her will is mine,' he said, 'and so mine is hers. Increase the tallies; I will have a thousand goats by autumn.'

Cha'Ensil's face had paled a little; yet he still spoke mildly. 'Perhaps,' he said, 'even Princes may overreach themselves, my Lord. Also, favours freely given may freely be repented.'

The boy spat contemptuously. 'Priest, I will tell you a riddle,' he said. 'I have a certain thing about me that is long and hard. With it I defend the favours that are mine; and yet I carry no sword. What do you think it could be?'

The other turned away, shuddering and making a very strange mouth; and for the time nothing more was said.

Later, Altrin had a novel idea. First he loved the Reborn with more than usual fervour, making her pant with pleasure; then he lay with his head against her breasts, feeling beneath him the swell of her belly that was so unlike the belly of a girl. 'My Lady,' he said, 'it has come to me that you have been more than generous in your gifts. Yet one thing I lack, and desire it most of all.'

She laughed, playing with his hair. 'The God is greedy,' she said. 'But that is the way with Gods; and I for one am very glad of it. What do you wish?'

He drew his dangling hair across her breasts, and felt her tense. 'Cha'Ensil, who is a priest, has many soldiers,' he said. 'They defend him, running to do his errands, and are at his beck and call. Yet I, in whom the God himself lives, have none. Surely my state should equal his, particularly if I am to ride abroad.'

She was still awhile, and he thought perhaps she was frowning. Finally she shook her head. 'A God needs no soldiers,' she said. 'His strength is his own, none dares to raise a hand. Soldiers are well enough for lesser folk; besides, Cha'Ensil is my oldest servant. I would not see him wronged.'

He sensed that he was on dangerous ground, and let the matter rest; but later he withheld himself, on pain of a certain promise. That she gave him finally, when she was tired and her body could no longer resist. He slept curled in her arms, and well conteno.

The party returned to the high house on the chalk. Once its walls would have been ritually breached; but that was in the old times, long since gone. In every room of the complex fires roared high, fighting the winter chill. The days closed in, howling and bitter; and the snow came, first a powdering then a steadier fall. Deep drifts gathered on the eaves of the God House, blanketing the demons that clung there. But rugs were hung round the walls of the inner chamber, a second fire lit before the wattle screens; and the Reborn and her Lord dined well enough night after night, on wild pig and wine. Sometimes too the priests of the household, or their women, arranged entertainments; at devising these last the Prince showed himself more than usually adroit, and in his Mistress's heart there stirred perhaps the first pang of doubt.

With the spring, Altrin rode out again. He took with him a dozen men of his new bodyguard, later recruiting as many Horsemen into his train. The party rode east, to where fishing villages clustered round a great bight of the sea and the Black Rock begins which none may cross, Divine or otherwise. Everywhere folk quailed before the young God with his cold, lovely eyes; and what those eyes happened on, he took. Grain he sent back and goats; and once a girl-child for his Mistress, to be trained in the rites of the God. Two weeks passed, three, before he turned back to the west. The Horsemen he dismissed, paying them with grain, hides and gold from his own supply; later that day he strode back into the hut on the Sacred Mound.

She was waiting for him, in a new gauzy dress of white and green. What expression her face held could not be told; but she was pacing forward and back along the beaten earth floor, her arms folded, her chin sunk on her chest. He hurried to her, taking her hands; but she snatched herself away. 'What is this?' he said, half-laughing. 'Are you not pleased to see me?'

She stamped her slim foot. 'Where have you been?' she

said. 'What are you thinking of? I cried for you for a week. Then I was angry, then I cried again. Now—I don't care if you've come back or not.'

A bowl and cup stood on an inlaid table, part of his winter spoil. He poured wine for himself, drank and wiped his mouth. 'I sent you a pretty child to play with,' he said. 'Wasn't that enough?'

'And I sent her back,' she said. 'I didn't want her. What use are girls to me now? It was you I wanted. *Oh* . . .'

He flung the wine away, angrily. 'You tell me I am a God,' he said. 'I wear a God's clothes, live in a God's house. Yet I must answer like a ploughboy for everything I do.'

'Not a ploughboy,' she said, 'a sheep herder. A peasant you were, a peasant you remain. *Ohh* . . .' He had turned on his heel; and she was clinging to him with desperate strength. 'I wanted you,' she said. 'I wanted you, I was so lonely. I wanted to die again. I didn't mean what I said, please don't go away. Do what you choose; but please don't go away . . .'

He stood frowning down, sensing his power. As ever, her nearness roused him; yet obscurely there was the need to hurt. His fingers curled on the edge of the brilliant mask; for an instant it seemed he would tear the thing aside, then he relaxed. 'Go to our chamber,' he said coldly. 'Make yourself ready; perhaps, if my greeting is more fitting, I shall come to you.'

Cha'Ensil, stepping to the doorway of the hut, heard the words and the sobs that answered them. He stood still a moment, face impassive; then turned, walking swiftly back the way he had come.

Some days afterward the hilltop began to bustle with activity. A new Hall was rising, below the God House and some forty paces distant; for the Reborn had decreed the older structure too chilly to serve another winter. Also extra accommodation was needed for the many hopefuls flocking to join the priesthood. The fame of the God was spreading; all were anxious to share his good fortune. The

Prince himself took a keen interest in the newcomers, selecting (or so it seemed) the comeliest virgins and the least prepossessing men; but Cha'Ensil held himself aloof from the entire affair. Later the Beautiful One rode north, and again. An extra granary was built, a new range of stables; and still the tribute waggons trundled down to the great gap in the chalk. The Horsemen bore hard upon the land; and where they rode, there also went the ensigns of the God. Smoke rose from a score of burning villages; and at last it was time, high time, to cry enough.

Cha'Ensil, seeking an audience with the Prince, found him in the New Hall, where he was accustomed to take his ease. He lay on a divan draped with yellow silk, a wine jug at his elbow and a cup. He greeted Cha'Ensil casually enough, waving him to a seat with a hand that flashed with gold. 'Well, priest,' he said, 'say what you have to quickly, and be gone. My Mistress waits; and tonight the strength of the God is more than usually in me. I shall take her several times.'

The priest swallowed but sat as he was bidden, gathering his robes about him. 'My Prince,' he began reasonably enough, 'I, who raised you to your estate, have every right to counsel you. We live, as you know full well, by the good will of the Horsemen. They fear the God; but they are children, and greed may outrun fear. This show of magnificence you seem so set on will end in ruin; for you, and for us all.'

The Prince drained the cup at a gulp, and poured another. 'This show, which is no more than my due, makes you uneasy,' he said. 'You lie jealous in your bed; and for more reasons than the ones you state. Now hear me. My strength may or may not come from the God; personally I think it does, but that is beside the point. Behind me stands One whose will is not lightly crossed; while I satisfy her, and satisfy her I think I do, your power is ended. Now leave me. Whine to your women, if you must; I am easily tired by foolishness.'

Cha'Ensil rose, his face white with rage. 'Shepherd

boy,' he said, 'I saved you for my Lady. For her sake have I borne with you; now I tell you this. I will not see her and her House destroyed. Take warning . . .'

He stopped, abruptly; for Altrin had also risen to his feet, swaying a little from the wine. A cloak, richly embroidered, hung from his shoulders; save for a little cloth, he was otherwise naked. 'And I tell you this, sower of winter wheat,' he said. 'That when the strength goes from me I may fall. But that is hardly likely yet.' He squeezed, insultingly, the great thrusting at his groin, then snatched at his hip. 'Priest,' he jeered, 'will you see the power of the God?'

But the other, mouth working, had blundered from the chamber. Behind him as he hurried away rose the mocking laughter of the Beautiful One.

The horse drummed across the Heath, raising behind it a thin plume of whitish dust. Its rider, cloaked and masked, carried a great Staff of Power. He crouched low in the saddle driving his heels at the beast's sides to urge it to even greater speed. While the fury gripped him Cha'Ensil made good time; later he slowed the weary animal to a walk. Midday found him clear of the Great Heath; at dusk he presented himself at the gates of a city of the Horsemen, a square, spike-walled fortress set above rolling woodland on a spur of chalk. There he instituted certain enquiries; while his status, and the gold he bore, secured him lodging for the night together with other services dearer to his heart. For the Chief Priest had by no means wasted his opportunities since taking service with the God of the great chalk pass. The morning brought answers to his questions. More gold changed hands; and Cha'Ensil rode north again, on a mount sounder in wind than the one on which he had arrived. Halfway through the day he bespoke a waggon train; the drivers waved him on, pointing with their whips. At nightfall, out in the vastness of the Great Plain, he reached his destination; the capital of the Horsemen's southern kingdom, a place resplendent with watchtowers and granaries, barracks and royal courts.

Here the power of the Corn Lord was less directly felt. Cha'Ensil fumed at the gates an hour or more before his purse, if not his master, secured admission. He made his way through rutted earth streets to the house of a Midsea merchant, a trader who for his unique services was tolerated even by the Horsemen. Once more, gold secured admission; and a slave with a torch conducted him to the chamber of his choice. A heavy door was unbolted, chains clinked back; and the priest stepped forward, wrinkling his nose at the odour that assailed him. To either side in the gloom stretched filthy straw pallets. All were occupied; some by women, some by young boys. The slave grunted, gesturing with the torch; and the other called, sharply.

Nothing.

Cha'Ensil spoke again; and a voice answered sullenly from the farther shadows. It said, 'What do you want with me?'

He took the torch, stepped forward and stared. Dull eyes, black-shadowed, watched up from a pallid face. The girl's hair sprawled lank on the straw; over her was thrown a ragged blanket. Cha'Ensil raised his brows, speaking gently; for answer she spat, turning her face from the glare.

The priest stooped, mouth puckered with distaste. Beneath the blanket she was naked; he searched her body swiftly for the signs of a certain disease. There were none; and he sat back on his heels with a sigh. 'Rise, and find yourself a cloth,' he said. 'I am your friend, and knew your father well. I have come to take you away from this place, back to your home.'

Cha'Ensil returned to the God House alone some few days later, and hastened to make obeisance to his mistress; but it seemed his absence had not been too much noticed. He served the Reborn well in the weeks that followed, and was unfailing in his courtesy to Altrin when chance placed the Beautiful One in his path; for his heart was more at rest.

Two months passed, and a third; the green of summer was changing to flaunting gold when he once more rode from the Sacred Mound. He headed south, to a village well enough known to him. Here, on a promontory overlooking the sparkling sweep of the sea, stood just such a Hall as the one he had quitted. He presented himself at the stockade, and was courteously received. Later he was conducted by tortuous paths to a tiny bay, closed on either side by headlands of tumbled rock. A dozen children played in the crash and surge of the water, watched over by a priest and a seamed-faced woman who was their instructress in the Mysteries. A purse changed hands; and the woman called, shrilly.

Cha'Ensil peered, shading his eyes. A lithe, brown-skinned girl waded from the water; she stood before him boldly, wearing neither cloth nor band, returning his scrutiny with a slow smile. He spoke, uncertainly; for answer she knelt before him, lowering her head as the ritual dictates.

He nodded, well pleased. 'You have worked excellently, Cha'Ilgo,' he said. 'The God defend and prosper you.' Then to the woman, 'See she is dressed, and readied for a journey. I leave inside the hour.'

That day a new priestess arrived at the Hall of the Reborn; and Cha'Ensil, whose office it was, conducted her to the Presence with pride. Altrin, seated grandly to one side, did not speak; but his eyes followed the girl as she moved through the forms of greeting and Cha'Ensil, watching sidelong, saw his brows furrow into a frown.

The opportunity for which the Chief Priest had waited was not long in coming. He was sent for, brusquely enough; a few minutes later, his face composed, he stooped into the presence of Altrin.

The Beautiful One, it seemed, was more than a little drunk. He eyed Cha'Ensil balefully before he spoke; then he said roughly, 'Who is she, husbandman?'

Cha'Ensil smiled soothingly. 'To whom,' he said, 'does my Lord refer?'

The other swore, reaching for the wine bowl. Its contents spilled; the Chief Priest hastened to assist him. The cup was recharged; Altrin, flushed, sat back and belched. He said again, 'Who is she?'

Cha'Ensil smiled once more. 'Some child of a chalk hill farmer,' he said. 'An apt pupil, as I have been told; she will no doubt prove an asset to the House.'

'Who is she?'

'Her name is Dareen,' said the Chief Priest steadily. 'The daughter of T'Sagro. Your father's neighbour, Prince.'

The other stared. He said huskily, 'How can this be?'

'I found her, in a certain place,' said Cha'Ensil. 'I freed her, thinking it would be your will.' He extended his arms. 'The emnity between us is ended,' he said. 'Let her happiness be my peace-gift to you, Lord.'

Altrin rose, his brows contracted to a scowl. He said, 'Bring her to me.'

Cha'Ensil lowered his eyes. 'Sir, it is hardly wise . . .'

'Bring her . . . !'

The other bowed. He said, 'It shall be as my Lord desires.'

The night was windy; the growing complex of wooden buildings groaned and shifted, alive with creaks and rustlings. Torches burned in sconces; by their light the pair negotiated a corridor hewn partly from the chalk, tapped at a door. A muffled answer; and the Chief Priest raised the latch, propelling the girl gently forward. He said, 'My Lord, the priestess Dareen.' He closed the door, waited a moment head cocked; then padded softly away.

She faced him across the room. She said in a low voice, 'Why did you send for me?'

He moved forward, seemingly dazed. He said, 'Dareen?' He reached to part the cloak she wore; and she knocked his arm away. She said furiously, *'Don't touch me.'*

He flushed at that, the wine buzzing in his brain. He said thickly, 'I touch who I please. I command who I please. I am the God.'

She stared, open-mouthed; then she began to laugh. 'You?' she said. 'You, a God? Who herded sheep on the hillside, and dare not lift eyes to me in the street? Now . . . a God . . . forgive me, my Lord Sheepdrover. This is too sudden . . .'

He glared at her. He said, 'I did not choose to raise my eyes to you. You were a child.'

She snarled at him. *'You did not choose . . .'* She swallowed, clenching her fists. 'Day after day I walked to where you lay,' she said. 'And day after day you watched me, like a silly little boy, and played with yourself in the grass because you were afraid. I humbled myself, in sight of you; because I wanted you, I wanted you to come and take me. But you never came. You never came because you dare not. Now leave me in peace. You are no man for me.'

He grabbed the cloak, wrenched. Beneath, she wore the green and gold of a priestess. Her waist was cinched by a glittering belt; her breasts jutted boldly at the thin cloth of her tunic. He gripped her; and she swung her hand flat-palmed. The slap rang in the little chamber; he doubled his fist, eyes swimming, and she staggered. Silence fell; in the quiet she probed at a wobbling tooth, rubbed her lips, stared at the smudge of red on the back of her hand. Then her bruised mouth smiled. 'I see,' she said. 'Now I suppose you will beat me. Perhaps you will kill me. How very brave that would be.' She circled, staring. 'Now you are a God,' she said. 'What happened to me, when you became a God? And Tamlin, and Sirri, and Merri, and all the others? Do you know?' Her eyes blazed at him. 'Tamlin died on a treadmill,' she said. 'Sirri was sold to the King of the Horsemen, who beat her till he broke her back. Merri has the sickness the Midsea people bring. I went to a whorehouse; while a certain God, whose name we will not speak, dressed in silk and called himself a man.' She wiped her mouth again. 'Well, go on,' she said. 'Beat me; or call your priests to do it for you. Then you can lie in peace, with your fat old woman who doesn't have a face . . .'

She got no further. His hands went to her throat; she tore an arm free, struck at him again. A wrestling; then her mouth was on his. She was groping for him, pulling and wrenching at his cloth.

Much later, when all was over, he began to cry. She cradled him then in the dark, pressing his mouth to her breast, calling him by a name his mother used when he was a tiny child.

He woke heavy with sleep, and she had rolled from him. He groped for her, needing her warmth after the many years. She nuzzled him, smiling and stroking; and the door of the chamber swung slowly inward.

He sat up, appalled. He saw the mask of glittering blue, the Chief Priest at her side. He sprang forward with a shout; but he was too late. The door banged shut; he wrenched it back, but the corridor beyond was empty. The Reborn and her minister were gone.

The light grew, across the Heath. Above him the high hill and its buildings lay deserted; and a drizzle was falling, drifting from the dull void of the sky.

He moved with a desperate urgency, stooping low, fingers clutched round the wrist of the frightened girl. The stockade was before him, and the high lashed gates. He climbed, scrambling, reached back to her. Her skirt tore; she landed beside him with a thud, glared back and up. He took her wrist again, slithering on the steep grass of the ditch, pushing aside the soaked branches of trees.

From a chamber high on the Mound, the Reborn stared down. No quiver, no movement betrayed her breathing; beside her, Cha'Ensil's face was set like stone. The fugitives vanished, reappeared on the farther slope. The woman stiffened; and the priest turned to her, head bowed. He said, 'My Lady?'

She turned away, hands to the feathered mask. She said, 'He must come back, Cha'Ensil.'

He waited; and her shoulders shook. He said gently, 'And if he will not?'

The muffled words seemed dragged from her. She said, 'Then none will sit beside me. None must know our secrets, priest. Or what power we have, is gone . . .' She waited then; till the latch clicked, the sound of his footsteps died. She dropped to her knees, crept to the corner of the little room. She pushed the bird-mask from her, and began to sob.

Beside the great mound the brook ran swift and silent between fern-hung banks. A fallen tree spanned it, stark in the early light. He crossed awkwardly, turned back to the girl. Sweat was on his face; he stared up at the Mound, plunged on again. Beyond the brook grew clumps of waist-high grass. He staggered between them, brown bog-water about his calves. There was a swell of rising ground; he fell to his knees, the girl beside him, hung his head and panted.

A voice said quietly, 'Where to now, my Lord?'

He raised his face, slowly. Round him the semicircle of figures stood grey against against the sky. A few paces beyond, masked and cloaked, was the priest. The Beautiful One glared, licking his mouth, and raised a shaking finger. 'Eldron, Melgro, Baath,' he said. 'You are my men. Save me from treachery . . .'

The man called Eldron stepped forward, stood looking down. 'Wake the thunder, Prince,' he muttered. He whirled the heavy club he carried, struck. The Prince collapsed, setting up a hoarse bawling.

Melgro wiped his face. 'Bow the trees down, Lord,' he said, and struck in turn.

Baath, smiling, drew a heavy-bladed knife. 'Rouse the lightning, ploughboy,' he said, 'and I will call you God.' He drove with the blade; and the little group closed in, hacking in silence. Bright drops flew, spattering the rough grass; the bawls changed to a high-pitched keening that was cut off in its turn. The body rolled a little way, back to the water; shook, and was still.

The girl crouched where she had fallen, unmoving. As

the priest approached she raised a face that was chalk-white beneath its tan. 'Why, priest?' she said, small voiced. 'Why?'

Cha'Ensil stooped above her, drawing a small dagger from his belt. He said, 'I loved him too.' He pulled her head back quickly, and used the knife.

FOUR

Rand, Rat and the Dancing Man

I

It had rained all night and on into the morning, so that long puddles lay everywhere about the wharves of Crab Gut and the crowd that had assembled to see the greatship leave plashed ankle-deep in oozing yellow mud. Drifts of vapour obscured the sea-filled cleft in which the village stood; above the huts with their roof-combs of painted wood the Tower of the Crab loomed its gaunt, pale silhouette. More than one of the watchers frowned at the omens, making beneath his cloak the sign that wards off evil luck.

Looker lay ready at her berth, as she had lain all night. Her bow and stern posts, tall and intricately carved, were rigged in their sockets, the great truss that was her strength strained to humming tightness, her yard in place above the tripod of spars that served her as a mast. Trim she was and beautiful, low in the water and broad in the beam, as fine a fighting vessel as any in Sealand; but the shields strapped to her bulwarks were whitened in sign of peace, white cloths covered her sides and fighting top so that she already looked like a ship of the dead. The crowd muttered, shuffling its feet, turning from time to time to stare up at the stockade surrounding the Tower.

It was from the stockade that the expected procession debouched. First came Matt the Navigator, burly and bearded, a bearskin draped across his shoulders, the curved lever of the steering oar carried like a staff of office. Behind him walked Egril Shipmaster, oldest servant of the House of the Crab, and his two tall sons. Then came Ranna the priest; at his elbow walked a boy with caged cockerels for the shipblessing. There followed the forty-odd rowers and crew, muffled and hooded against the downpour. Last of all strode Rand the Solitary, onetime Prince of Crabland, with Elgro the Dancing Man at his side.

Alone of all the company, Rand was bareheaded; also the watchers saw he carried neither axe nor sword. The rain plastered the long fair hair to his skull, gleamed on cheekbones and throat. He held his face high, seeming unaware of the downpour; his eyes looked grey and vague as the sky.

Drums thudded on the wharf. Matt swung to the platform above *Looker*'s stern cabin, shipped his lever, drove home the wedges that secured it to the great shaft of the oar. Clattering rose from amidships as the rowers took their places, eased the blades of the long oars through the ports. *Looker* rolled slowly, shedding water in streams from the awnings rigged above her deck. Men ran forward skidding and slipping; ropes splashed into the sea.

The drums stopped. Ranna, knife in hand, held up a struggling cockerel; and Rand spoke quickly, from the greatship's stern. 'No blood,' he said. 'Wine if the Gods must have it, or water; but spill no blood, Ranna. It is not my will.'

In the stillness, the hiss of rain sounded clearly. The greatship surged and creaked, feeling already the lift of the open sea. A rope groaned, tightening. Egril swore, circling finger and thumb beneath his cloak; Elgro shrugged, and spat. The priest turned his masked face to the ship; and a shout from Matt brought the oars crashing down. The last lines snaked away; the blades rose once in salute, dipped again. *Looker* steadied and began to gather way, trailing a greyish sheen of wake. The last the villagers saw of her was the rhythmic flash of her rowing banks, the last they heard the thudding of her drum. Then she was gone, vanished like a spirit into the shadowy sea.

She pulled hard and steady the rest of the day, following the vague loom of the nearer shore. All day till evening, the rain roared unceasing. The bows fell and rose, slicing the sea; spray flew back in stinging sheets, mingled with the slosh of rainwater on the decks. The drum beat, timing the strokes; the rowers leaned their weight forward and back, monotonously, faces blank. Their passage was unobserved; no fishing boat would put from shore in weather such as this, no warlord in his proper mind leave the shelter of his haven.

Below decks, the little cabin stank of wet leather and cloth. Rand groaned and tossed, the hammock in which he lay swaying to the movements of the ship. The timbers of *Looker* creaked and squeaked and talked; the drumbeats echoed in the tiny space, becoming the ringing of a fearsome gong, the smashing of an iron-clad ram against an oaken door. He muttered, rubbing at his face, fumbling for the amulet round his neck. In time, the fever that had gripped him abated; he fell into a troubled sleep.

A strange thing happened. It seemed the stout sides of *Looker* grew clear as glass, so that through them he could see the waves and restless sky. The waves lapped and hissed, foam gleaming on their crests; through and between them a nightmare swam, trailing its complex body, holding up long skinned arms.

His shout, ringing through the ship, startled the rowers on their benches. He sat up convulsively, crashed his head with bruising force against a deck beam. Hands gripped his upper arms. He threshed, wildly; and intelligence came back to his eyes. He lay panting and sweating; and the Dancing Man smiled. 'The rain has eased, my Lord,' he said. 'We have made a good offing; will it please you to set a course?'

The greatship lay motionless in the water, steadied by her oars. Rand stared round him blinking, feeling the evening air move cool against his skin. Astern, dimly visible in the growing night, were the ragged mountains of Sealand. Ahead the edge of the cloud-pall loomed low across the water, seeming more solid than the land. The sun was setting, in a miles-long tumble of copper light; the sea was calm, and empty.

He climbed to the forward grating, stood clinging to the stempost. He ran a hand across his face, swallowed. 'South,' he said. 'South and west, Elgro. Take me to the Islands of Ghosts.'

Men scurried into *Looker*'s rigging. Her sail, with the great red Mark of the House, fell and bellied; ropes flew and cracked as the canvas was sheeted home. Water bubbled under her stem; and at last the long oars came dripping inboard. The breeze blew steadily; she gathered speed, on course for the Lands of the Dead.

Rand stayed on the lookout platform, feet apart, one hand gripping the stempost, the wind moving his hair. The sun sank crimson and angry, the mountains veiled themselves in dark. The rowers prepared their evening meal, stretched tired limbs, rolled beneath the benches. Once Elgro brought food for his lord, a bowl of rich-smelling soup; but Rand refused it, gently, turned his eyes back to the sea. Elgro, cursing under his breath, padded the way he had come; and overheard the seaman Dendril mutter to his friend Cultrinn Barehead. 'The nights are full of wonders,' he said, 'When the favoured of the Gods turn their hands to wetnursing. Who can tell; when we return to Sealand, perhaps we shall find all the nursemaids have become priests.'

Elgro tripped over the butt of an ill-stowed oar, flinging the contents of the bowl with some accuracy at the speaker's head. Dendril swore, clawing the scalding mess from his face and beard; when he could see again Elgro's vicelike fingers were gripping his shoulder, the pale eyes of the Dancing Man staring into his own.

'I heard you curse the spilled soup, friend, and that is all,' said Elgro softly. 'Which is as well for you . . .'

The rigging of *Looker* creaked in the night wind. The rowers snored, wrapped in their sealskin cloaks; and the drum was quiet. For Rand, the great ram had ceased to beat.

Her eyes were blue; light, clear blue like the horizon of the summer sea. Her hair hung to her waist, pale as foam, garlanded with flowers and berries. Her hands were slender, her hips broad. She broke bread for him, laughing, at ease in her husband's Hall, while the kept-men of King Engor snored with the dogs on the rush-piled floor. The firelight flickered, bronzing her skin; her hand brushed his arm, cool and soft as a moth. She raised her cup to drink; his lips shaped her name, Deandi.

He moved in the hammock, muttering.

He had been Prince of the Crab, in that far-off time; a tall, inward, powerful young man, given to strange fits of brooding, to hunting and wandering by himself, to little company. On feast days, when mead and metheglin and beer ran like water, when the great Hall of the Crab shone red and smoky with the glare of torches and big-breasted girls pranced and jiggled on the table-tops, Rand sat apart, listening as like as not to the tales of fishermen. He had never been known to pay attention to any woman, much less seek her bed; so that his father the King put scorn on him, taunting his cowardice, calling him less than a man. He sent him finally to tend the crab pots for a month, saying they seemed to be his greatest love; and folk grinned behind their hands to see the Prince in the trews and apron of a fisherman. Rand performed his duties gravely, neither sad nor gay, rising early on misty mornings, sculling out in a borrowed coracle to haul at the rough black lines, fill his fish tubs with the wriggling catch. The warboats passed him, on their great way to and from Crab Gut. Sometimes their crews hailed him, much amused at his expense; but Rand merely smiled and waved back, balanced in the rocking chip of a boat, showing his even white teeth. He was without doubt a very strange young man, particularly for the son of a King.

Cedda, though powerful, was old, nearing his sixtieth year. His health was not what it had been; so that when he laid siege to the tower of his neighbour Fenrick many shook their heads, declaring it would be the last war he would wage. In that they were correct; for after a month Cedda, cursing feebly, was carried on a great litter from the scene of his endeavours, a marsh fever in his bones. He lived long enough to see the stronghold breached, its defenders sworded and its cattle driven to new fields; then he passed to the Gods, leaving Rand as patrimony a Kingdom and a blood feud, neither of which it seemed the young man much desired. For the halfbrother of Fenrick was Engor the Wolf; and the wife of Engor was Deandi, of the cool white arms.

He called her from the hammock, time and again, beating his fist on the cabin's wooden side.

He opened his eyes. Grey light seeped into the little space; in his mouth was a taste like blood. He swung his legs down, stood gripping a stanchion. *Looker* rolled slowly. The tension of the great truss thrilled in the woodwork; timber creaked and shifted, whispering.

He pulled a cloak round himself, unlatched the cabin door. He stepped into a shadowed world. The water lapped and bubbled; the sky was grey as new iron. The rowers clustered on their benches, still wrapped in their cloaks; the sail slapped idly at the mast. Astern, the land had vanished; *Looker* was a speck, in the great waste of the sea.

He walked forward, stood shivering a little and chafing his hands. A touch at his arm made him turn; he stared into the Dancing Man's long eyes, seeing the strange head with its frizz of hair, half red, half badger-grey. Elgro said, 'Good morning, my Lord.'

He looked back at the water, and smiled. He said, 'It's

like the frozen world the priests talk about, where men are as old as mountains.' He leaned his back to the stempost, stared up at the tall mast struts. He let his eyes move down to the truss and the long ash poles that tightened it, the awnings rolled on their spars, the cramped complexity of the deck. He said, 'Elgro, how old is this ship?'

Elgro considered, running blunt fingers through his thatch. 'Your father built her, in his own youth,' he said, 'to fight a war. That was two seasons before the great flood, when the roof blew off the Tower and the sea monster came ashore. And five years before he took the throne himself, and made a war with Dendril and the sons of Erol of the Fen.' He shrugged. 'Many years, my Lord,' he said. 'Too many to count in the head.'

Rand nodded, slowly. His skull felt hollow and empty, as though he had been drinking Midsea wine. He closed his eyes; and the rocking of the vessel seemed intensified. He said, 'It all comes back. I dreamed again last night. Elgro, was it right? For such a little sin?'

The other pursed his lips. He said, 'I danced the ghosts away the night you were born. Don't ask me to answer for Gods.'

Rand frowned, as if at some effort of memory. He said, 'We stand close enough; yet we are so far apart. Sometimes it seems I stand apart from all men; even you, Elgro. As if there's no one in the entire world but me. At others . . . it's as if we were ghosts ourselves. Wailing and chattering, none able to hear the next.'

Elgro watched stolidly, not answering. A silence; then Rand sighed. He said, 'I remember the first time I sailed with my father. I was five. We went to Seal Hold, where Tenril had his Tower. Do you remember?'

The Dancing Man nodded.

Rand said, 'It was summer, so the sun never set. There was a big tent, on the shore. You could hear the shouting from it, and the dancers' bells. I sat and watched the seals out on the rocks. The light was strange. It was as if it came from inside things. From everything.'

Elgro waited.

Rand said, 'Later, the sea was blue. You could smell the land, miles out across the water. Like hay, and flowers. That was the night she came with me.'

Elgro said, 'My Lord, you must eat now.'

Rand shook his head, eyes vague. He said, 'She wanted to sail north, for ever. To see the Ice Giants, and find the Bear King's Hall.' He turned. He said, 'What do they say of these Ghost Islands? Tell me again.'

Elgro shrugged. 'They say the spirits fly there, after death. And that the cliffs are lined with wailing Gods; and Kings from old time thick as sprouting grass.'

Rand smiled again. 'And you?'

Elgro shook his head. 'I say most lands are much the same, my Lord. The sun sets and rises, the people wake and sleep. Some scratch the ground, some fish. Others make war.'

Rand said, 'And we do none of these.' He leaned his elbows on the greatship's curving side, stared at the sea. He said, 'When she came with me, it was all new again. I thought I could live for ever.'

Astern, the sun was like a blind bright eye. The rowers stretched, scratching themselves. Somebody laughed; a crewman swaggered to the ship's side to piddle in the sea. Rand straightened. He said, 'To have such nights, as make you pray for dawn. Elgro, dance one Ghost for me. I'd give you half the world.'

The wind rose, through the day. *Looker* made good speed, hissing her way south, trailing a wake of brilliant foam. Once mountains showed high and faint to the east; once the lookout called for a strange sail. The greatship stood well clear. By nightfall, the sea was empty again. The wind still blew from the north, strong and cold.

A medley of sounds roused Rand from sleep. Water boomed and seethed, timbers groaned, spray flew rattling across the planking overhead. *Looker* was in wild motion; rising, rolling, sliding headlong into the troughs of waves. He reeled his way on deck, stood clinging to a mast strut.

Away to the west stretched a ragged coast. He screwed his eyes, shouted a question; at his side Egril nodded sombrely, the long hair flying round his face. He said, 'The Ghost Islands, my Lord. But we make no landfall here.'

By midday the weather had worsened. Squall after squall swept down; the greatship laboured, rolling lee scuppers under, pitching in a welter of white. Twice Egril ordered the crewmen aloft to take in sail. The wind yelled in the rigging, plucking at their backs as they climbed. *Looker* fled south, under a rag of canvas; and still the wind increased. The yard was braced round, and again; but the tide was setting now toward the coast, sweeping the vessel to leeward. Egril called for the oars to be unshipped; and a weary struggle began. Rand set himself to row with the rest, the Dancing Man at his side.

The drum throbbed, urgently; he flung his weight forward and back, hearing the hammer blows beneath the hull, feeling the planking shake under his feet. Blisters formed and broke on his palms; but the pain and labour were antidotes to memory. For a time, he felt nearly happy.

Through the day, the vessel held her own; but toward nightfall the wind, gusting as violently as ever, veered to the east. Matt and Egril held anxious counsel, clinging to the lee of the wildly tossing poop. To the south, dim in the fading light, stretched a long spit of land. Beyond, if *Looker* could weather the point, lay the deepwater channel separating the north and south Ghost Islands. Once through it a vessel might run for days; to the edge of the world, if need be.

The crewmen scurried again. The sail was furled, the great yard lowered inches at a time to the deck. The feat accomplished, *Looker* lay a little easier. Her truss was tautened; and the rowers bent themselves once more, wearily, to their task.

For an hour or more the issue stood in doubt. Across the sea, above the medley of other sounds, could be heard the boom of surf. The moon, gliding between ragged clouds, gave glimpses of close rock. *Looker* pitched and rolled, falling off into the troughs of waves, rising through a welter of spray. A sea carried away the sternpost, another half the shields of the weather rack; the cloths with which she had been draped had long since flogged themselves to tatters. In time, the roar to leeward seemed to grow less. The rowers stared, unwilling at first to believe their senses; and the land was falling away, ahead showed a waste of sparkling water. The greatship yawed again, swept sideways by the crabbing of an enormous tide.

The respite was brief. The wind blew now from dead astern; and the channel was narrowing. Once a cliff-wall reared to larboard, its top lost in darkness. Waves crashed at its base, seething upward two or three times the height of *Looker*'s mast. The vessel jarred and shook, caught in a yeasty boiling, before the undertow plucked her clear. The channel widened once more, narrowed again. The look-outs clung to prow and masthead, eyes red-rimmed, glaring into darkness. The greatship rolled, water gurgling and sloshing in her hold. Her crew, bone-weary, lost all track of time; they groaned and muttered, praying for the dawn.

The sky lightened, by imperceptible degrees. The masthead became visible, black against scarcely darker grey, and the battered length of the deck. Men slumped across the oars, gasping with relief. Elgro, his hair caked and spiky, gripped his young master's shoulder and grinned; Egril, relaxing for the first time in many hours, permitted himself the ghost of a smile. The strange tide, still flowing, bore the greatship effortlessly to the west; it was as if the storm, blowing so long and violently, had piled up untold masses of water, which now must find release.

The voice of the masthead lookout was as thin and desperate as the cry of a bird.

Ahead, growing from the dark, stretched a long mounded spit. At its base the sea frothed round jagged teeth of rock; beyond, a beach of smooth grey sand sloped to low cliffs. The current, setting across the channel, drove the vessel down fast as a running horse.

A fresh ship, with a fresh crew, might have weathered the hazard; but the seconds that were lost while the rowers struggled with the oars were irreplaceable. The blades rose and flashed; but the pull was ragged. *Looker* surged sideways, recovered, wallowed again. Then it was too late; she swept forward helplessly, already among the rocks.

A bellow from Egril brought the blades down once more. In every place save one the reef thrust up grey and dripping, pounded by spray. Matt swung his weight at the steering oar; the greatship steadied, rushed for the gap.

For an instant, it seemed the manoeuvre would succeed. Black water slid past, bubbling; then the oars of the larboard rank struck rock. The butts swept forward across the packed thwarts; a concerted shriek, and the benches were empty. *Looker* slewed, struck with a pounding roar.

For Rand, it was as if time was slowed. The impact flung him headlong across the deck; he gripped a tangle of rigging while water surged round his waist. Something struck his thigh; an oar-shaft rose end over end, hung turning. The vessel rolled, pounded again. The truss flexed; and the long levers that tightened it spun from their crotches. He saw a man hurled backward, a bright mash where his face had been; then the bow planking rippled and burst.

The dissolution of the greatship was bizarre in its suddenness. Lacking the tension of the truss, the hull seemed to explode on the instant into its component fragments. The mast-spars, wrenched apart by the springing of the bulwarks, crashed into the sea. Oars, benches, gratings, hatch covers, tossed in confusion. A wave creamed forward, dotted with casks, planks and bobbing human heads. A bird wheeled, its voice lost in the noise of the surf; the wave licked the foot of the cliff, expended itself in a fading fringe of lace.

Water rushed into the lungs of the King. His ears

roared; he rcse flailing, sank again toward stillness. He was aware, vaguely, that hands gripped his arms; then his knees struck sand. He staggered forward, rolled full length, lay groaning and retching salt. Over him, chest heaving, stood the red and grey, bow-legged man who had snatched him from the Gods.

The survivors huddled moodily on the beach. Of forty men, just twenty-one remained; and of those Cultrinn crouched whimpering, glowing rags clutched to the splinters of an arm. Below the cliff Egril lay grey-faced and coughing. His sons stooped over him; at his side knelt Rand, and the Dancing Man.

Dendril walked slowly to the group. He stood feet spread, hand on the pommel of his sword. 'King of the Crab you are called,' he said, staring down contemptuously. 'But I see no King worthy of the name.' He raised his voice. 'I see a fisherman,' he said. 'Who fished too long and well, robbing among other things his neighbour's pots. Who in his arrogance denied the Gods their due, and now expects us all to share his punishment. Half of us are gone already; shall those that are left die with him? Rather we will leave him here to mope, and I will lead you. His kept-man will bring him soup.'

Rand turned, shaking his head as if in pain; and Elgro stepped forward smiling. 'Now, Dendril,' he said. 'And all you others sworn to follow the Crab. A new tune has come into my head. I feel my feet begin to itch; will one of you partner me? For ghosts are hovering just above our heads; a sacrifice will soothe them.' He crouched, eyes raw-rimmed with salt, flexing his long arms. A silence; then one of the rowers, a burly blond-bearded man called Egrith, spoke up. 'Well you know I make no cause against you, Elgro,' he said. 'Also what vows I take, I keep. But this much is true. We sailed with neither mark nor sacrifice, which is contrary to any priestly law I ever heard; and see where it has led us.'

'Why, Egrith,' said the Dancing Man, 'I see indeed

where it has led you; through a time of mortal peril to a most well-found beach, where we shall shortly dry our clothes and gather some food, and conduct ourselves like Sealanders rather than squabbling children. If you are dissatisfied with that you should perhaps walk back into the sea; or come with me and I will hold your head under water till your honour is appeased.'

Somebody laughed, abruptly; and the tension broke. Dendril, turning to rally the rest, saw his support already melting away. He clenched his fists angrily, and stalked off.

'This is well,' said Elgro after a pause. 'Now, all the rest of you; fetch wood to build a fire. And Egrith, climb the cliff a little way and watch. My spirits tell me there are many tribes in this land, not all of them friendly.'

The party set to work. Timber from the wreck abounded; sparks were coaxed from flint and steel, a blaze kindled in the shelter of the rocks. An iron pot had been salvaged from the water; and Matt, wading out, secured a cask of salt meat and another of Sealand herrings. They lolled on the beach more cheerfully while their sealskin cloaks, propped on sticks round the warmth, steamed and stank. An hour passed; then Galbritt and Ensor called from below the cliff. Rand, hurrying to them, saw the Shipmaster raise himself. Twice he made to speak, extending his arm; then the coughing shook him again. He fell back, eyes fixed and blank. Blood showed between his teeth, and he was dead.

'This too was well,' said Elgro quietly. 'Now, we will make a cairn here for him. He can lie in sight of the sea; and no fox or bird will visit him, annoying his sleep. Also I will dance the strongest dance I know, so his rest will be the sweeter.' He turned, quickly, to the sons. 'Will you be satisfied?'

They stood frowning, pulling at their lips; and Galbritt, the elder, answered. 'He spoke strangely, before he died,' he said. 'We didn't understand him. Something there was of witchcraft, and a Fairy woman who entranced the King;

but he called for no blood in vengeance. We shall be satisfied.'

The Sealanders scurried again. A mound of rocks was raised above the Shipmaster, twenty feet or more long and six feet high. At its head they set the great stempost of *Looker*, which the waves had washed up on the beach. Elgro, inspecting the work, pronounced it satisfactory. He danced a wild, stamping song, forward and back across the How; when it was done he walked to Rand, who stood as ever a little apart, his chin sunk on his chest. 'Now, my Lord,' he said softly. 'We are twenty strong, and in better temper than before; though one of us, it is certain, would be best elsewhere.' He jerked his head to where Dendril sat scowling by his injured friend, and whetted a knife significantly on his palm.

Rand stared, and shook his head. 'Elgro,' he said, 'you know the vow I took. I have spilled blood enough; now more lives are on my head. Let it be.' He pulled his cloak round him, looked at the sea. 'We will leave this place,' he said. 'Let the men take what they can carry, from the wreck; it may be some time before we can find shelter.'

The party wound upward slowly, Rand leading with the sons of Egril. Matt followed, taciturn as ever; then came the rowers, well hung about with weapons, some with bulky packs on their backs. In the rear Cultrinn, white-faced and moaning, was half carried, half dragged up the steep cliff path.

The sun was high by the time they reached the crest. Behind them the sea stretched into distance, calm now and mockingly blue; to the south the land ran broken and rolling, hill after hill dotted with bracken and carpeted with heather. No smoke rose, anywhere; there were no sounds, no signs of human habitation.

Rand shaded his eyes, uncertainly. 'Elgro, I lean on your counsel again,' he said. 'You know my need; which way shall I go?'

Elgro scowled. 'I know the ways of ghosts to some extent,' he said. 'I dance for life, and death. But your business is with the Gods. For that you need the priests we left behind.'

Rand glanced at him sharply, and shrugged. 'In that case,' he said, 'one way is as good as the next.' He struck out across the short turf, head bowed, not looking back. The Sealanders followed, in a straggling line.

At midday they rested in a sheltered hollow, eating a little of the food they had brought with them. Rand, now, was impatient to be gone. They rose without undue complaint, and once more shouldered their loads.

The sun dropped toward the west. Their shadows lengthened; and still the empty hills marched to either side. The sky was reddening when they came on a curious sight. At the crest of a sweep of grassland was set a little stone hut, no more than waist high. Round it at a distance of twenty paces or so stood a circle of upright stones. The wind had dropped, through the day; now no leaf stirred. The place was utterly still.

Elgro approached sniffing like a dog, as was his custom when puzzled or suspicious. 'This place stinks of Gods,' he said finally. 'So some sort of folk live in these hills.' He walked forward carefully, setting his feet in line, squatted at the entrance to the shrine. He stared a while; then straightened, with a short laugh. 'A fine spirit,' he said. 'If he is the greatest the land can offer, I think we shall come to no harm.'

Rand, stooping, made out an image in the shadows. Eyes of polished stone winked at him; above were two tall ears. He shook his head, frowning. Wild and ragged though the carving was, the figure was undoubtedly a hare.

'Now,' said Elgro, 'people who worship hares must be very odd folk to meet.'

At Rand's side, Galbritt touched his arm. He drew, with a scrape of steel.

Facing them some twenty paces off, where a moment before had been empty heather, was a little group of men. They were short, barely reaching to the shoulders of the

Sealanders, but sturdy and powerfully built. They carried light spears, no thicker at the tips than twigs; and three or four held drawn bows.

The Sealanders bunched, muttering; but Rand raised an arm. He walked forward slowly, palms spread. 'We are sailors, shipwrecked on your coast,' he said. 'We come in peace, desiring only shelter for the night. Also one of us is very sick. If your priests can bring him to health, we will pay with gold.'

The strangers stared, stolidly; then one, who seemed to be their leader, grunted. 'Those are very peaceful swords I see in your folk's hands,' he said. 'And peaceful axes and spears. Also you have defiled a holy place, the punishment for which is death.'

Rand said mildly, 'We meant no harm; we approached not knowing it was the house of a God. Show us how he will best be pleased, and we will make an atonement. Also I will sit at your fire and talk, for I see you are an old folk, and very wise.'

The strangers grunted together; then the leader turned back. 'Sealanders seeking peace are wonderful folk,' he said. 'Yesterday at noon the sun turned cold, hanging the land with icicles. Tonight, undoubtedly, the moon will become green.'

Rand turned. He said, 'Elgro, tell them to put their swords away.'

The weapons were sheathed, unwillingly. The little people jabbered once more among themselves; in time it seemed a decision was reached. The bows were lowered; and a guard formed up, at a circumspect distance from the Sealanders. The party moved on, following a well-trodden track across the shoulder of the hill.

The village they eventually reached was curious in the extreme. There were no fine buildings, no Chief's hut or High Priest's Lodge; in fact from a distance no dwellings were visible at all, so well did the low roofs, overgrown with bracken and turf, blend with the valley floor on which they stood. Smoke rose here and there; at the hut doorways as they passed, women with babies at their hips stood staring sullenly. All were unclothed to the waist, and as dumpy and unlovely as their menfolk.

There was a council hut of sorts; a long, low structure, as overgrown as the rest. Outside it the Sealanders waited suspiciously, it seemed an interminable time. Within, voices could be heard raised in argument. Finally their guide reappeared. 'I, who am called Magro, bid you welcome,' he said importantly. 'Our God, who is very wise, has evidently sent you to be his guests and keep him company. In one week's time, we hold his high festival. Then you will worship him; and your promise will be fulfilled.'

He led the way to a hut taller and longer than the rest, set a little apart on a mound overlooking the shallow stream that supplied the place with water. 'Here you will rest,' he said. 'Food will be brought you, and drink; but we use no skill in healing. I will speak of your friend to the Fleet One; after that, if he dies it is the God's own will.'

Soup of a sort was brought, and jugs of flat, stale-smelling beer. Elgro, sitting moodily at the doorway of the hut, took a mouthful and spat it at the grass. 'Well, my King,' he said, 'I hope your penance has so far brought you joy. It would seem to have cost us a ship and half a company, and very nearly our lives into the bargain; and I think others of us will not see Crab Gut again. For my part, I would trade heartsearching for one mouthful of Sealand mead, drunk at ease in our own Hall, with folk we can trust at our backs and within sound of the sea.'

Rand made no answer; just jabbed at the turf with a pointed stick, and frowned.

Later that night they sought out Magro in his hut. The little chief sat swigging beer in front of a smoky fire, surrounded by his women. He scowled as the Sealanders entered, greeting them with a belch; but Rand squatted beside him in the ashes humbly enough. 'Here is gold,' he said, 'for my people are grateful. Also a great treasure; a magic stone, by which we cross the sea. It points always to

108

our homeland, wishing to fly back across the water.'

The chief took the needle on its slender thread, glanced at it incuriously and tossed it aside. 'The gold we will keep,' he said. 'Magic stones are of no particular use. We are an old people, too wise to trouble with toys. It can hang from the neck of one of our babies, or a woman.'

At Rand's side, Elgro hissed like a snake. The Prince laid a hand on his arm. 'First I will tell you how we were shipwrecked,' he said. 'We sailed from Sealand with peace-cloths on our sides; for I had heard there are many Gods in this country. I am a King in my own land; this is my Dancing Man, a friend of ghosts. We came for counsel.'

'Then you are fools,' said the little man frankly. 'As befits Sealanders, and pirates. There are such Gods, as I know very well; but their land lies to the south, many days' journey away. You will not live to reach it; if you do, it will be the worse for you.' He shouted, harshly; and more beer was brought. 'Drink,' he said. 'We are kindly people, returning good for evil; whatever you may or may not have heard.'

Later he condescended to discuss the subject of Gods.

'Once there were many Gods, and ghosts too,' he said. 'Some lived in rocks, some in trees and streams, some in hollows in the ground. Then we were one people throughout the islands; living in peace, harming no man, remembering the wisdom of the Giants.' He cleared his nose, coarsely. 'Then the Horse Warriors came,' he said. 'From where, nobody can tell. They took the North Land; our cities, which were wonderful, were destroyed. Then they came here. Our cities were destroyed. Some of us fled, to where the pasture is thin and the ground bad for the plough. With us we brought one God, the oldest and strongest of all.' He held up the figurine that hung round his neck, and burst into a singsong chant. 'The Hare fights no man, being fleet and wise,' he said. 'The Hare strikes down his enemies, being cunning in the night. The Hare is Lord of the hills, and the high pastures by the sea.'

He reapplied himself to the beer. 'Now the Sealanders come in their turn,' he said. 'They fight the Horse Warriors on land, and harry their ships. Like them, they burn and kill. You, who are Sealanders, we have no cause to love. Yet we have taken you in, and sheltered you. Here you will remain. In one week, it is the festival of our God. You will worship him.'

Rand frowned, drawing with a finger in the ashes. 'Chief,' he said, 'how will this be?'

But Magro merely belched again, and shrugged. 'In your own way,' he said, 'you will worship him.'

Later Elgro spoke bitterly, in the darkness of the communal hut. 'With regard to wisdom,' he said, 'I should have taken that sawn-off little viper's neck between my fingers, to teach him if nothing else the wisdom of civility.'

Rand lay wide-eyed, staring into the blackness. 'I came for peace, not killing, Elgro,' he said. 'For peace.'

Elgro snorted. 'Your desire for peace, I have no doubt, will be fulfilled,' he said. 'For it will end in the deaths of us all.'

Rand turned, crackling the bracken bed. He lay a long time, hearing the steady breathing of the rowers, the whimpering of the wounded man. Toward dawn, the sounds ceased. In the morning light they saw the Hare had made his answer; Cultrinn was dead.

In the days that followed, they learned the ways of Magro's folk and their God. His shrines abounded, dotted everywhere about the surrounding hills. From hollowed trees, from caves, from the little huts, the tiny mask winked and glinted at the light. He was fleet, and weak, and watchful; and he owned the land.

On the fourth morning people from the surrounding countryside began flocking into the little moss-grown town. There was a great coming and going, a clattering and splashing by the brook. Dogs barked, women chattered, children yelled. Tents sprang up by the score, rough affairs of hides slung over bending willow poles. Stacks of fuel were cut and transported; and a vast fire built, on the outskirts of the village. Elgro viewed the proceedings with growing distrust. 'As to this business of worship,' he said, 'it seems to me we have enough Gods already. Also the way of the thing has not been made clear enough for my taste. Some modes of adoration can be less than comfortable; as you, my Lord, are very well aware.'

But Rand shook his head. 'These are hospitable folk,' he said. 'Their manners are not all that could be desired, but they have offered us no harm. We should be churlish to leave now, or refuse to see their God-rites. Besides'—he smiled, gently—'a Dancing Man of Sealand has little to fear, surely, from a Hare.'

Elgro scowled, and shrugged; but for the remainder of the day, and the day that followed, he went conspicuously well armed.

By the fifth morning, the tents sprawled to the valley rim; and by nightfall a strange procession had begun. Everywhere, the hare images were gathered from their niches. More arrived and more, each propped in a litter of cloth and willow poles, in charge of a chanting group of men with torches and flutes. The fire was lit; round it clustered a growing congregation, a sea of alert ears, unblinking yellow eyes. Drums set up a pounding; beer jugs were passed more and more freely, and the dancing began. Priests, naked save for furred headdresses, whirled and shrieked; chanting girls, the hare-symbol swinging between their breasts, wound in and out among the seated people, scattering drops of blood and honey.

The noise redoubled. Heat from the fire beat back; and Rand felt his own head begin to throb. The ram was swinging again; he grabbed for beer, gulping eagerly, anxious for oblivion. Sweat burst out on his body; the dancers swayed, surging forward and back, hair flying, faces orange-lit by the flames. Then it seemed the whole world spun. He rose with a cry; plunged headlong, barely felt the hands that dragged him to the hut. He sprawled across the bed, shaking and groaning, the noise still in his

111

ears like a distant sea. In time the sounds receded. The dance went on all night, till earliest dawn; but he was far away.

They crowned him King, in the great Hall of the Crab, setting him on the painted wooden throne. A day and night he sat, his father's sword across his knees, while round him the drinking and feasting went on. The greatships creaked and tossed, clustering in the harbour and along the wharves of Crab Gut; on the hill the Tower blazed with light, where Rand the Solitary held open house for all the world. To him came messengers from every court of Sealand; from Seal Hold to the Blue Fen, Orm Rock to the scattered Lakes of the Bear. Each swore friendship in the ancient way, with blood and salt; he received them smiling, giving a golden ring to every man. But as the night wore on his eyes turned more and more to the windows set beneath the high roof-eaves. Vat after vat was broached, and jar after jar of Midsea wine; and still the voice he wanted most to hear was silent.

They came with the dawn; a dozen grim-faced men, stamping up from the harbour to pound at the stockade gates. Beer was sent for and meat, the King's advisers summoned or shaken rudely from their snoring. He received the messengers in state, seated with Elgro and Ranna the High Priest. They strode in haughtily enough, armour jangling, glancing neither to left nor right; and the Staff of the Wolf was planted in Cedda's Hall.

For a further day and night the King withdrew himself, ordering the strangers cared for with all courtesy. He sat in his high chamber, watching the sun patterns move on the rug-hung walls, hearing the clank of milkpails from the sheds, the shouts of children at play. At length his decision was reached, and the Council reconvened.

The messengers chose to hear him fully armed, each with a red war-lanyard on his belt. Hubbub rose, in the Hall; the King stilled it, holding up his hands. 'Let us be patient,' he said. 'Wrong has been done; blood will not wash out blood. Now, let our friends approach.'

He stared at each man thoughtfully before he went on. 'Hear me well,' he said, 'and take back careful word to your master. Fenrick put shame on my father, Cedda King, claiming certain grazing lands, and rights of chase in others owned by the Crab. For this we went to war, and Fenrick's Tower was breached. With Engor we made no quarrel; nor do we seek one now. Yet a blood price was incurred, which the Wolf has every right to claim.'

Muttering rose again; once more, he stilled it. 'The Tower of Fenrick we keep, by right of conquest,' he said. 'This by all Sealand laws is just. Also those of his lands adjoining ours, from the Tower to Steffa's Rock. Let a line be drawn between these points, and clearly marked with posts. The lands beyond, to his own borders, we give to our brother Engor. Let his people possess them in peace. The cattle taken I cannot return, for they are spoils of war. But for my part . . .'

Uproar, in the hall. He rose; and by degrees it stilled.

'For my own part,' he said, 'I give my father's spoil. The cloth from the Yellow Lands, the Midsea wine; the chest of spices, and eight bars of gold. Also the weapons from the armoury, both axes and swords; and the greatship *Seasnake*, with her shields and fittings of war. This I will put in writing for your King. The lesser things you may take with you when you go; we will prepare *Seasnake* for her voyage, and provision her for one week at sea. If your master will send a crew to man her, it will be honourably received.' He smiled down at the messengers. He said, 'Will this be pleasing to King Engor?'

They looked at each other in stunned silence, and shrugged.

Later, from the rampart walk, the Dancing Man watched the last of the waggons jolt down toward the harbour. Then he turned, showing his teeth. 'My Lord,' he said, 'remember what I say. This day's work will be paid for many times, in blood.'

Rand shook his head, frowning. 'Elgro,' he said, 'can

we not live in peace? The sun is free for all; and the mountains, the green things in the spring, fish in the sea. I have put my hand out, which no King before me did. Let us enjoy these things, while we can. The days are short enough, for all of us; and darkened with shadows, whether we will or no.'

Elgro shrugged and turned away, muttering.

For Rand's people, they were troubled times; for word of the giftmaking spread, from the southern marshes to the bleakest northern Tower, where the aurora flickers and the Ice Folk come to trade. Everywhere men shook their heads, and solemnly agreed the King of the Crab was mad. But mad folk who are rich make useful friends; and delegation after delegation presented itself at the Tower, armed with demands for this and that. Sometimes Rand chided them and sent them packing; but usually, he gave. He sent tapestries to the Prince of White Bear Lake, gold to Ulm of the Fishgard, a dancing woman to the Lord of the Nine Isles. Meanwhile, the boundary stakes were planted. Engor occupied the ceded lands, with a conspicuous show of force. Two days later news was brought that the fence was down, the standard of the Wolf advanced to the very edge of Rand's territory. He frowned, but made no move against his neighbour.

Warboats took to sailing Crab Gut in broad daylight, robbing the fishermen of their catch, adding insults to the injury of theft. Rand soothed his people's indignation, from his own pocket. Armed strangers appeared on the pastures of the Crab, frightening the field-thralls from their work, stealing cattle, trampling the standing grain. To their Kings, Rand sent remonstrances couched in the mildest terms; and more gifts, to ensure the peace he craved. In this way the uneasy summer passed. Autumn gales lashed the coasts of Sealand; and for a time, the Kingdoms were quiet.

Spring brought the disaster Elgro had foretold. For days, while the sun grew slowly in strength, news came in of raids and pillagings, the murder of peasants, burning of outlying huts. Engor, parading Rand's boundaries with all his strength, made no secret of a boast that before another winter he himself would sit in the Hall of the Crab. Rand spent a night in noisy council. Ranna spoke bitterly and at length; Elgro chided; Egril stamped the floor of the Hall, swearing before he stomached further insult he would sell his services to a foreign lord. Through it all, Rand remained immoveable. Wolfhold held all he found dear; for Deandi's sake, he would make no war with Engor.

The people muttered, darkly. There was talk of defiance, of rebellion; even, at the end, of the raising of a new King. Then one morning matters came to a head. A band of refugees presented itself at Rand's gate; women and some men, bloodied and in fear of their lives. The tale they told, of torture and killing and rape, sent Rand stumbling grey-faced to his room, calling for Elgro and a scribe. An ultimatum was sent out by the hand of a Midsea trader, a swarthy little man who it seemed valued gold more than he feared his life. The village by Crab Gut settled uneasily to wait its answer.

It wasn't long in coming; for Engor had camped a bare dozen miles from the fortress of his enemy. A shout was raised that very night; and a grim-faced Elgro summoned the King from his room. Rand rose without a word, and followed; down the winding wooden steps, across the Hall to the stockade.

Round the great gates stood it seemed all the people of the town. The crowd opened silently, for the King to pass. He stood staring, the wind moving his hair and cloak, while his skin turned white as salt-crusted rock.

At the gates stood a cart, drawn by a span of bony oxen. On it had been erected a stout wooden post. The thing bound to it was reddened from head to foot. Its tunic, tied up soddenly above the waist, displayed the ruined groin. The eyes of the messenger glared appalled above a mask of flesh. From the mask the manhood swung, and dripped.

Drums beat, in every village of the Crab. Fires burned, and torches; by their light men polished armour, honed axes and swords. The messages flew, to Orm Rock and White Bear Lake and the satrapies that clustered round Long Fen. Fighting ships rode at Crab Key, patrolled the mouth of the Gut. The land seethed, like a boiling pot. Day and night, the soldiers streamed in; and finally, Rand was ready. He showed himself to his people; and folk marvelled, seeing Cedda come again in youthful glory. Then the gates creaked back, the King and his bodyguard rode through. Behind them, an army streamed north to war.

The din, the shouting and crack of whips, creak and rumble of wheels, faded. His shoulder was shaken, and again. He groaned, rolled over, tried to stand.

Grey light was in the sky. Outside the hut, in silence, stood the Sealanders, drawn swords in their hands. Six of them would not rise again; they lay stark in the dawn, their eyes rolled up beneath the lids. Beside them was the body of a priest. In his hand he still gripped a furry paw, its claws dipped in some brownish substance. Long scratches on the faces of the dead showed where the Hare had taken his revenge.

Round them, the village slept.

'Now,' said Elgro, 'I hope your thirst for wisdom is slaked, my Lord. Before we leave, we will show some skills of our own. I will speak with this little Chief.'

In Rand's brain the drugged fumes of the beer still spun. He stared round him, at the dull eyes and trembling hands, and shook his head. He said bitterly, 'Do that and we are all dead, Elgro. All we can save is our lives.'

The little party straggled grimly, in the growing light. No further words were spoken till the valley was behind them. By midday they were deep among the hills. For an hour or more clouds had been thickening on the higher slopes; now they crept lower, bringing a thin, chilling rain.

The mist saved them. Twice they heard the voices of pursuers below them; twice the shouts, and jangling of weapons and harness, passed them by. That night they sprawled beneath an overhanging rock, too weary to seek proper shelter. At dawn some sixth sense roused the Dancing Man. He rose quietly, narrowing his eyes. One place in the heather was empty; Dendril had gone.

The weather worsened. The rain fell steadily, day after day. Above and to every side sounded the roar of waterfalls, invisible in the driving mist. The Sealanders moved south blindly, living as best they could on stream fish, eggs of wild birds. They would have starved; but on the fourth morning they came on the ruins of a town.

It had been of considerable extent. They wandered uneasily along paved, grass-grown streets, between shells of ragged stone. Watchtowers reared gaunt and desolate, the dim sky showing through their windows; to either side, stretching into the mist, ran a great ditch and mound, once topped by a palisade of sharpened stakes. It was the finest and highest fortification they had seen; but like the city it had been overthrown. More watchtowers had stood at intervals along it; now their stones lay tumbled and fire-blackened on the grass.

On the outskirts of the place Egrith made a discovery; a patch of curious fleshy-stemmed plants, tubers growing thickly round their roots. Raw, the things had a sweetish, earthy taste; cooked, they were better. A fire was coaxed into life in one of the roofless buildings; the Sealanders sat all day boiling pan after pan of the strange earth-fruits, burning fingers and mouths in their haste to gulp the things down. Their hunger appeased, they stoked the fire again, making some shift to dry their clothes. They passed an uneasy night in the ruins, starting at the slightest sounds; the splash and drip of water, calls of night-flying birds. The desolate place seemed thronged with ghosts; even the Dancing Man sat frowning, a drawn sword by his side, a spear laid ready to hand.

Morning brought a cheering gleam of sunlight. They gathered the last of the tubers, cramming what they couldn't eat into their packs. At last it seemed their luck was changing; for they were leaving the hills. Beyond the ruins the land swept down to a great green plain. Along the horizon ran a strange dusky band; beyond, very sharp and clear, peaks jutted into the sky, laced with the rolling blue and silver of clouds. The sight further heartened them; and Elgro smiled, gripping Rand's arm. 'There, my Lord,' he said, pointing, 'is as fine a place as I have seen, to search for Gods.'

They started down, in good spirits; but the promise of the morning was not sustained. Before they had cleared the hills, clouds were once more climbing to obscure the sun. The distant mountains vanished; and rain began to fall, as heavily as before. They plodded on dourly, pausing once to eat. Shortly after Matt, who was leading, stopped and pointed. Rand joined him, and Egrith and the Dancing Man. They stood staring, frowning up at the obstruction that blocked their path.

It looked like nothing so much as the crest of a vast, frozen wave, twenty feet or more in height and as black and shiny as polished jet. It seemed the land sloped up to the lip of the bluff; in places too the rock of which it was composed overhung slightly, heightening the curious impression. Elgro, approaching carefully, struck with his spear-tip; gently at first, then harder. Chips flew; he picked one up, stood turning it in his palm. Its edges were sharp as the blade of a knife.

The party moved to the right, seeking a way round or over the obstacle. A mile or so farther on, the cliff edge was split by a series of deep cracks. They climbed, carefully, one of the little ravines so formed, stood once more staring. In every direction save the one from which they had come the rock lay bare and glittering. No tree grew, no blade of grass; the wind, rushing across the emptiness, made a thin, persistent moan. Stretching into distance were more of the curious wave-like forms, like ripples on a gigantic pond, each crest the height of a man. It was as if the land itself had burned, flowing outward from some focus of unspeakable heat.

Rand pushed the wet hair from his eyes and frowned.

He said slowly, 'The Hare King told me, there were once Giants. Elgro, could this be?'

The Dancing Man pulled a face. 'That I do not know,' he said. 'But if this was their work, I shouldn't have cared to meet them.'

The party trudged south, through the grey void of the still-falling rain.

The strange place was vaster in extent than they had realised. Water had collected in every dip and hollow of the rock; they splashed knee-deep through lake after lake, some of them scores of paces wide. Darkness overtook them far from shelter. Lacking fuel, they could build no fire; they ate the remainder of the tubers raw, huddled miserably in the lee of one of the curious ridges. Round them the wind howled and zipped like an entire legion of spirits.

The rain eased toward morning. The sun climbed blind and red, throwing long spiky shadows across the rock. To the south rose the peaks they had struggled to reach. They drank a little water from the pools, squeezed out their cloaks as best they could and staggered on.

The hours that followed were torture of a different kind. The sun, strengthening, brought steam boiling from the rocks; the strange landscape blurred and shook, hazed with vapour. Also the ridges to the south were steeper than any they had seen. The land rose in swell after swell, each terminating in a vicious, jagged little cliff. They detoured and backtracked wearily, stumbling and skidding, gashing hands and knees on the sharp rock. The place, most certainly, was cursed; for strive as they might, the hills drew no closer.

It was past midday before they reached the final crest; and another hour before a safe descent was discovered. They ran and leaped the last few yards, rolled gasping in unbelievable grass. They lay a time seeing the high rock they had quitted cut the sky like an edge of night; then Elgro snorted disgustedly, and delivered his opinion. 'Giants I cannot speak of, or Gods,' he said. 'But I have had some small experience of demons. And demons it was beyond a doubt that shaped that place, to be their own.'

Beyond their resting place a track led through a little wood. Bluebells hazed the grass. It was as if the tree boles rose from a vivid lake; between them shone the sunlit flank of a hill. They climbed, slowly. At the crest they turned, saw the place they had left lie black and shimmering like a miles-long scab of pitch.

That night they came on a scattered flock of sheep, grazing untended at the head of a tree-filled valley. At the base of a rocky outcrop showed the mouths of several caves. They built a fire in the largest, slept comfortably for the first time in weeks, and with full bellies.

Elgro roused his master early next morning. Rand sat up, grunting and rubbing his face. Outside the cave mouth, sunlight dazzled through a screen of leaves. The morning was golden, and still. Somewhere a bird piped; close at hand was the tinkle of running water. Rand turned, frowning; and the Dancing Man tilted his head, laid a finger to his lips. He heard it then, distant but clear; a high fluting, mixed with the steady thudding of a drum.

The others were already awake; they stood chafing their hands and frowning. The noise faded, eddied closer. The Dancing Man ducked under the cave mouth, cautiously parted the bushes. He stiffened then and wriggled back, beckoning the others to join him.

Along the valley bottom moved an odd procession. First came the musicians, leaping and gyrating; then a little knot of white-robed men; then a cart drawn by oxen, an elegant affair with slender gilded wheels. On it, bound upright to a post, stood a black-haired, bare-legged girl in a short yellow tunic. She was wrenching at the cords that held her, trying to break free. Cymbal men followed, and more dancers and priests; bringing up the rear was a procession of folk in multicoloured trews and tunics, for the most part carrying bows or spears.

The Sealanders watched in silence. The procession passed not much more than a stone's throw away, moved on up the little coombe. At the head of the valley the track climbed steeply. The cart was halted, the girl released. She was bundled roughly forward; and the whole group of people vanished from sight over the crest.

Rand, staring, met Elgro's puzzled frown. He ran stooping, along the high side of the valley, darting cautiously from rock to rock. The others followed, keeping below the skyline.

Beyond the ridge the land sloped with unexpected steepness. Hills ringed the horizon, blue and grand; closer, immediately below their vantage point, was a great tongue-shaped depression, its sides thickly overgrown. In it a lake lay black and utterly still.

The procession was once more visible, descending the last few yards of a rocky path. At the water's edge grew a stout, gnarled tree. The strangers clustered round it, with much shouting and gesticulating. A wait; and horns blew across the water, their voices clear and glittering. The party began to retreat, it seemed with more haste than dignity; behind them, tethered at the lake edge, they left the girl. The cart was turned, the oxen prodded into a trot; and the procession headed back the way it had come, vanishing finally between the sloping shoulders of the hills.

Elgro watched it go, and shrugged. 'This,' he said, 'is extremely odd. Either these folk are mad, which seems most likely, or my eyes have been deceiving me.' He rose; and there drifted from below a single piercing cry.

'Eyes and ears both,' said Elgro dryly. 'Now that I cannot have. *My Lord* . . .'

He was too late. Rand had risen without a word, set off down the hillside at a fast run. Elgro swore his loudest and loped in pursuit, waving to the rest to follow.

By the time they gained the lip of the depression their leader was halfway to the water, running with great leaps. Elgro pulled up, panting; and Matt gripped his shoulder, pointed silently. Across the loch, speeding toward the opposite bank, ran a smooth vee-shaped ripple. For an instant, a pale bulk might have showed behind it; then it was gone. The water swirled, and was still again.

Elgro tackled the descent, still cursing. When he reached the tree, Rand had already slashed through the cords. The girl sagged forward, knee-deep in water; the Dancing Man caught her roughly, pulled her to the bank. 'What is your tribe?' he demanded. 'This is my Lord Rand, a King of Sealand. What is this place called?'

She could only shake, and whimper.

Galbritt said, 'Something was in the fjord.'

They stared at the water, gripping their sword hilts. Orms were not unknown in Sealand. Egrith said apprehensively, 'Perhaps we should have left her where she was. The monster will be angry.'

Elgro snorted derisively. He said, 'The water horse eats no maiden's flesh. Salmon he will take in season, and browse among the deep weed. These people are fools. In any case, better use can be made of this.' He shoved the girl's kilt up with his foot, stared appraisingly, then hauled her to her feet. He said, 'To ease a sickness, we would all risk much.'

Galbritt said, frowning, 'What sickness, Dancing Man?'

Elgro inclined his head, and grinned. He said beneath his breath, 'The sickness of our Lord the King.'

From above came a high-pitched shout. Elgro jerked his head up; and something bright and rushing flicked past his eyes. A thud; and Galbritt staggered. He said, 'Our Lord the King.' Then he dropped to his knees, sagged forward. From his neck protruded six inches of gaily-feathered shaft.

Elgro took his captive's wrist, and ran. Missiles hummed past him. Another man flung his arms up with a shriek, toppled into the lake.

Ahead, the valley side steepened. A great rock thrust out above the water. The Dancing Man ducked underneath, Rand at his elbow. A yell from behind; the Sealanders turned, stared back appalled.

The figure, howling defiance, was running swiftly up the steep path to where a fringe of heads above the valley rim marked the attackers. They saw an arrow strike it, and another. It staggered; and a volley of shafts hissed down the cliff. Ensor rolled, fell headlong. The body struck the sloping ground beyond the path, rolled again with a flailing of arms and legs, lay still. Silence fell; and Egrith groaned, beating his fists on rock. 'King Rand,' he said, 'you have killed us all.'

The path was filling now with jostling men. Thirty or forty were visible, and others still crowding to the brink. The Sealanders backed, frowning; and Rand exclaimed. Beneath the overhand, what had seemed a dense shadow was in fact the mouth of a considerable cave. He rolled sideways, wriggled; they heard him thump down inside. His voice called again, hollowly, from the ground.

Elgro followed, shoving the girl ahead of him. The others crowded after, straightened staring. They were in the shaft of a ragged tunnel. It sloped down steeply, into blackness. Somewhere close could be heard the splashing of water.

There were voices at the cave mouth. They edged back instinctively, further into the dark. The voices jabbered excitedly. A spear glanced from the rock wall; but none of the pursuers made to enter.

The girl was dragging back, desperately. Elgro shook her, like a dog with a rat. 'Be still, you little idiot,' he said. 'Or I shall put my sword into you.'

Rand frowned behind him at the darkness. He said, 'Elgro, where could this lead?'

Elgro shook his victim again. He said, 'To all the Hells, for all I know.'

Egrith said shakily, 'I would not care to go down into Hell.'

Elgro nodded at the cave mouth. 'Go back the way you came then,' he said, 'and take the quicker route.' He ducked into the gloom, towing the girl behind him.

The passage wound and twisted, in places barely an

armspan wide. Fifty paces from the entrance the darkness was complete; the air was filled with a sharp, fishy stench that caught Rand's throat, making him cough and gag. The girl moaned, wordlessly.

Elgro grunted, prodding with a spear tip, setting each foot carefully. For a while the rock trended steeply down in blackness; then the passage widened. He straightened, and blinked. From somewhere ahead came ghostly grey light.

The light increased. They emerged in a little round chamber, like a room hewn from stone. In the far wall the tunnel plunged down again, gaping like a throat; above, a shaft rose to a circle of pale sky. Rand, staring up, saw translucent fronds of bracken; as he watched, the lip was eclipsed by a sailing edge of white. He said, 'Elgro, we could climb.'

The Dancing Man frowned, nostrils dilated. He said, 'Listen.'

At first there was nothing but the omnipresent splash and drip of water. Then they heard a far-off gurgling, ending in a noise like a great sucking gasp. It came again; and with it a slithering and rasping, as of some huge weight dragging itself over rock. The girl screamed. In the enclosed space, the sound was deafening.

Elgro grabbed Rand's elbow. He said urgently, 'Up . . .'

A yard or more above the cavern floor ran a rock ledge, green with algae. The party scrambled hastily, stood tensed on the insecure footing; and Rand, staring, saw the opposing tunnel fill and bulge. A pale mass rose into the chamber, grew a great glistening tip that waved and quested. He saw liver-coloured rings of muscle, a raw mouth that opened, snapped.

Instantly the place was full of din. The girl cried out again, scrabbling at him. Rubble showered, crashing; Egrith, brushed from his perch, vanished with a despairing shout. The mass swelled, ballooning to fill the chamber; and Elgro raised his sword double-handed, struck.

The effect was appalling. The keen blade, with all the Dancing Man's strength behind it, sheared cleanly through the horror. The body-tip fell, mouth still gaping. The monster writhed, geysering foam and blood; then the whole great bulk subsided. The thing extended itself, weaving in blind pain; and as slowly began to stream past, yard after yard, groping into the tunnel they had quitted. They stared down, eyes bulging, and saw it clearly for what it was. It was obscene, gigantic; and it was a worm.

Egrith lay still at the bottom of the pit. Elgro, his face contorted, stepped down, turned the body with the butt of a spear. What flesh the slime had touched was white and scalded, as if by boiling water; the head lolled grotesquely to one side. The Dancing Man stared up. He said, 'He broke his neck.'

Rand turned to the rock wall, shuddering, and began to climb.

That night as they lay in the heather the Dancing Man crawled to where the girl was huddled, pulled the cloak they had given her roughly aside. She began to writhe and mew; and he clapped a hand impatiently across her mouth. 'Be still, little Rat,' he said. 'And for the sake of all the Gods, be quiet. I mean no harm, but to keep you from a chill. Now lie close, and stop your snivelling; for you are for my Lord the King.'

II

His dog's sense roused him at first light. He frowned, sniffed and was instantly awake. His hands, groping beside him, touched nothing but grass. He sat up, with an oath. There was no sign of her. The little dell in which they had slept lay empty and still, mist-streaks drifting between the trunks of trees.

He stared round him, narrowing his eyes; then rose, buckling his sword belt. A path wound through the copse; he followed it, stepping silently, and paused. Somewhere ahead, a twig snapped; and again.

He flattened himself to the bole of a tree, stayed waiting. The figure came cautiously, muffled in its cloak, a silhouette in the early light. It stepped past; and Elgro pounced, knife in hand. The blade was poised when a muffled squeak checked the stroke. He half-overbalanced, grunting.

She said furiously, 'Let me go, you Sealand oaf. You'll make me drop the eggs.'

Elgro said, 'Eh? What?'

She said, 'These.' Beneath the cloak she held a wicker basket. The Dancing Man, staring, saw it was filled to the brim. Beside the eggs were a loaf of bread, a pitcher of milk, a great round of cheese. He frowned at them. He said, 'Where did you get these?'

She sniffed. She said, 'That's my affair. In any case they're not for you. They're for the Prince.'

He fell into step with her. He said, 'He's not a Prince. He's the King of Crabland.'

She tossed her head. She said, 'If I am a Rat, I will call you what I choose. Are you his servant?'

Elgro drew himself up. He said quietly, 'I am his Dancing Man.'

She looked at him curiously, from black-rimmed hazel eyes. She said, 'I have heard of such people. Can you raise the dead?'

He snapped, 'If needs be, child.'

She sniffed again. She said, 'I doubt it. If last night was an example, you cannot raise the living. I thought you Sealanders boasted of your prowess.'

He stopped, staring; and she glanced up at him amusedly. 'Go on,' she said. 'Now beat me, to prove your manhood. And make me drop your Lord's breakfast.'

'Last night,' he said grimly, 'when you were whimpering with fright, you were glad enough of company.'

'Last night,' she said, 'I whimpered with the cold. I needed a man to warm me.'

He growled. He said, 'You were warmed.'

'Aye,' she said composedly. 'By your cloak.'

She turned aside; and he gripped her arm. He said, 'This is the way we came.'

She pulled away, disdainfully. She said, 'And this is the way I go.' She laughed. 'Sealander, if I were to run, you and your great feet would never catch me.'

He said tartly, 'Why don't you?'

'Because my folk live far away,' she said. 'And you at least, as I have seen, can use a sword.' She pushed aside an overhanging branch, let it spring back. He caught it, and swore.

The path wound down to a little glade, hazed with the blue flowers. The sun, striking between the tall saplings that lined it, made shafts of misty light. A brook chattered over stones, ran clear and deep between overhanging banks.

She thrust the basket into his arms. She said, 'Orm killer, with that great weapon of yours, do you think you can guard my eggs?' She walked to the middle of the stream, stood fiddling with the neck of her dress, raised it quickly over her head. She said, 'I have a certain odour clinging to me. I think it's Sealand sweat.'

The tunic thumped into his arms. She walked forward to where the water deepened. She knelt, panting, began splashing herself vigorously. She said, 'Why are you so far from your homeland? You and your fine King?'

He stared. Her body was slender, with high, firm breasts. Beneath her arms were crisp curls of black hair.

She looked over her shoulder. She said, 'I asked a question, Dancing Man.'

He shrugged. He said, 'It's a long tale. Not one you would understand.'

She said sharply, 'What makes you so sure?'

He stayed silent.

She ducked her head; then rose, flinging water drops from her hair. She said, 'If you have seen enough, put your eyes back in your head and undo that bundle. Also, give me back my tunic.'

The bundle contained trews and a woollen jerkin; the

clothes a sheepherder might use, up in the hills. The tunic she employed to dry herself. She waded to the bank, dressed quickly. She said, 'In Sealand, do the women wear fine clothes?'

He frowned, remembering a certain Queen. He said, 'It has been known.'

She examined herself, critically. She said, 'You sound gruff. I think you are displeased.'

He smiled, and made no answer.

In the clearing, Rand sat quietly on a rock. Beside him was Matt. There was no sign of the others.

Elgro ran to him. He said. 'What happened, my Lord?'

Rand withdrew his eyes from a high tree branch, where a lone bird sat and piped. He said, 'They found me unworthy to be their King. So I released them.'

Elgro flushed deep red, pulling his lips back from his teeth. In his rage he ran a little way up the side of the coombe, and back. He said, 'Had I been with you, this would not have happened.'

Rand shook his head mildly. He said, 'It was their choice. Also they came honourably, when they could have killed me as I slept. Who was I to tell them no?'

Elgro snarled, and turned on the one-time Navigator. He said, 'You could have prevented them.'

Matt, whittling at a stick, stared up with his little black wide-spaced eyes. 'Use your head, Dancing Man,' he said bluntly. 'What could I have done, against six? As things stand, at least I spared one pair of hands to serve the King.'

Elgro stood glaring at the empty hillside, clenching and unclenching his fists; but the girl shrugged. 'Good,' she said. 'There will be that much more for us. Dancing Man, if I gather sticks, will your powers extend to the kindling of a flame?'

Elgro stared at her darkly, pulling at his badger-striped hair; but Rand smiled. He said, 'Can this be the little thing we stole from the Worm?'

Elgro grunted. He said shortly, 'It is.'

She walked quickly to the King, knelt with unexpected

humility and reached to touch his wrists. She said, 'These hands saved my life. Now it is yours, to do with as you choose.'

Rand shook his head, and pushed her hair back gently. He said, 'Your life is your own, child. And my Champion struck the blow, not I. How are you called?'

She hung her head. 'Rat,' she said meekly.

He frowned, and rubbed his mouth. He said, 'That is no sort of name.'

She blushed. 'If it please you,' she said, 'it will serve, till my Lord bestows another on what he owns.'

Rand looked up, surprised. 'She speaks well, Elgro,' he said. 'Also, see these shapely hands. She is a pretty child; she will make someone a fine wife one day.'

But the Dancing Man was still too angry to answer.

A fire was built; and the girl prepared a meal, quickly and deftly. When they had eaten, and the pots were scoured and packed, she ventured a question. Elgro answered curtly that they had come from the north, from the country of the Hare People; and she frowned. 'Then you crossed the Black Rock,' she said. 'How long did you spend on it?'

Elgro, more soothed by a good breakfast than he would have cared to admit, shrugged. 'A night,' he said carelessly. 'And parts of two days.'

She frowned again, biting her lip. 'That was badly done,' she said. 'As you love your King, do not be so foolish again. I would not have the devils rot his teeth.'

Elgro sniffed. 'We saw no devils,' he said. 'Or if we had, I have powers to overcome them. I do not fear your stories, child; the Rock is empty.'

'Oh, la,' said the Rat, turning up her short nose. 'Then do you return there, friend of ghosts, and sit a week with them. Come back to me blind and hairless, and tell these things again.' She stared intently, eyes glowing beneath her thick brows; and Elgro grunted and turned away, impressed despite himself.

Later the question of a direction was raised. Rat was

once more informative. 'All this land,' she said, waving a slim arm, 'the Land of the Hundred Lakes, was taken by the Horse Warriors in my grandfather's time. Their great castle lies to the south. Beyond is the sea, and my father's country. Where people sit in safety, and are not fed to Worms.'

Rand said quickly, 'Do you have strong Gods?'

She pulled at her lip. 'We have Gods,' she said. 'But I cannot answer for their strength. Every year the Horse Warriors oppress us worse, raiding for slaves and sacrifices.' She brightened. 'We do have a Cunning Man though,' she said. 'He lives in a cave in a mountain, and is older than the trees. They say he remembers the Fire Giants, and fighting-ships like iron islands. If my Lord pleases, I will take you to him.'

So the matter was settled; and the diminished party struck south, through a land of purple hills and bitter blue waters. They travelled by night, hiding during the day. Villages there were in plenty; and farms and stockaded Towers, stony roads that carried a traffic of lumbering ox carts. Everywhere too were soldiers; dark faced, steel-capped men riding proud, tall horses. Left to themselves, the Sealanders would have fared badly; but mornings and evenings the girl flitted away, invariably returning loaded with provisions. Salt fish she brought and flour, eggs, goat cheese, milk. At Elgro's questionings she merely tossed her head. 'Rats live by stealth,' she said, 'and are accomplished thieves. Would you expect less of me?'

On the fourth morning they saw on the horizon a remembered band of pearly light. They pressed on swiftly, crossing great fells, always in sight of the sea. Evening found them once more clear of the hills; and by dusk they reached the coast. The sun, sinking in a yellow blaze, showed the outlines of a huge earthwork, brooding humpbacked over a shadowy foreland. Nearer stretched a desolate beach. Sand dunes were laced with wiry grass, through which the wind sang mournfully.

Rat walked to the water's edge and pointed. 'That is the

castle I told you of,' she said. 'The Lake King sits there, with a thousand men to guard him. Beyond is Long Spit.' She chewed a knuckle thoughtfully. 'I was captured on a fishing boat,' she said. 'There are villages somewhere to the west here. We are too few to man a warship, even if we could steal one; a fishing boat it must be.' She glanced up sidelong at Elgro. 'Unless your magic can grow us fins and tails,' she said, 'and swim us home in comfort.'

They walked some distance before coming on signs of habitation. The villages they finally reached were ramshackle and dirty. Boats there were, certainly; but all were drawn up firmly, and watchfires burned close by. Also dogs set up a shrill chorus at the party's approach. They saw what they wanted finally; a chubby, unhandy-looking little vessel, beached by herself in saltings a mile or so from the castle mound. Close by, smoke rose from a low hovel built of turves. There were no other signs of life.

Elgro circled away, pressing a finger to his lips. They saw him flit across the mud; moments later, straining ears might have caught a dull thump, the faintest of splashes. Then the Dancing Man was back. He squatted, driving his knife-blade into the ground to clean it. He said, 'She has a sail and oars, and water in the casks.'

Launching the vessel proved nearly beyond their strength. They strained and splashed, panting. A rising tide helped them; eventually, the boat slid clear. They sculled cautiously half an hour or more before hoisting the sail. A light breeze blew, steady to the south. Matt took the tiller; Long Spit, and the castle with its torchlit walls, faded in the gloom astern. The boat rolled, water chuckling and slapping under her blunt bows; and Elgro felt his spirits rise at the tang of salt.

He stood in the bows, muffled in his cloak, Rand at his side. 'My Lord,' he said softly, 'you have seen by now, surely, how the world goes. The crops spring, fish swim in the sea, there are men and women and towns. As in our own country, so in this; there is no Land of Ghosts. Also'—he jerked his head amidships, to where Rat dutifully tended the sail—'you have, to my eyes at least, replaced all you have lost. Let us stand further from the coast. Smaller ships than this have sailed to Sealand.'

But Rand turned a shocked face in the gloom. 'Elgro,' he said, 'that would be a shameful thing. She is no more than a child; also my word is given. What sort of men would we be, to save her from a Worm then bring her to more grief?'

Elgro opened his mouth again, closed it with a snap. He groaned inwardly, and held his peace.

They made good time. In the dawn they saw, stretching to the left, a great steely estuary; and Rat, crowing, called for Matt to alter course to the west. They sailed through the morning, closing slowly with the land. At midday she pointed again. Blue hills rose inland; beyond, ghost-pale against the sky, was a great massif. 'Snow Mountain,' she said. 'The highest hill in our country. My Lord, you will very soon be safe.'

Rand turned absentmindedly, and squeezed her shoulder.

They stood in once more toward the coast. To right and left, bobbing specks resolved themselves into fishing boats. The Lakeland vessel creamed between them, Rat capering and shouting in the bow. Shouts answered her, from every little ship.

They rounded a great snake-like promontory. Beyond was a narrowing estuary. Rat pointed excitedly. 'The Old Ones had a castle there,' she said. 'Then the Fire Giants came, blasting the land. Only we survived. We are the People of the Dragon, the oldest folk in the world.'

They passed the ruins, rising amid a green tide of trees. Beyond was a well-built town. A harbour was guarded by watchtowers and high earth walls; above, on the hill, reared a white-painted Hall. Boats were tied up at the quays, and greatships of unfamiliar design. Elgro, frowning, nudged his Lord's arm. He said, 'They have no trusses. How can that be?'

She turned to him scornfully. 'It is our secret,' she said.

'Our scribes wrote many secrets, hiding them in magic caves.' Then to Matt, 'Hold the centre of the channel, Sealander; the water shoals fast here.'

The sail came down at the run. The vessel rolled, bumped alongside the quay. Ropes were thrown and caught; and a surge of men came running, some with swords in their hands, some with spears. Elgro clawed at his belt, cursing; but the Rat jumped ashore, shouting delightedly. 'Dyserth, Cilcain,' she said. 'Put your weapons down this instant, and help my friends; or my father will have your ears.'

Consternation, on the quay. A man prostrated himself; others leaped to steady the boat. The noise spread; a crowd began to form, jostling and shoving. Elgro sheathed his sword, stood staring up. 'Rat,' he said gravely, 'who might your father be?'

She turned jauntily, hands on her ragged hips. 'Talsarno King,' she said. 'Lord of the Western Hills.'

Lines of torches lit the Hall with a warm orange glow. The light gleamed from glassware and brooches, costly silver plate. Board after board was piled with delicacies; trays of spiced meat, pastry, fresh-baked fish. Sucking pigs smoked, garnished with herbs and apples; lobsters reared blood-red, their claws locked in mock battle. Musicians played and jangled on a gallery; servingpeople moved among the many guests, replenishing horns and drinking cups from jar after jar of yellow Midsea wine. Sweet-smelling rushes covered the floor of the place; on the walls tapestries, heavy with golden thread, showed dogs and fishes and dragons. Mer-things swam and dolphins; the Great Orm reared its fearsome bulk, in a shower of glistening spray.

It was a feast such as the Sealanders had never seen. They lolled at ease, winepots in their hands, while a minstrel sang the tale of the great fight, repeated already a dozen times or more. Men roared their approval, banging cups and goblets; but Rand shook his head. 'It was a sad thing, living underground,' he said. 'I think it meant no harm.'

The song ended; and Talsarno clapped his hands. He sat at the head of the great table, the Rat beside him in a dress of blue and green, her hair bound with flowers and silver leaves.

'Now, King Rand,' he said, 'name what gift you choose. A woman here or there is nothing much; but a daughter is a different thing, more so as one grows old.'

Rand smiled. 'Honour my men,' he said, 'and it will please me well, my Lord. Elgro here struck the blow; and the Navigator brought us safely through our many troubles.'

'This is true,' said the Rat brightly. 'Also the Magician guarded me very well, taking me under his cloak to shield me from the cold. Yet for the love he bears our House, he offered me no harm.'

Rand toyed with his cup. 'I seek nothing save wisdom,' he said. 'Among ourselves we call these lands the Isles of Ghosts. If the dead in their country can be visited, then I must journey there; or know no rest.'

The King pulled at his beard. 'It saddens me to hear of such a wish,' he said. He lowered his voice. 'If I may counsel you,' he said, 'from greater years if not from greater wisdom, then I say this; that sorrows pass. All sorrows. King Rand, you are still young. Nothing endures.'

Rand said gravely, 'This will endure.'

Talsarno shrugged, and drained his cup. 'I have no skill in these matters,' he said. 'But there is a Sage, of whom my daughter spoke. For forty years and more he has shunned the light, communing only with the Gods. Old he was in my father's time; and his father before him, so they say. My seal will part his lips, if this is truly what you desire; but my spirits tell me no joy will come of it.' He laid a hand earnestly on Rand's arm. 'My Lord,' he said. 'Let me equip a greatship, to carry you to your homeland. Gold you can have in plenty, and wine and cloth; a dowry, for my daughter's life. You will sit in your own high Hall again; and the years will bring you peace.'

But Rand stayed silent, staring down; and the other sighed. 'More wine,' he said. 'In the morning, my daughter will guide you to the Sage. For the rest, we have no cause to love your countrymen; but between my house and the people of the Crab shall be eternal friendship. This my scribes will write and this I swear; by the White Hill and the Dragon, by Talgarrec and the Sons of Osin, who founded this kingdom when the Giants died and Time began afresh.'

The party was lodged for the night, richly enough; but Rand turned and tossed, waiting for the dawn. In another part of the place Rat too lay sleepless, wetting the new silk sheets with tears.

The track led up through a green valley, set thickly with lilac and tall spikes of delphinium. Higher, the hill slopes flamed with gorse and poppies. Rat led the way, astride a shaggy, goat-footed little pony. Myrnith, chief priest of the Dragon, followed; Rand and his Sealanders brought up the rear, with a file of Talsarno's soldiers. From time to time the Dancing Man swore, slapping at his arms and neck. The heat was intense; above each rider buzzed a cloud of stinging flies.

Beyond the treeline the air was cooler. They crossed screes of naked grey rock. The sun shone from a deep blue sky; a buzzard circled, a dot in the vast emptiness. Ahead were peaks and rock-walls, drenched in light. A breeze blew, lifting Rand's hair, bringing the scents of summer from the rich valleys below.

The girl reined. Beside the path was set a tall square post, outlandishly carved and painted. The party halted, uncertainly; and Myrnith turned, his round dark face impassive. 'Your men will wait here,' he said in his lilting voice. 'The ground beyond is holy; only priests may enter.'

Elgro dismounted awkwardly, hitching at his belt. 'I am

135

holy too,' he said, 'having danced away greater ghosts than any in this country. Also, I serve the King. Where he goes, I go.'

The soldiers muttered, frowning; and Myrnith shook his head. He said stonily, 'It is forbidden. It is the Law of the Dragon.'

The Dancing Man dropped a hand to his sword hilt. 'When one Law meets another,' he said equably, 'a test of strength is customary. Which of you will discuss the matter with me?'

A pause, that lengthened; then the priest shrugged. 'Defy the Gods if you choose,' he said. 'On your head be it, friend.'

Rat swung her legs from the pony, hitched his reins to the totem. 'I also claim my right,' she said. 'I am a priest, by privilege of birth.'

Myrnith stared down at her gravely. He said, 'You will not like what you see.'

They climbed again. The path steepened, angling across a great slope of granite. Above, the shoulder of the mountain rose in soaring buttresses. The priest stepped to the cliff face, raised a hand. 'Wait here,' he said. 'Perhaps the Old One will speak, perhaps not.' He moved forward, vanished behind a projecting spur of rock. He was gone some time. 'The Gods favour you,' he said when he returned. 'Also he knows your errand, by some skill of his own. Listen, but do not question. If you question him, he will not answer.'

Rand stepped forward, the girl at his elbow, the Dancing Man close behind. The spur concealed a cleft in the apparently solid rock. Within it, the air struck chill. The cliff walls closed, gleaming with damp. A dozen paces, and the way widened again. The King stopped involuntarily, the girl clinging to his arm.

It was as if at some time gigantic forces had split the entire mountain. The walls of the fissure in which he stood soared to an unguessed height. Above, all that was left of the sky was a ragged silver thread. What light reached the floor of the place was grey and dim. The wind bawled, over the distant peak; the chasm responded, uttering a single note that shook the rock, passed to silence.

Some fifty paces ahead the walls of the place swept together. He made out a flight of rough-hewn steps, bowls piled with rotted offerings. Above, the rock was pierced by a single hole, no more than a handspan wide. A heavy stench came from it; round it roughly mortared blocks showed where the anchorite had been sealed alive. They were stained and blotched, as if over the years the thing had become a filthy throat.

His stomach rebelled. He choked, and would have turned away; but a voice spoke from the cell, thin and reedy as a ghost.

'In the old times,' it said, 'the Giants came. Elwin Mydroylin was King in the west. The warboats came, the boats of floating iron. Forests grew on their decks. Others sailed beneath the water, hurling javelins that scorched the earth. The crops were withered, and trees in the passes next the sea. The cities of the Giants were destroyed. Elwin Mydroylin went down to night, and his sons who killed the Dragon on Brondin Mere. The Wanderer came to the White Hill. He saw the love of women, and it was false. He saw the love of men, and it was false. The Dragons came in the north. The hills were shaken.'

Elgro's voice ran in the cleft. *'Seer, where is the Land of Ghosts?'* The rock-walls caught the words, flinging them mockingly forward and back; and the wind roared, playing the place like a gigantic pitch-pipe.

The noise faded. The voice went on, inexorably. 'Elwin went down to night. The House of Mydroylin was extinguished. Haern came, and Morfa, and Amlwych Penoleu. The Dragons fought in the north, and the sea was let in. The indivisible was divided.'

The stink gusted. Rand swayed, feeling sweat start out on him coldly. The voice came again. 'The Mere People took the south, loosing the devils of the Fen. Beyond, the Forest grew. The seeker after Gods must pass it. None succeeds. After the realm of Gods, there may be Ghosts.'

A pause; and a scrabbling, at the hole. A hand appeared, and forearm; mired with filth, streaked with bright sores. The sores moved and throbbed. The voice rose in a shout of laughter. 'Approach, Sealander,' it said. 'Receive my blessing.'

Rand's sight flickered. He reeled, felt the Dancing Man grip his arms. He turned, hands to his face; when he could see again the sun was hot on his back. Above rose the cliff; below, a great distance away, were the horses and waiting men. He panted, shuddering; and Elgro took his shoulders. 'Now we have seen wisdom,' said the Dancing Man between his teeth. 'Where to next, my Lord?' The guide reined, pointing. 'Follow the track,' he said. 'The way is clear enough. Beyond the woods, the Mere People have their towns. No Kermi deals with them; they are a jealous folk, not to be trusted. The Horse Warriors hold the south, from the Great Plain to the sea. If you must journey in their lands, journey by night. They love no strangers.'

He turned his horse. 'I have brought you as the King ordered me,' he said. 'Here, Talsarno's writ ends. Trust no man beyond the woods; and the Gods be with you.' He raised his arm briefly in salute; and the Dragon staffs wheeled, the little escort clattered back the way it had come.

Rand clicked to his mount, moved on down the winding track. Matt followed, slumped unhandily in the painted saddle; Elgro, grumbling, brought up the rear.

They were leaving the high hills now. They crossed long slopes bright with speedwell, set with heather tufts and clumps of bilberry. Beyond, pines rose from thickets of rhododendron. There were no apparent signs of life; but twice Elgro turned, watching back fixedly at the skyline.

On the lower ground the pines gave way to a dense forest of beech. They rode an hour or more, through tilted green glades; it was early evening before they reached the forest edge, and reined. A last slope led to a meandering, shallow stream; beyond, a blue plain lifted to the horizon.

Elgro ranged his horse beside his lord. Rand turned, enquiringly; and the Dancing Man smiled. 'We should camp there, by the stream,' he said, pointing. He glanced once more over his shoulder. 'I saw some mushrooms a little way back,' he said, 'that will make a tasty supper. I will be with you presently.'

He drove his heels at his pony's sides, jogged back the way he had come. Rand stared after him with troubled eyes, but made no comment. He walked his horse forward, to the stream.

The Dancing Man waited, eyes narrowed, till his companions were out of sight. He turned his mount then, at an angle from the path, crashed into the undergrowth.

The rider came slowly, letting the pony pick its own way. To either side, the forest was still and warm; the late sun, slanting through the leaves, spread a canopy of gold.

At one point the track angled sharply beside a massive smooth trunk. A branch as thick as a man's body hung above the way. The pony passed beneath; and a figure dropped with a swift thud. The animal squealed, kicking its heels with fright. Its rider, borne from the saddle, rolled threshing. She tried to rise; but the weight of the attacker kept her pinned. She writhed, desperate; and a broad-bladed dagger was pushed between her teeth. 'Answer me quickly,' hissed Elgro, 'and tell no lies. Are you alone?'

She nodded, whimpering; and he twined his fingers in her short hair. 'Now know,' he said, 'women are my bane. A Fairy woman it was that cursed my Lord, making him the child he is. Twice you have shamed me, and many more than twice times mocked my words. Now in your silliness you follow us again. Is it to mock?'

She moaned, terrified, and tried to shake her head.

'Oh, la,' said Elgro, 'This is a different song. Who sent you, Rat? Was it your father, to spy?'

The merest headshake. She closed her eyes, panting.

'Why then,' said the Dancing Man, 'perhaps you love the King. Is that the tale?'

She tried to cough, and choked.

'I have seen this business of love,' said Elgro. 'And a curse and plague it is, when women get their hands on it. Love there is, as we Magicians know; it leaps between the stars, and drives the whole green world. Yet foolish men pine for a face or thigh, with bone beneath no prettier than their own, swearing for lack of them the sun will fade; and this you know full well. So you run to one and to the next, saying "Oh la, behold and worship me;" or, "You are a King, and this your Dancing Man; how quaint he seems".' He groped for her, with his free hand; and she groaned. 'Now hear a Mystery,' he said. 'That these, and this, and this beneath your kilt, were given you by God. Yet women, who are bags of blood, are vain as little babes, and price the shape that Heaven only lent. So kingdoms fall, and men run mad, because you squat to piss.'

The knife-blade shook. 'No man followed me, in all my life, and lived,' he said. 'Yet for my lord's sake, I bear with you. This perhaps is love; and high above your understanding.' He flung her from him, with a great heave. She rolled across the leaves, lay shaking. He sheathed the dagger, walked to stand over her. 'You chose the road,' he said. 'Now follow it. Be faithful to my lord; or my ghost will find you, if I no longer breathe.'

She got to her knees, wearily; hung her head, and was very sick. When she had finished she raised an ashen face. She said in a low voice, 'Dancing Man, now may I catch my horse?'

He stepped aside, impassively. She walked to where the animal stood; mounted and rode with icy dignity, down toward the Plain.

The sun rose, and set. They walked to the south, steadily. Rand led, his chin sunk on his chest; after him came Matt, jogging stolidly, gripping the saddle horns in front of him. The girl led the packhorses; Elgro Dancing Man brought up the rear. Duck and heron rose at their approach, honking and wheeling. They forded shallow streams, paced by the hour beside desolate fens, flecked all over with the fluffy white of marsh grass. Sometimes they passed rough settlements, once an entire lake city, built from the shore on a forest of stiltlike legs. The inhabitants of the region were numerous; but they neither approached nor offered harm. One and all seemed content to watch from a distance, standing in sullen little knots as the Sealanders passed.

The girl rode for the most part silently, bearing the discomforts of the journey without complaint. Each night she boiled the party's drinking water, setting the pannikins carefully aside to cool. A pouch at her belt contained delicate bone hooks. She set traps for the water birds, tieing the baited hooks to wooden floats; and once she stole some little wicker pots, with them caught a yard-long eel. The Sealanders wouldn't touch it, to a man; she cleaned the fish and ate a part herself, sitting a little distance away, her dark eyes fixed on Rand.

The following day they came on an ancient road, its surface cracked and broken. In places chunks had been levered up entire by the springing of bushes and weeds. They were of stone chips set in a black, tarry matrix. Such roads existed here and there in Sealand, though the art of making them had long been lost. To Rand it seemed strange to come upon one here; but it ran south, straight as an arrow, vanishing into distance. He turned his horse on to it, calling to the others to follow.

The road dipped and rose, flooded for much of its length. The horses splashed knee-deep, sidling and snorting. Ahead the lake stretched to the horizon, dotted by clumps of reed, islands crowned with stunted, unhealthy-looking trees. The party rode in silence, eyes screwed against the dazzle of sunlight; till at midday the girl reined. Rand, glancing back, saw she sat the pony rigidly, staring down.

He walked his mount back, and stared in turn. Beside the road, the water was crystal clear. In it, pinned to the drowned grass, lay the body of a girl. She was naked, her flesh white as Midsea marble. Her eyes were open, watching up with a curious intentness; her hair, dark and long, flowed slowly round her face, graceful as fern. At knees and elbows, forked stakes had been driven into the earth to hold her firm.

Twice the King spoke, gently; but Rat, it seemed, could no longer hear. He took the pony's bridle finally, led her away. She came unprotesting, staring back at the death place as it receded. He spoke twice more, receiving no answer. He shook his head, and let her be.

They camped, unhappily, on the driest part of a swampy islet. Rat moved about her duties quietly, cleaning and preparing the game they had brought with them, setting out her baited lines. Later she slipped away, walked to the water's edge. She sat awhile, rocking dully on her heels, staring to the north while the sunset flared and faded. Then she reached to her belt, took out the little knife she carried. She laid her hand on the ground, pressed the blade without fuss into her palm, dragged it down her forearm.

It was Rand who missed her from the camp. He walked, frowning, to where she still sat huddled. He stooped then with a cry, tried to take her arm; but she wrenched away. 'Leave me alone,' she said unsteadily. 'It's my blood; I can drop it where I choose.'

He scooped her up despite her struggles, blundered back shouting for Elgro and Matt. A linen shirt, her father's gift, was brought from one of the packs, torn into strips for bandages. He washed the long wound carefully, binding her arm and wrist; when it was done, and the fire stoked and blazing, he regarded her sternly. 'Why did you do it?' he demanded. 'Have we become so terrible to you, that you must creep off and take your life?'

She sat shivering, huddled in a blanket. 'It wasn't for me,' she said bitterly. 'It was to quiet a ghost. Myrnith would have known the proper way; but all I had was blood.'

'Whose ghost?'

'Bethan,' she said. 'Who the Marsh Gods took.'

He stared, in dawning understanding. He said, 'Was she a Kermi?'

She grimaced, cradling the injured arm. 'We played together,' she said. 'Afterwards, we were in love. She vanished a month ago. We thought it was a wolf.' She swallowed. 'There was a storm,' she said. 'I took a boat. I hoped I would be drowned. But the Gods didn't want me. The Horse Warriors caught me instead.'

She stared at the fire. 'If we go north,' she said, 'they take us to feed to Worms. If we go south, the Marsh is always hungry. The Sealanders raid from the west and the people from Green Island, who drink seal blood and cut their fingers off when their chieftains die. And all the time the Horsemen want our land. Soon, if my father doesn't stop singing and being wise, there will be no more Kermi. The world will be at peace again.' She turned to stare at Elgro, for the first time in days. 'She did not ask to be nailed into a bog,' she said. 'But doubtless as a woman she deserved it.'

Rand frowned at her, shaking his head; and the Dancing Man rose, stalked off into the dark.

That night she lay beside the King, wrapped in his blankets. Twice in the still watches he woke to hear her sobbing. He drew her to him finally, stroking her hair. 'You should not have followed us,' he said gently. 'Your debt was paid already; I go to the Land of Ghosts, where there is nothing but sorrow.'

In time her head grew heavy against his shoulder. He lay till dawn, watching the white mists crawl, hearing the sighs and gurglings of the marsh. He dozed at first light, woke bleary-eyed and heavy. The party saddled up and mounted, headed once more south. Rat looked as blenched as the water girl, while the usually silent Matt complained of pains in the head and back. Only the Dancing Man, splashing grimly in the rear, seemed unaffected.

By late afternoon they were clear of the marsh; but the Navigator's condition was worse. He rode wild-eyed, ranting and muttering, breaking into snatches of song. They camped before nightfall, improvised a couch for him from the packs and their contents. The girl sat beside him, raising his head from time to time to drink. He moaned and shouted far into the night, talking nonsense about Crabland, and fishing, and drinking Midsea wine. A very little wine they had with them, brought from Talsarno's Hall; they gave it him, and it seemed he dozed at last. To Rand's anxious questionings, the girl shook her head. 'He has a marsh fever,' she said. 'Twice I saw him drink bad water, in spite of what I asked; this has come of it.' She stared at Elgro, with her disturbing eyes. 'The time has come for your skill, Dancing Man,' she said. 'You who know the secrets of the stars.'

But Elgro turned away, his face set darkly. Later, while the girl slept, he spoke bitterly to Rand. 'In Crabland,' he said, 'when I was your father's man, I danced more fevers than my body has bones. I danced you into the world, though the midwives doubted your life. Now the power has gone. My legs no longer seem to belong to me, I see things several times over.' He spread his hands, regarded them gloomily. 'The Gods do this for shame, or mockery,' he said. 'Or this business of enchantment is more widespread than I thought.' He spoke as if to himself, frowning at the fire. 'What I said was true,' he muttered. 'And is true, through the world. And yet I sinned. How can this be?'

Rand reached to grip his shoulder. 'It will come back,' he said. 'When we are out of this place, and breathe clean air again.'

But Elgro shook his head, his eyes opaque. 'The times are altering,' he said. 'My Lord, I have the oddest thought; that one day Sealanders will own this country too. There will be no ghosts then, or need of Dancing Men.' He rubbed his face, wearily. 'It's my conceit,' he said. 'We think as we grow old, the world is ageing with us. Get yourself some rest, my Lord; I will watch for now.'

By morning, Matt had fallen into a slumber from which

none of their efforts could rouse him. They talked together, anxiously; then Elgro cut two saplings, lashed them to the harness of the packhorse, wove branches for a makeshift stretcher. On it the Navigator was tied, still breathing stertorously; and the grim march was resumed. They climbed steadily, into rolling green hills. By midday the sick man was awake, wrestling with the straps that held him, calling on all manner of Gods and spirits. When they stopped, to give him water and breathe the horses, he barely recognised them.

Deep in the hills, they came on the Black Rock again.

Rand would have ridden forward; but the girl clung to his arm. 'My Lord,' she said, 'there is death there. No one goes twice on the Rock, and lives.' She appealed to Elgro. 'Dancing Man,' she said, 'this isn't for myself. But if you go on, then think of a promise you made. I would as soon rest here and sleep, as see the King with the flesh boiled off his bones.'

Elgro stared at her for a time, setting his mouth and pulling his hair; then he turned his horse. 'My spirits tell me she is right, my Lord,' he said. 'Many demons live on the rock. We must pass it by.'

They turned east, thinking that offered the easier route. For most of the day the black band shimmered on the horizon. Finally it curved away, ending in a great ragged crest. They turned the horses thankfully, riding due south.

The land to which they came was the strangest they had seen. For mile after mile, the little hills were coated with hectic green. The grass grew limp and brilliant, the stems pulpy, the leaf blades a handspan broad. Crowning the hills were trees of proportionate vastness. Their shapes were bizarre. Some flung their branches straight as spear-shafts, a hundred feet and more into the sky; others writhed and twisted, springing in great knots and curves, thrusting out fists of root wherever they touched the ground. The horses shied and snorted; and the Rat looked concerned. 'I think,' she said, 'we should go east again, my Lord. This is bad land too; the winds from the Black

Rock make these things happen. I have heard it said that men grow monstrous too.'

But Rand shook his head. 'We will go south till nightfall,' he said. 'If the taint is in the air as you believe, then we have breathed enough already. We shall take no greater harm.'

Toward evening Matt, who had quietened, began to sing and shout once more. His bawling floated into the sky, among the appalling trunks and limbs; and the Dancing Man pulled at his lip. 'I wish the Gods would take him,' he said frankly. 'At least he would be at rest; here it seems he lives in Hell.'

The sun dropped toward the horizon. They topped a hill and bunched, instinctively. Facing them across the intervening slope was the strangest monster of all that strange land. Its limbs, bone white and stripped, raged and squirmed for yard after yard, stooping to brush the grass, flinging out roots thicker than the body of a man. The light struck through the sea of branches, luridly; and Elgro jerked a hand from beneath his cloak, fingers circled in the sign that wards off death. They sat the horses, staring; and a voice beside them made them leap with shock.

It was Matt. He stood swaying wildly, his face suffused. 'Behold,' he said. 'I see the World Tree, that stands at the end of Time. Under its roots the sea-Orms sit, and the Wolf that will eat the sun; and there are the Gods all in a row, with their eyes on fire and their pricks like a greatship's truss. Can you not see them?'

Rat cringed, hands to her mouth; and the others turned, climbing quietly from their horses. 'Matt, old friend,' said Elgro gently, 'we will let these matters be. We will sit down now, and eat; for these Gods, who I see very clearly, are tired and do not want to chatter. In the morning, you can talk to them; meanwhile tell me about the Great Storm again, when we rowed King Cedda to Blue Fen and saw the water snake. That is a better tale.' He nodded to Rand; and they leaped.

The other hunched his shoulders with surprising speed,

and thrust out his arms. He had always been noted for his strength; now it seemed redoubled. Rand, for all his bulk, was hurled across the grass; Elgro rolled cursing between the horses' feet. He was up in an instant, but the Navigator was quicker; he cried out, raising his arms, set off toward the monster calling at the top of his voice. They fled after him, appalled.

The branches were overhead, swooping and curving. Matt howled at the trunk, beating his fists. They reached him, and were flung away again. Red marks appeared before him, on the blenched white wood; then he fell, arching his body. They grabbed him, hauled him back somehow the way they had come. They laid him on the grass, prised at the locked jaws; but it was too late. His tongue was in his throat, and he was dead.

Rand straightened slowly. 'We will put him back in the harness,' he said. 'We will not leave him here; his ghost would never rest.'

They walked the horses silently, circling well clear of the great tree. In the last of the light, the girl reined. Beneath the pony's hooves was normal grass; they had passed the Forest.

Next day the sun was hidden. Cloud masses drove low overhead; it seemed they trapped the heat close to the earth, so that they sweated as they rode. Thunder shook and muttered, but no rain fell. Toward evening they reached the edge of a great plain. It soared away in the dull light, its ridges crowned by wind-smoothed crests of trees. To right and left tall posts were planted in the grass. They rode to the nearest. Plumes of dark hair moved in the rising wind; topping the thing was a great bleached skull. Lightning flickered, above the clouds; and Rand turned. 'This is the place they spoke of,' he said. 'The edge of the Horse Warriors' land.' He walked his mount forward, into the emptiness.

The storm broke toward nightfall. Rain fell in torrents; the blazing and din were continuous. They were far from shelter; they plodded grimly, cloaks flapping, hair and leggings streaming. An hour after dark they reached a village, huddled in a fold of downs. It was a poor enough looking place; but fires were burning here and there, there was a watchtower of sorts. They rode to the stockade, too weary for caution. Their hammerings finally produced a response. Questions were shouted, and answered; the gates creaked back. It seemed the Dragon's name carried some force, even in the south.

The huts were miserable affairs for the most part, mere holes scraped in the ground and thatched with reed. In one they were lodged, and Rat saw to the stabling of the horses. They lay restlessly, huddled in damp cloaks, while the storm grumbled into silence. Rand dozed eventually, only to be visited by monstrous dreams. It seemed the Orm-child floated to him, time and again, holding out her white arms. He lifted his own arms to her; and the whiteness changed on the instant to another thing, that woke him shaking in the first light of dawn.

He rose, stood swaying. Her breasts rose and fell in the dimness; the lashes brushed her cheek. She slept quietly, as though her ghost had made no journeyings. Beside her, the Dancing Man's face looked pale and drawn as a corpse. He left the hut, walked to the southern stockade. Hills showed on the horizon; the air was cold, and sweet.

Later they took counsel with the headman of the place; a grey-headed, embittered old creature, frail and much bent. 'The horses we will keep,' he said. 'Also their packs, to pay the trouble we have been to. The Horsemen do not like strangers in their country; heads have rolled, and villages been burned, for less than we have done. If you go south, and I say you are mad to think of it, you must go as slaves; for we are all slaves here. The Horsemen own the land.'

Rand said slowly, 'What do you know of their Gods?'

The other spat. 'Gods they have in plenty,' he said. 'Some ask for grain, and so they steal our crops. Others call for blood, and then they take our children. There is a great God in the south, or so I hear. His Priestess came of our people; but so holy was she that they let her be. And once she visited the Land of Ghosts, wandering there some time.'

Rand gripped his shoulder. 'Chief,' he said, 'is this the truth?'

The other shrugged tiredly. 'What should I know of truth?' he said. 'Once we were free, to farm our grain and feed our flocks in the valleys. Now we are slaves, and kiss the ground if a Horseman happens by. These are truths. If there are Gods, they have no thought of us. More than this I neither know nor care.'

Clothes were found for them; trews and coarse tunics of unbleached cloth. 'Now, surely, your heart's desire is achieved,' said Elgro grimly to the King. 'Lands you had, and they are gone. A Tower, that you left behind; a ship, and men to follow you. A ransom was in our saddlebags; and that we paid to lodge a night in a wet hole in the earth. Now we must bend our necks, wear cloth that stinks of farmers' sweat. If this is wisdom, then the world is on its head; and time enough for me to leave it.' He stared at his swordbelt lovingly, laid it aside. He hung the weapon from a lanyard round his neck, arranging the folds of his cloak to hide the blade. 'Some dirt on our faces would not I suppose come amiss,' he said. 'And while the thought is on me, my nose tells me there are pigs herded close by. I think I will go and roll in one of their sties; if I am to play a part, I must play it well.'

They left the village, tramping along a stony white road. A final slope took the place from sight. At the crest the girl turned, tears shining on her face. Rand, approaching awkwardly, laid a hand on her shoulder. He said, 'What is it?'

She pulled away, brushing her lashes with the back of her knuckles. 'It's nothing,' she said. 'It's only for my pony. They can't sell him; it would be dangerous.'

He frowned. He said, 'What will they do?'

She shrugged. 'Kill him and eat him, I suppose,' she said. 'My Lord, we must go on.'

The land was populous. They passed lines of ox carts,

file after file of the dark-faced, steel-capped soldiers. Here and there were ramshackle villages like the one in which they had lodged, and chequer-patterns of small square fields. Between them, palisaded towns clustered beneath Towers not unlike the castles of Sealand. Suspicious looks were cast at them a score of times; but they passed unmolested. In time the villages became less frequent. The road climbed and climbed again, crossing the great chalk backbone of the country. Hills reared in the emptiness, topped by the gaunt shapes of beacons; farmhouses huddled in the valleys, cattle no bigger than toys cropped the sparse grey grass. At one such place they bargained for their supper, paying with the last of the gold from Rand's belt. They slept the night in a rustling, hay-filled barn. In the morning a troop of soldiers passed, in charge of a dozen heavily loaded carts. Behind the tailboard of the last staggered four or five weary-looking men. Rand, frowning, saw one of the prisoners fall. The cart rumbled on indifferently, towing him in the dust.

They were nearing the sea. They entered an area of heathland, a flat, sour expanse laced by little watercourses, splashed with bogs. Pine trees rose in clumps above the endless rhododendron thickets. Across the horizon ran a curving line of hills; closer, chalk headlands showed eroded rivers of white. They left the road, striking directly across the heath.

The sun climbed, gathering intensity; the bracken shimmered and swam. They rested through the heat of the day, crawling into the heart of one of the bright-flowered clumps. Toward evening they moved off once more, striking the road again where it swung back toward the hills. Along it they plodded, thirsty and footsore, till the girl stopped, gripping Rand's arm. Beside the road lay the body of a man, one of the prisoners they had seen pass. A gaping wound showed in his back; round him the magpies were working already, scolding and flapping on the stained grass. They passed the spot grim-faced, and hurried on.

The sun was levelling when the Dancing Man turned. He narrowed his eyes, staring back the way they had come. Along the road behind them galloped a troop of men. The pouring light struck sparks from harness and weapons, the riders' bright steel caps.

To either side the heath stretched empty and flat; there was nowhere to run. They drew to one side, humbly, stood heads bowed for the column to pass. Instead, it reined; and the leader a strapping, hook-nosed man with flowing hair and beard, rode forward. 'You, I think, are the people we seek,' he said without preamble. 'Which of you is the Sealand Lord?'

Rand shook his head. 'I don't understand you, sir,' he said. 'We came from the coast to the villages by the Great Plain, to sell sheep for our master. Now our task is finished, and we are on our way home. Please let us go on; for it is late already, we shall be beaten.'

A man rode forward from the column, smiling. He wore a gaily-patterned surcoat; and his long fair hair was carefully dressed and tied, 'Well spoken, King of the Crab,' he said. 'But you must put aside your modesty this once. We are honest folk here in the south, and anxious to entertain you.'

The Dancing Man's hand flew to his neck, but for once he was too slow; a swordtip was already pricking his throat. The Horseman spoke gutturally. He said, 'Let your weapons fall.'

He did as he was bidden slowly, his grey eyes hard as stone. 'Why, Dendril,' he said, 'this is a strange affair. In Lakeland I killed a Worm; it seems a lesser escaped me, to dress in fine clothes and speak ill of its betters.'

The Sealander swung from his horse, unconcerned. 'When I raise me in my Tower of the Crab,' he said, 'with these my friends to help me, my dress will be finer yet. But you will not be there to see it.' He stooped to retrieve the sword, and turned away. 'Kill him,' he said. 'The others will give no trouble.'

Rand stepped forward quickly. 'Hear me,' he said. 'We

came in peace, with white cloths on our ship. We would have sailed to your great towns, bringing gifts; but our boat was wrecked, as our friend here can tell. We brought no harm; we came to worship your Gods, and learn wisdom from your priests.'

Dendril walked forward. 'No harm?' he said. 'No harm? Then where is Cultrinn? Where is Egril? Where are Galbritt, and Ensor, and all the rest?' He weighed the weapon in his hands, swung it viciously. The crosspiece, heavy and rough, caught Rand across the temples. Light burst, inside his head; when he could see again, he was staring at a horse's feet. He made to rise; and the Warrior spoke distantly. 'On your knees to a Horseman, Sea-lander,' he said. 'Or I will cut your heels.'

He put a hand to his forehead. It came away red and wet. The Rat knelt by him, pressed a cloth to his face.

Elgro had crouched, eyes blazing; now he relaxed. 'Well,' he said, 'so much for Kings. When they fall, the time has come to seek new masters.' He turned to the Horsemen, spreading his arms. 'My Lords,' he said, 'you need have no concern for me. I have no wish to die before my time. Also, I have powers undreamed of. In my own land, I was a notable Magician.'

Dendril said narrowly, 'Kill him.'

A sword was raised; but Elgro lifted a hand. 'Wait,' he said. He turned to the black-bearded leader. 'Kill me and you make a great mistake,' he said. 'I could serve you well. When I dance men grow big with vigour, taking twenty maidens in a night, and still demanding more. Others pine and falter, developing great pains. My enemies sit down and groan, sending quickly for a priest. All this I bring about, by steps in the dust.'

Dendril said, 'Do not trust him.' But the leader frowned, eyes narrowed curiously. 'I have heard of these Dancing Men,' he said. 'Let him show his skill.' He stared at Elgro. 'Dance a pain, pirate,' he said. 'Fling it from distance, and perhaps I will let you live. Fail, and you die this minute.'

Elgro bowed his head. 'Lord,' he said humbly, 'it will be as you wish.'

The Horsemen circled, grinning. He stepped into the ring made for him, and began to dance. He danced such a dance as had surely never been seen. He howled and roared, twisting his supple body into knot after knot. He bent till his forehead touched the ground between his heels; he leaped and capered and spun cartwheels. Dust rose round him; and the smiles of the Horsemen turned to laughter. 'Do your magic quickly, Sealander,' shouted the leader. 'This leaping is for children.'

Elgro climaxed his performance with a dozen gigantic standing somersaults. The last brought him alongside the Horseman's mount. By his knee hung a dagger in a decorated sheath. The Dancing Man snatched it, quick as a snake, and threw. A thud; and Dendril stared down appalled. His face turned grey, and then a blazing white. His legs gave way; he sat in the dust, hands gripped to his stomach, and began to shriek.

Elgro straightened, snarling. 'There is your pain,' he said. 'Is it enough, for one small Dance?'

A frozen moment; then the ring of Horsemen closed in.

The column trotted slowly, in the gathering dusk. Rand stared up, swaying with weariness. Ahead, the hills swept down to a pass carved through the chalk. In the pass rose a great steep-sided mound, its summit crowned with nubs and spikes of stone. High on the crest stood a fantastic Hall. Its windows blazed with light; on its ridge pole, dim against the night, monstrous shapes of rushes clambered and loomed. Round it torches burned, and many fires; the terraces thronged with figures that were cloaked and horned.

There was a gatehouse, built of crumbling stone. The horse to which he was tied clattered through. Inside were more soldiers. Challenges were shouted, and answered. The bridle was seized, the lashings cut from his ankles. Beside him the girl was dragged from the saddle; he saw the Dancing Man dumped on the ground like a sack of grain. Hands gripped him; he swung his legs clumsily, and the grass rose to meet his knees. He rolled sideways, felt the hill sway. The hands came again and faces, mouthing red-lit. He closed his eyes, and sank away from them.

The crash and rumble of wheels shook the ground. The tip of the great ram swayed and lurched; beyond, the face of the Tower was brightly lit. Flames rose, above the rampart walk; he saw arrows fly blazing, strike the wooden walls. A man plunged, screaming. Water cascaded; the twinkling spots of light were extinguished.

The wheels pounded. He pressed his chest to the axle, driving his feet at the packed earth of the compound. A roar from the Crablanders; and the pace increased. Something rang on his shield, bounded into the dark. In front of him a man shrieked and fell, hands to his face. He stumbled, and ran on.

Another shout; and the engine brought up against the Tower door, with a jerk that fetched him to his knees. Missiles rained on the roof of stout stitched hides; beneath it the Sealanders, stripped to the waist, frantically cast the lashings from the great shaft. He stared, through the slits of his battle helmet. Arrows hissed overhead once more. Frantic activity, on Engor's battlements; and a leather mattress began to jerk and sway down the Tower front.

Men scrambled to lay hands on the ram. Something smashed and patterned on the hides. Fire ran, streaming; and the chanting began. *'Way . . . and ho . . . Way . . . and ho . . . '* He leaned his weight with the rest; and the ram swung. The head, wedge-shaped and shod with iron, struck the door with a noise of thunder; and again. Creaks and snappings sounded; the mattress danced and leaped.

Flamelight showed through cracks that broadened. He let go the shaft and ran, sword in hand, shield held slanting above his head.

'Way . . . and ho . . . Way . . . and ho . . . '

Light poured from the Tower. The door crashed

inwards, torn bodily from its hinges. The ram swung free; he ducked beneath it, leaped. A spear glanced from his shoulder armour; he gripped the shaft, drove with the blade, wrenched it free, struck again. His voice roared in the mask; behind him the Crablanders burst into the Hall like a flood.

There were steps, of sounding wood. He bounded at them, swung his sword again. A man shrieked, toppled past him. There was a remembered door. He drove at it, shoulder and shield; and the latch-thongs parted. Beyond were crying women. He flung them aside, strode to the bedchamber. The couch was tousled, and the room empty.

There was a further door. He wrenched at it, reeled back. Night air moved against his skin; below was the flame-lit compound.

It seemed the nightmare was continued. The masks pressed closer, jostling; and the hands were on him again, gripping shoulders and arms. The hill-top was a great confused mass of building, roofs and chambers clustering round the high central Hall. He was dragged through room after room, orange-lit by torches, full of a pungent, sweetish scent that made his brain spin. The masks whirled and bobbed; masks of stone and wood masks of metal and bone, masks of feathers glimmering on girls who wore nothing else at all. The torches swayed; somewhere drums pounded, mixed with the pounding in his ears.

In the Hall a great fire burned. He saw, in darts and flashes, the trestles laid for a feast, the rush-strewn floor, walls hung with trophies of the God; his lances and spears and swords, his axes and chariot wheels and bolts of silk. He was hustled to a place, the girl banged down beside him. Weals showed on her face and neck. The bandage had been pulled from her arm; the cuts had bled again, spattering her clothes.

His wrists had been bound with a rawhide strip. He placed his hands on the trestle, palms together; and a cup was jammed against his teeth. He drank perforce, feeling the stuff flood across his chest. The wine woke new and burning images; the long room spun once more.

Horns sounded, close and harsh. The doors were flung back; and a procession debouched into the Hall. First came dancers and hornmen, girls with cymbals and bells; next creatures in rustling costumes of straw; and finally a covered, gaily-decked chair, borne on the shoulders of four burly priests. Above it rose nodding heads of maize and wheat; and the Sign of the God, a phallus of bound green rushes. The horns blared; the chair was set down and silence fell, broken only by the crackle of the flames.

A voice spoke querulously from behind the drapes. 'Bring me closer,' it said. 'How can I see them, from here?'

The bearers hurried, deferentially. The chair was raised again, the curtains parted; and Rand stared, trying to stop the spinning in his head. He saw what at first seemed nothing more than a mound of brilliant feathers; then the cape moved, rustling. Black eyes glittered through the mask slits; and the voice spoke again. 'Why did you come to my land, and to my House?' it asked. 'Do you bring the Touch that Heals? For this, I saved you from my Horsemen.'

He swallowed, shaping his lips round words. 'Where is my Dancing Man?' he said. 'Is he alive, or dead?'

The mask quivered. 'What is life?' it said. 'What is death? I, who died on the hill, knew both.' The voice wavered, seeming to lose the thread of its thoughts. 'What has happened?' it asked plaintively. 'Where is the God? For seven times seven years, I was his Bride. Never did he fail me . . . Sealander, where are the years? Can you answer?'

He lowered his eyes. He said, 'I came seeking wisdom, not to give it.'

The mask bobbed again. The crone said abruptly, 'Is this your woman?'

He shook his head, in pain. 'Do not harm her,' he said.

'Her father is a King in the west. He will give the God rich gifts.'

It seemed he went unheard. 'How red her blood runs,' said the priestess. 'The blood of the young . . . Show me, child, there is no shame. Show me and I will tell you how the God went with me, seven times seven years . . .' The voice sank to a mutter, rose again. 'Where is the God?' it asked. 'What has happened to me?' Then in a thin shout, 'I burn . . .'

Rand groaned, bringing his fists down on the table. 'Mother,' he said, 'this is age . . .'

She shrieked, 'The Favoured cannot age . . .' She snatched at the mask, with a thin brown hand; and he turned away. The face had withered, falling in round the smashed nose, the cicatrice of a great scar. 'We have searched,' said the creature. 'First we sought the touch that heals all ills; but no man brought it to my Hall. Now, we search again. For the soul lives in the flesh, like a silver worm. Who finds that worm, and swallows, will be young; but it is quick, and shy.' She called, rattling the feathered cape; and a great wooden wheel was carried into the Hall, set down.

The King rose slowly, arms extended, face like a man suddenly blind. He swayed; then the thing before him spoke. Little enough remained, to show that it was Elgro; but the voice was the Dancing Man's. *'My Lord,'* it whispered slowly, *'I think now, your penance is done.'*

In Engor's Tower, the noise had died away. He ran, feet pounding, back the way he had come. He took a woman by the throat, shouting for the Queen; but she could only wail. He hurled her from him, ran again.

In the Great Hall, the dead lay sprawled and heaped. Blood mapped the flags with brilliant traceries. A man sat on the door edge, patiently holding up the remnant of a hand; beyond, in a silent semicircle, stood the Crablanders. In their midst the leather mattress swung, still cradled in its web of ropes. Bulging it was, and sodden; and its corner as it moved traced a thin pattern on the sill.

He was unaware that he slashed and screamed; but the leather parted, before his face. He turned away, hands to his skull; but not before he had seen, above the red and white, the coils of ash-pale hair.

The cry that came from him was the noise of a wolf. He raised his arms, the fingers crooked; and the bonds that held him snapped. The trestle barred his way; he laid a great hand to it, flung it aside. Screams sounded; the masks swirled and fell. He seized the wheel and raised it, ran staggering to jam it at the flames. Logs spilled and rolled, blazing; and Elgro's ghost fled from him, with a shriek.

A sword was in his hands. Foam flecked his mouth; he struck, not knowing that he swung the blade. He struck for Egril and Cultrinn, Galbritt and Ensor and Matt. He struck for Cedda, and Engor, and Deandi the Fay; and each blow was a life. The fight swayed round him, surging; the noise doubled and redoubled, till the rafters rang. Then it seemed there were none to oppose him; so he struck the trestles and chairs, the drapes on the walls, the rushes, the jars of wine. Lastly, he struck the litter of the priestess. The gilded grasses flew, and tatters of drenched silk. He stamped and trampled, screaming; and a thin wail rose. Then the thing inside was young again.

The redness faded. He ran to where the girl was crouched, seized her arm. He raised her; and the doors of the Hall burst inwards. Faces poured forward, shouting; and the bronze-strapped shields of Sealand, swords, the tips of spears.

He ran again, crouching. Behind him the Hall was hazed with smoke. The flames spread swiftly, licking at the drapes, leaping to the roof. Thatch fell, blazing; the smoke swirled, thicker than before.

There was a low door, iron-barred. He smashed his foot against it. Night air blew round him; he stumbled, dragging the girl behind him across a slope of grass.

The blazing thatch of the God House lit the hill-top with an orange glare. He ran swerving, between tall pillars of stone. A roof section caved in; the flames roared up, brightening. Yells sounded from where the raiding party engaged fresh troops of Horsemen. There was a crumbling wall; he tumbled the girl over it, heard her land with a crackling of branches. A man was close behind him. He turned, parried the mace-swing, drove upward. The blade passed below the God-mask, burst out through the skull. The body convulsed; he tore the weapon free, vaulted to the wall-top and dropped into the dark.

The side of the mound was thickly overgrown with bushes and young trees. He half-ran, half-skidded down a cliff of grass, still towing the girl. The slope steepened. He tripped, rolled. The girl yelped; he landed in a smother of bushes, lay staring up. High above, over the great shoulder of the mound, the Hall roared like a furnace.

There was a stream, running cool and swift between tall fern-hung banks. He stepped into it, pulling her after him. Trees arched overhead, velvet-black in the night; he waded groaning, hands to his temples, and heard her cry.

He turned back, floundering. She was crouched below the bank, head down, arm gripped across her chest. He glared, face working; then he stooped. He raised her carefully, feeling her shake and sob; and waded on again, into the dark.

The two figures moved slowly, down the long rough slope of grass. Beyond was the sea. The dawn was in the sky, washing the land with pale grey light.

Bushes fringed the edge of a low cliff. Rand crouched, parted the branches carefully. Below, greatships were drawn up on the beach. Fires burned at intervals; closer, tall standards were thrust into the grass. He stared, narrowing his eyes; and let his held breath escape. 'Ulm of the Fishgard,' he said. 'Crenlec, from Long Fen. Friends of the Crab.'

She sat staring dully at the water, still gripping her arm.

159

He turned her wrist gently, pulled her fingers away. 'They are all gone,' he said. 'Matt, and Egrith, and Egril and his sons. If she is in Hell, she knows I tried to follow. I sent my best before, to tell her so.'

He scooped his arms beneath the girl, raised her once more. She laid her head on his shoulder wearily, eyes closed. 'We are all dead,' he said. 'The Rat is dead. Child, how are you called?'

The lips moved, in the drawn face. 'Mavri,' she said. 'Of the White Rock.'

He frowned. 'There is a Tower, in my country,' he said. 'If I sit there again, I will try to be a King.'

She made no answer; and he stepped forward heavily, climbing the zigzag path down to the ships.

FIVE

Usk the Jokeman

I

Once more the year had turned. A spring breeze blew, drying the harsh earth, swaying twiglets in their haze of golden-green. The same wind pressed against the tower in the high chalk pass, as against a sail; and the tower responded, with a medley of squeaks and groans. Other sounds rose from the complex of buildings that surrounded it; clank and scrape of pails, clatter of churns from the buttery, heavier grumble of the cornmill from the lower ward. A herdboy yodelled, whacking the flanks of his sway-bellied charges; the heifers bellowed mournfully, cramming their way through the narrow entrance with its jettied wooden gatehouse.

From the Great Chamber atop the rustling edifice King Marck stared vaguely down. The casements, ajar to the bright sky, admitted sunlight that striped the rough floor with gold; but the King seemed unaware. In one hand he gripped a sheaf of parchments; in his other he held a fine goose quill, the tip of which he employed alternately to scratch forehead and nose. He noted, unseeing, the progress of the little herd; then turned back, frowning, to the trestle table on which his work was spread. He drew his shabby gown about him, scotched on his stiff-backed chair. 'The Devils take our ancestors for their wandering ways,' he said, half to himself. 'Here, clear enough, is the tale of Rand son of Cedda, son of Ceorn; the same who was Rand Wolfkiller in the Saga of Usgeard. This much is plain; that he fought with Fenricca, whose clan bears the Wolf-staff to this day. But what of this other tale, that he sailed to the lands of the dead and met with ghosts? Also he saved a Princess from a dragon of the Northern Fens. "Sea Worm" is given in the Usgeard. Now the Sea Worm was the Mark of the Fishgard tribes; what are we to make of this?'

'That the Devils already have thy ancestors for their own,' said a dry voice over his head. 'For their minds surely wandered farther than their feet; and their tongues' wanderings were such as to put both to shame.'

Marck looked up, his frown deepening to a scowl. Usk, Jokeman to the House of the Gate, was a strangely fashioned creature; thick in the body and spindly in the shanks, with a swarthy, slab-sided face fixed now in an elaborate leer. His eyes were deep-set and black, his nose imposingly hooked. His cap, with its swastikas and bells, was as usual rammed slant-wise on his cropped head; he tweaked it in mock obeisance before swinging by one leg from the beam on which he perched, to swipe the air above his master. Golden motes rained thickly; and he sneezed and cackled. 'Library dust, my King,' he said. 'Thick it lies, where learning most abounds; and thickest of all'— he fielded a missile hurled up from below—'thickest of all, I say, round genealogists of Sealand.' He regained his perch, seemingly without effort. 'But what's the matter, Lord?' he said. 'What is so sore amiss, that thou repayest thy Fool, who ever honoured thee, with naught but brick-bats?' He spoke winningly, offsetting by his tone the malice of the words; for the Old Tongue was little pleasing to those who boasted Sealand blood.

His estimation of his master's mood was sound. The bright morning, it seemed, had lightened even Marck; the royal scribe merely smiled, and began ticking points on his fingers. 'Rand it was who came south, through the Narrow

Sea to the Land of Rocks,' he said. 'With him he brought the Mark of the Crab, which my house still bears; the blood lines are clear enough. Arco was Rock King then, Arco the White, whose folk also had been kings in Sealand. This Arco gave in mockery the land a hide might cover; but Rand and his women—Rand the Cunning, he is called in the Edva Rigg—sliced the hide so finely, the thong they made circled a mighty hill. This is the part of the tale that likes me best.'

Usk, who had sunk his head between his hands, heaved his most lugubrious sigh; but his master, once embarked, was not to be checked by trifles. Marck rose, running his fingers through his unkempt yellow-grey hair. 'Daughters Rand had in plenty, but no sons,' he said. 'So Crab Hold passed to Renlac, by marriage to Ellean the Fair. This Renlac fathered Bralt, my great grandsire, taking the Mark in honour of his wife. When Arco came here with a mighty host, Renlac was his Shiplord. Arco honoured him, after the Battle of the Sandhills where the Midsea power broke; and so the Crab was restored to its ancient place. Renlac took the Southguard where we sit, holding it for Arco and his sons; after which . . .' A thought struck him, and he paused. 'I have heard in jugglers' stories,' he said, 'that this land, and the Misty Isles, were once the Islands of Ghosts. Could that mean . . .' He scrabbled among the papers with which the trestle was strewn. 'Could that mean merely this, that Rand Wolfkiller came here for his bride? Is the old tale true?'

Usk dropped neatly from the beam. He swung his feet on the table edge, watching their pointed shadows flit across the boards. 'There was a People of the Dragon in the west,' he said. 'Or so I heard my father tell. These the Horsemen broke in foolish pride, before they bowed the proper knee to Sealand.'

The gibe, if gibe it was, went unremarked. Marck chewed the quill tip, frowning again. 'If that were true,' he said musingly. 'Ellean, Rand's daughter, did take a Dragon for her Mark. Why, that would mean . . .' He

163

glanced up, sharply; but the Jokeman, with a return to his former mood, interrupted him. 'That thou might stretch thy hand to western hills,' he said. 'Yet there thou sittest, Marck of the Gate, like breathing stone or a statue of thyself, blotting a fair day with ink. These dusty things with which thou strive will be thy death.' He ran to bound at the windowsill, checked dangerously on the lip of the sheer drop. 'The air trembles, every live thing stirs,' he said. 'Fowls in the frith, the fishes in the flood . . . Why sit thou there, my King? Up, and ride . . .'

For a moment a curious expression, almost of yearning, might have flitted across Marck's drawn face; then he shook his head. 'Be silent, fool,' he said. 'Soon, under Atha King, all these lands will be one. There will be need then for libraries; and books to fill them, telling how we came by greatness. If you cannot be silent, at least be still.'

The other swung a carrot-coloured shank across the sill, and pulled a face. 'My Lord,' he said, 'Out of thy wisdom, what makes a man a fool?'

Marck raised his head, with a grimace. 'Ceaseless babbling,' he said.

'Then answer this,' said Usk. 'And I babble not, how may I show myself a fool, and worthy of my keep? Speak, sir; for when a fool babbles, wise men from their charity answer him. Else are they not wise, and he no fool.'

He caught the coin the other flung him, nimbly. 'Also I have heard, that wise men live for ever,' he said. 'Pray tell me, master, if thou think'st this true?'

The King stared thoughtfully. 'No man lives for ever,' he said. 'Neither King nor commoner. Which is well enough known, even to fools. What is your meaning?'

'For that you must excuse me,' said Usk, equally grave. 'For a fool can have no meaning. I say but this; that two doors, both as dark, stand close upon each other. That we must pass between them, it being the will of certain Gods. That fish swim in streams, and birds call close to palaces; that kingdoms of linen are but chilly lands, an they be desert.' He bit the coin insultingly, stowed it in his belt. 'A fool's words have no wit,' he said. 'Or I might further ask; who follows thee, King, in thy high chair? For whom are coffers stacked? This little matter of the flesh stands between thee, and immortality.' He skipped to the door. 'I leave thee to thy labours,' he said. 'Perhaps the birds will quiet their song, in honour of thy wit; but that I doubt.'

The door thudded behind him. Marck once more ran his fingers through his hair; he turned the papers on the table, made to write, threw down the quill. He rose, seemingly with irritation, stood at the window. The breeze gusted, bringing with it the scents of earth and fresh grass. The tower creaked; and he saw, as if for the first time, the clear blue sky, dotted with puffy clouds that sailed like ships.

The spring night was chilly; so that fires crackled in the kitchens and lower halls of the place, throwing orange reflections on ceilings of limewashed wood. Above, the Tower stood austere and dark; save for a glimmer, faint as a marsh spirit, where the Lord of the Gate still busied himself at his tasks.

Round the largest of the fires, and sweating a little from its heat, sat a varied group of retainers: a Serjeant of the Wardrobe, a couple of handlers from the royal mews, a soldier of the standing garrison; and a plump-faced kitchen maid, black hair straggling beneath her grubby cap. Beside her, lolling at ease, reposed the great bulk of Thoma, Marck's seneschal. At his feet squatted the Jokeman. He was prodding at the fire with a long metal spit, and as usual talking with some animation. 'Why, man,' he said, 'a hair will turn the matter, one way or the next; as thou shalt see.'

Thoma, whose thoughts never ran far from food, had possessed himself of the part-carved carcass of a chicken. He sucked a legbone noisily, and licked his wrist. 'A hair is a poor thing on which to hang our fates,' he said. 'I for one would not see a Mistress of the Gate. I hold we get by well enough, and keep our state, without a woman to oversee our lives.'

'No woman, surely, would care to see much of thine,' said Usk tartly. 'As for hairs; they are very potent, and oft enough hath answered for folk's lives. With hairs I would attempt this Tower; aye, and hear the wailing for the dead ere dawn.'

Thoma laughed rumblingly, and belched. 'Thy tongue could ever turn my wits,' he said good-naturedly. 'But this once I will dispute with you. Make that good.'

The Jokeman sprang to his feet with curious elation, danced a step in the ashes. 'For shame, good captain,' he said. 'Thoma, thou bladder of valiance, did'st thou not sit outboasting the cocks not three nights since, about thy service with King Atha's train?'

'That I did,' said Thoma. 'At Long Creek, and Great Grange, and Morwenton when we put down the pretender Astrid. Aye, and burned his Hall.'

'What breached that Hall, to let in thy sweaty feet?' asked the Jokeman sardonically.

'The catapulta, certainly,' said Thoma. 'But this is from the point.'

'The Gods forgive,' said Usk. 'Thy wit grows short in breath.' He danced another jig. 'What, bound among its ropes, gives an engine strength? What lends power to its skein, that else would burst? I hear Queen Maert was first to shear her locks, to give great Atha victory.'

The soldier spat at the fire. 'Your wit is hollow, Jokeman,' he said. 'It rings like a cracked pot.'

'And yours is earth,' muttered the other, forgetting in his annoyance his habitual mode of speech. He turned back to Thoma. 'Was not thy grandsire of Horseman stock?'

Thoma waved a large hand. 'These things are long gone,' he said. 'Long dead.'

'And well dead,' said the soldier, rising. 'The Sealanders own this country, Jokeman; as you had best remember.' He turned on his heel, and stalked away.

Usk watched him go with narrowed eyes. 'Well,' he said lightly. 'Those who make heart's matter of the babble of a fool are fools indeed.' He sat back beside Thoma, securing a portion of the chicken. 'Yet this is true,' he said, watching up. 'Our fathers took this land; took it and were lords of it, before the sea-folk came.'

Thoma shrugged. 'What's gone is gone,' he said philosophically. 'And I for one have no complaints. But tell me these thoughts you have of the King.'

The other nodded, his dark face sombre. 'Many years have I served him, seneschal,' he said. 'Wishing naught but his good, as do we all. Yet still it grieves me to see him solitary; the rareness of his person cries out for a mate. So I have wound my skein, hair by hair; a twist here and a tweak, to win him to my thought. Now I must seek thy help; for married he must be, and that ere further winters fall.'

'And to whom would you marry him, rogue?' asked the kitchen girl, yawning. 'Or is such high policy not for common ears?'

'Not for thine, certes,' snapped the Jokeman. He pushed his cap further to the back of his head, and smirked. 'I know a Maid, not of this common earth,' he said. 'Of high blood, and most ancient line; most fitting, for a King.

The kitchenwoman, and the others, attempted to draw him further; but Usk, for once, held his peace. He twirled his cap, jangling the bells, and smiled again; till one by one they sought their beds, and let him be.

Sometime in the night a contraption of ropes and levers, set high on the wall of the little hall, moved briefly. A bell jangled, and again. The Jokeman, still sitting beside the barely glowing embers, stared up, eyes white in the gloom. 'Ring till thou burst,' he muttered balefully. 'Call Demons or the Gods, for all I care; for Usk is with his ancestors . . .' He stretched, curled himself in the corner farthest from the fire, and was quiet. In time, the bell ceased to move.

Marck could not have been said to wake. Rather, he

became aware; of the dim light diffusing through the high chamber, the brighter grey of the single window-slit, stark as cut lead. The air of the room was cold, and still.

He turned his head, listening. The silence seemed to suggest by its completeness the immensity of the sleeping land. No bird, no voice. No snore. The grey light, he knew, lay across heath and tillage, forest and sea; across the Great Plain with its crests of wind-carved trees, across the marshes far to the north where the unknown country stretched out for ever. His mind, free-ranging, saw the villages huddled beneath their thatch, hill-tops crowned with their ramparts. On each a stockade, pale gatehouses criss-crossed with timbering; crowning each a Tower, ragged in the early light. Gaunt-eyed, and still. Utterly still.

Increasingly it seemed his life was lived in these dawn watches. Almost it was as if his days, the activity, the petty irritations that filled them, were in reality brief as dreams, meaningless interruptions of a vigil that was in itself endless. He wondered at this vigil; and at the Fate that, creeping by still degrees, had placed him so apart from life. Once, surely, there had been wine and warmth, laughter and good company. When had these things ceased to be?

As ever, there was no answer. It seemed he had grown to silence, like an ageing tree.

There were many dreams. Once—not he, surely, but another—had sat in Midsea palaces, at the feet of learned men. There also had been women, veiled, swaying creatures with the eyes of deer; and a fire in the blood, long cold, that marred his studies of the wheeling stars. He remembered these women, like creatures from another world; and the palaces, their towers bright in sunlight, topped by domes like sharp-tipped onions, red and yellow and green. The dry voices scraped, down the years; while his hands made the dots and squirls, the runes and flowing curves, that are the Midsea tongue.

The dream was interrupted by another. This echoed

with battle noise, the thunder of siege trains, the roar of flames. Altred was overlord when his father's death called Marck from his studies, back to a troubled land; Altred who took his brother's wife, and split a new-found kingdom to its roots. In that great war the Crab Shield followed the gonfalon of Atha, from the Marshes to the eastern fens, Southguard to the Great Black Rock where remnants of the Horsemen lingered out their lives in wind-scorched keeps. Towns burned, ringed by the lesser spots of siege fires; battles were fought on parching plains, amid reddened winter wheat. Finally, in a river valley hemmed by endless woods, the last great siege was laid; and Altred died, his life the price of peace.

And there were the Towers on their hills, the great Hall Marck's father raised in a chalk gap next the sea; quietness, and armour hanging dusty on the walls, the martens nesting under the high eaves.

Yet the war-sounds still clamoured in his dreams; so to buy his rest Marck wrote the tale of battles, the Shields that had gathered to Altred and to the House of the White Horse. Those who had lived, and those who had died. Later—and this was an unheard-of thing—scribes were summoned to copy out the work. Few enough there were, in all the White Island; but the word spread, first to the Land of Rocks, later to the Middle Sea itself. So the clerks came flocking, to sit in lines in the Great Hall of Marck's Tower while the royal writing-master strode forward and back, intoning the story that had come to him. A scroll was sent to Atha King, in his palace by the narrow sea; and Atha, delighted, heaped honours on the scholar of the Gate. Fine horses came to Southguard; hunting dogs, a brace of white sea-eagles and a purse of gold. Marck, moved by such royal favour, redoubled his efforts. His fame grew; so that minstrels and wandering sages took to calling at his Hall, in hope of refreshment and reward. They were seldom disappointed; and the King found new material constantly to hand. He traced the wanderings of the Horse Warriors from their Midsea home, penning the epics the minstrels carried in their heads. The Horsemen too brought with them Gods and ghosts, peopling the Mound on which Marck's Tower was raised; the Mound that was blood and flesh and standing stones, bones of old folk from the start of time. Magic obsessed him; trolls and Marsh monsters, reed-women haunting the noonday pools and red-eared phantom hares. Behind them all, discernible yet, stalked a vast golden shade. From his Tower the King looked out on a bulging hill of chalk; at certain times, in summer evenings and at dawn, lines might be discerned on its surface. Sometimes one saw an upraised club, sometimes the head and shoulders of a great Man; the marks a God himself might make, rusting on the grass. Marck, in learned argument, dismissed the fables that were told; yet still from time to time the hill drew his curious gaze. Chalk carvings were unknown to his Sealand forbears; he produced a monograph on the subject nonetheless, verifying by experiment the ease with which the green skin of grass might be stripped away. Atha, sensing the means for a fresh demonstration of his power, ordered that his Mark be inscribed on all his boundaries, wherever suitable subsoil could be found; so white horses, and sometimes red and brown, once more came to inhabit the land.

It was at this point that a strange malaise gripped Marck, born of the laughter of a carter's child. The shout, vibrant and innocent, came winging up to the Tower one bright day, sending him mumbling from his work to stare into a mirror, pull at the straggling hair the years had turned to grey. The child's voice pierced him; he knew that he was old, and the Tower rooms were chill, and his audience was a jester with cap and bells. The days of joy were done; now he saw the passing of the seasons, snow and fresh spring, the world turning its strange circles under moon and sun. He was oppressed by futility; his food was soured, and his rest destroyed.

He had begun his greatest project, a history of the conquests and journeyings of all the Sealand tribes. Once the tales would have joined beneath his fingers to make patterns undreamed-of; now, the work was stale. Days and nights he spent in sightless staring, a pen in his fingers, the pages spread before him. He took to riding, sometimes at curious hours; a shabby, restless King in breeches and homespun, muttering and dull-eyed. Those of his subjects who met with him bowed the knee, wondering and a little fearful; but Marck was unaware. He brooded by high woods, in lightning flash and summer rain; smelled the wet earth, uncaring.

In time, the sickness passed. A fragment of the former joy returned, buoyed by returning skill; but the shadow that had swept down that bright day was never wholly lifted. Scholars came to the Southguard, some with gifts, some from the Middle Sea itself. Marck received them courteously, as of old, delighting in learned talk; but constantly his eyes and mind would wander. It was at this time that Usk began his wheedling; and strange thoughts flickered in the mind of the King.

The sky was brighter now; and sleep had fled, for yet another day. Marck pushed back his blankets, felt the washing of cold against his skin. A drain, ill-smelling, projected from the wall; he used it, sighing. Over his breechcloth he hung a knee-length riding tunic; he buckled the heavy leather belt, and stamped into his boots. He took down his thickest woollen cloak, and eased open the chamber door.

The guards on duty at the gatehouse clashed to attention, grounding their spears on the turf. A Serjeant, still bleary with sleep, began bawling for an escort; but the King stilled him with an upraised hand. 'Leave me,' he said simply. 'I ride but a little way; none will molest me.'

The other eyed him dubiously; but he was used by now to his master's queerish habits. The gates creaked back; and Marck passed through with a muffled stamping of hooves, the champ and jangle of the charger's bit.

At the foot of the Mound a village had grown up over the years. He paced silently before the white-walled dwellings with their roofs of heavy thatch. Once a dog yapped briefly; a child wailed, and was quieted. Beyond the sleeping houses a steepening way led to a little brook, arched over by tall trees. Mist moved round the belly of the horse; the water-scent was powerful and cold. Beyond the brook the path once more began to rise, climbing the shoulder of the flanking hill. Marck urged his mount, impatiently. When at length he reined, the Tower was small with distance. Below him the mist stretched out like a sea, hiding the real sea beyond. Over its surface ran ripples and fading flashes of light, now here, now gone; and the whole, he saw, was in stealthy, steady motion, flowing inland to the great chalk pass. The sight arrested him. It was as if he, and he alone, had glimpsed a Mystery; the ancient, inscrutable life of the hills themselves.

He rode on, engrossed with the fancy; and feeling too the rise of an excitement he had thought stilled for ever. Once before, in another lifetime, he had ridden thus. Then as now, the chill air lanced at face and arms; then as now some Presence, older than the wandering lanterns, older it seemed than the ghosts that thronged the Southguard, moved before him. The hills stretched westward, shadowy still, humped rampart-like against the sea. The hidden waves seethed to his left; the track rose, fell and rose again. He clicked to the horse, shaking the broad rein, feeling the creature's swaying, hearing the creak of harness, the snort of breath. He knew himself at one with the land, the land that itself was awake and watchful. The spirit, the very essence of the place breathed out some message in a tongue as powerful as it was strange; and he saw, or sensed, all the folk who had known the hills since time began. The Giants, still unforgotten, with their glistening engines; after them the growers of corn, the spinners of wool, the makers of butter and beer. The Horsemen, spreading like a stain; and the New Men, the Sealanders, threshing the water in their many-legged ships. Last of all his own folk, Altred Brothercutter and Atha whom he loved, who set him on his own great chair and placed the sword across his knees, the ring of ancient yellow on his head. All this there was and more, much more; a tale that, could it but be told, would be the greatest in the world.

The slope he climbed was easing. Before him glowed a cloud of light; he panted, driving in his heels. The warhorse scrambled the last yard to the crest; and King Marck blinked, rubbing dazzled eyes.

He had come miles; much farther than he had intended. He stood now on a broad, smooth ridge of chalk. To his left, a marker rose above a tall cairn of stones; the sun, mounting the sea's rim, touched the rough iron with gold. The shadow of the Crab was flung across the mist; the land to westward was a haze of brightness, in which shapes of fancy moved.

He dismounted, walking to the cairn. The horse, left to itself, wandered a pace or two, dropped its head to crop the close-knit grass. Marck drew the cloak more tightly, laid his head against the great piled stones and closed his eyes. Somewhere a sea bird called; the light, refracted by the mist, burned at his lids. In more prosaic mood, he might have said he slept; but certainly the strangest vision came to him.

It seemed the spirit of the place, the Thing that had plagued him on the way, once more returned. Her limbs, he saw, were the creamy brown of tide-washed sand. Her hair shone rich and dark as jet; her eyes, deep pools, reflected headlands and seas. She towered, all-encompassing; yet the hands she placed in his were slight and warm as the hands of the carter's child. He wondered how such things might be; and she laughed, knowing his thought. *'I am she you sought,'* she said. *'I am the land and sea, snow on far hills; summer mist, the hot bright grain. I am the reed-pool woman, sun on green water . . .'*

Warmth coursed through him then, the blood raced in his veins. He would have risen, joyful and light; but the Spirit laughed, pressing a finger to his lips. She spoke much, of many things, and later showed him Mysteries;

cities and towers beyond imagining, great roads that thronged with folk, ships of floating iron. For there too she had lived, in the time of the Giants; and worn bright short clothes and laughed, and served men beer in a room of amber light where a stone fish swam in a case of priceless glass. And once she lay on a hillside, and wore a kilt of doeskin and a necklace of coral and jet. She who died in silk and flames was born again a Princess of the West; while Dragons fought, and the magic ships roared, and Gods and cities fell and rose. *'And once,'* she said, *'I lay in a house with round white towers. I walked in a deep green marsh, and wonderful things were done. These things you shall do, for a need; for a King must wed his land. Once I was Mata. Then I was the Reborn. Now my name is . . .'*

But Marck, rousing with a great start, already knew.

At times during the long ride back, he sang snatches of song. At others fear and guilt came on him, so that he wrung his hands. He addressed arguments to the rocks, colloquies to the wheeling gulls. Once, hands to his temples, he cried, 'It is not fitting . . .' Then the warmth her touch had brought once more flooded him. Riding a green stretch of turf, his mind was eased; crossing a tumbled scree he roared that a King could feel no desire. He pulled at his hair and beard, plucked his sleeves; then he laughed again and said, 'Thoma is my man, and will perform my offices.' He also wept; but by the time his Tower once more came into sight, gleaming in the early sun, he was calm again. The hooves of his horse rang hollow on the outer bridge; as the Serjeant ran to grip the rein, he raised his head. He said, 'It will be for my people.'

'And that,' said Thoma heavily, 'is the tale of it. Or as near as man may judge. So Scatha take all smooth-tongued schemers, all wearers of motley, all dabblers in matters of high estate; and above all Usk, who I verily believe has turned our good King's head with his prattle. Were there such times, in memory? Once, in faith, we were content enough; now we must wear . . . *ahh* . . . fineries that chafe the skin, constrict our persons to the shape of . . . village wenchels, on the word of some God-forsworn tailor, whom the Nightrunners may as willingly keep.' He wrenched at the collar of his tunic, and groaned with relief. 'As for the rest,' he said, 'we must take what comfort remains . . .' He swigged deeply from a pot-bellied flagon, and wiped his mouth with the back of his hand.

His companion, a strapping young Captain of the Royal Guard, stared round him dubiously. Certainly the chamber in which they were lodged, and in which for a week they had waited the pleasure of King Odann of the Plain, seemed little calculated to promote cheerfulness. Apart from the two narrow beds it was empty of furniture, and its gloomy walls were unrelieved by paint or drapery. A single arrowslit, unshuttered, admitted grey light and the piercing wind of the Plain. The door was massive, studded with iron and barred, ominously, from the outside. From beyond it now came the tramp of feet, a shouted order. The wind rose again, with a sigh and rumble; and the Captain grinned, turning back to his companion.

No finery, certainly, could have constricted the sene-schal's ample person to the dimensions of which he com-plained; but if the thought crossed the other's mind he forbore comment. Instead he shrugged. 'By the Gods, Thoma,' he said, 'but when Jokemen control Kings, the world is upside down. Or we should all wear motley, and make our fortunes presently. But what was this other tale you spoke of, that the King met with a Fairy woman who promised him great riches?'

Thoma scowled, and made a sign with his fingers. 'As for that,' he said, 'I'd as lief be ruled by our lord Usk. His scrawny neck I could at least take between my hands.' He shuddered, and readdressed himself to the flagon. 'If it was true,' he said, 'and our lord not touched in his wits with riding in sea mists, then there was power there; more than Usk and all his marshalled ancestors might command. But witchcrafts are for priests, Briand, not for us. Talk no more of it.'

The other frowned in turn, rubbing at his lip. 'But did he say aught else?' he persisted. 'What were these prophecies she made him?'

'Aught else,' groaned Thoma. 'What did he not say . . .' He shook his head, running blunt fingers through his thatch; then it seemed the desire for confidence overcame his instinct for caution. 'All night I sat with him,' he said, 'and on into the dawn. The half of what he spoke, I own, has gone out of my head; for much of the time I dozed. Something there was of Gods most certainly, and a Great One reborn as a carter's child; but the manner of that is past the telling. In this much the Jokeman spoke truth; that fuddling with old books, and older stories, waters a man's brains, an he hold to it enough. For my part I could wish us home again, out of this stinking place. And this whole business ended, or not begun.'

But the other rose and punched him cheerfully. 'For shame, Thoma,' he said. 'What, a courtier of thy proved mettle to leave the game half played? Thou hast worked mightily for our Lord in this matter, and will ere yet bring him handsome winnings. Though I must own, if Goddesses are in question he has perhaps sent thee to shop in the wrong market . . .'

Almost certainly he would have said more; but the sudden sideways glint of Thoma's eye warned him to silence.

An hour passed, draggingly. Thoma had emptied the flagon, and begun once more to complain, when the doorbolts were withdrawn with heavy creaks. Both men rose, hands to their sword hilts. The door swung inward; and a cowled priest faced them in the gloom. 'My Lord Odann bids me tell you his decision is reached,' he muttered. 'He requests you to attend him.'

They followed the other's flapping gown down ill-lit steps. The Great Hall was as dank and gloomy as the rest of the place. The windowslits, deep-set between massive timbers, were muffled with smoke-stained cloth. Lamps burned here and there in niches, crude wicks floating in saucers of stinking oil. At the end of the high chamber, on a dais flanked by torchbearers, sat Odann King. In one hand he held the great staff of his house, with its snarling wolf's head; his other was hidden amid the dark folds of his robe, but it seemed he gripped himself as if to ease a pain. Round him clustered priests and nobles. Bronzed skin was much in evidence, and hooked noses, black-browed eyes; for the Horseman blood was strong here on the Plain.

To the King's right stood a cloaked and hooded woman. Little could be seen of her face save the dark eyes, the finely arched brows; but her figure was slender and desirably formed. Behind her and a little to one side stood Dendra, brother to the King. His feet were set apart on the rushes, his thumbs hooked in his belt; and he scowled at the ambassadors with little favour. Round him lounged some dozen heavily armed men. They made no move to salute the newcomers, but stared like their leader in silence.

Thoma sensed well enough the tension in the Hall. He stepped forward, sweating slightly, grounded his staff and began to speak. 'Greetings,' he said, 'to Odann of the Plain and to his House, from his brother Marck of the Gate, Keeper of the Southguard, Lord of the Seaward Hills.'

The raised hand of the King cut short the formal speech. A spasm crossed his face. He arched his back, pressing with his elbows against the arms of the throne. The moment passed; and he turned to stare at the girl beside him. A wait; then she put the hood back, with a quick movement. Her hair was black, they saw, her skin clear and brown, her arms and shoulders gracefully made.

'This,' said Odann, 'is my daughter, much beloved. What does the Gate King give, for such a prize?'

Thoma's eyes moved round the company, finding little

comfort. He cleared his throat, and smiled. 'My master is a simple man,' he said. 'Yet his coffers are rich, and for this blessing he has opened them. He offers thirty horses, each strong-backed and trained for war. Also a chest of gold, such as two strong men might carry; three of silks, and yet another of spice. A waggon of fine wine from the Midsea lands, both yellow and red . . .'

Dendra swore, loudly. Odann once more raised his hand; but the other went on unchecked.

'Silks,' he said. 'And spices. The Gate insults us, brother.' Then to Thoma, 'We have no use, here on the Plain, for women's toys. Go home, chalkdweller, while yet thy legs can bear thee.'

A burst of laughter from the soldiery; and Thoma stepped forward, neck reddening. The glances that passed between Dendra and his brother, and between Odann and the girl, were lost on him; for the Plainsman had spoken in the Old Tongue, in which 'chalkdweller' and 'barbarian' are one. He would have drawn, regardless of his mission; but Odann had risen, stood racked and swaying. His daughter clung to him; but he put her gently aside. 'You will forgive my brother's words,' he said wearily. 'When he sits here on this throne he will speak as he chooses; then if you wish, you may answer him.' He turned back to the girl, staring a great time; then he raised his voice. 'Hear me,' he said. 'All you within this Hall. The gold we will take, and the spices. Also fifty horses, sound in wind and limb, with their saddles and all trappings of war. This, and nothing less; I do not barter, Hill Men, for what is without price. Will you answer for your King?'

Thoma, dry-mouthed, gifted his master's stable. The girl turned on him a blazing white face; then drew the hood about her and hurried from the Hall. The King stepped from the dais, taking the arm of a priest; and Dendra turned with a final glare and stalked from the place, his followers at his heels. Servingmen scurried with the trestles for a feast; and Thoma, slowly relaxing, grimly caught the Captain's eye.

From a chamber high in the Tower the girl stared down. Beyond the outworks of the place, the baileys and barbican with its steps and gantries, clustered the banners of the Crab. The stamp of horses carried to her and a bawled order from Thoma, bulky in a cape of fur. The little column formed itself, turned and trotted away, vague in the early light; became a darker smudge that receded against the vast blurred greyness of the Plain.

She turned, her face pale and set, and gripped the wrap tighter round her shoulders. She said in a small voice, 'I will not go to him.'

Beside the royal bed a flask of wine stood on an inlaid table. Odann reached clumsily and poured, held the cup to his lips. He drank, and sighed. 'Miri,' he said, 'sit with me. Come here.' She did as she was bidden, silently. His fingers touched her hair, where it lay coiled against her shoulder; then he pulled his hand away. 'Listen,' he said, 'and hear me well. Soon, Dendra will sit in my chair. There is no place for you here.'

She had turned, lips parted; and he took her hand. His sight blurred; and a part of him was nearly glad of the pain that made her increasingly remote. 'Miri,' he said gently, 'try to understand. This man, this Marck, will use you honourably. Once, many years ago, I knew him well; and he you. A child, at your mother's knee . . .' He drew his breath, sharply; grimaced, and went on. 'There is no place for you,' he said again. 'The Southguard lands are richer than our own; his Tower is well-founded, and he stands high with Atha King. In one month, you will go. You must take the chests of cloth, and the things that were your mother's . . .'

She threw herself down abruptly, hiding her face. She began to sob; and his hand once more found her hair. 'My child,' he said, 'do this for me. Do not make my pain the worse.'

She said in a muffled voice, 'I will never serve him.'

The King lay awhile watching up at the ceiling, his face drawn and grey. 'Do as you will,' he said finally. 'If you

179

cannot honour him as a husband, perhaps you will learn to love him as . . . a father.'

She raised her head then slowly, staring at him with her great dark eyes.

Throughout the day, Thoma refused to slacken pace. The party muttered, Briand complained more loudly; but the seneschal pressed on grimly, his face to the south. At last, toward nightfall, the desolation of the Great Plain was left behind; and a village showed ahead, a well-found place with high watchtowers and a stockade on which torches burned at intervals. Only then did the leader rein, to stare back narrow-eyed at the heights still visible in the growing dark. The Captain, his spirits rising at the prospect of warmth and food, ranged up beside him. 'Well, my Lord,' he said, 'in spite of thy complaints, thou hast discharged thy duty fairly. And gained for the King a most comely bride.'

But Thoma was not to be soothed. 'A devil, from a place of devils,' he said. He touched heels to his exhausted horse. 'Worse is to come of this,' he growled. 'Mark me, my friend.'

Yet later to the King he said, 'She is a pretty brown child.'

Then began a house-cleaning such as the folk of the Gate had never known; for Marck, the most industrious of clerks, had ever been the most indulgent of rulers. Now, all was changed; and men stared to see their liege lord resplendent in scarlet and gold, stepping briskly about his affairs. Small whirlwinds swept the kitchens of the Tower; and its pantries and buttery, its stables, dormitories and mews. In their wake they left stone flags gleaming, cooking vessels scoured and bright. Cartload after cartload of rushes, scraped from the floors, made their way down the Mound, to be dumped in heaps on the banks of the little brook; in their place, floors were strewn with precious hay. It became a commonplace to see Marck perched dangerously on a tottering stool, personally supervising the removal of some high cobweb that had offended the Royal eye; for the King brought to his new preoccupation the same meticulousness that had earned him fame as a scholar, and many a night the household got to its rest with groans and aching backs. Nor was this all; for craftsmen were summoned, some from as far off as Great Grange, to beautify the chambers and Hall. The walls of the Tower dazzled white in the sun before they were through, while the Great Hall acquired a ceiling of vivid green, pricked all over with golden stars. It was in fact, as Thoma heavily remarked, no longer a fit place to drink in; he took refuge in the farthest and meanest of the kitchens, only to be evicted in turn by a small army of limewash-wielding workmen.

Meanwhile the formal business of the marriage must be attended to. Clerks drew up the contract, working under the direction of the sorely-baffled seneschal; for Marck, in a state of high alarm, refused to bring his scholarly wits to bear on the matter in any way. A messenger despatched to Atha's court returned not merely with the royal assent but with a rich gift, a furlined robe and necklet of gold, fit wearing for a Queen. The following day an armed contingent of Plainsmen presented itself at Marck's gate; when the warriors left it was with twenty-five mares and stud animals, and a massive chest of plate. After which the tailors reappeared, to fit the housefolk with fresh livery. Everyone, from the meanest turnspit to the most dignified Serjeant, became resplendent in yellow and green; such expense was unheard-of, hitherto unimagined. Usk, it seemed, profited from the changed circumstances most of all; so that plump Maia, coming upon him one day in the inner courtyard of the Tower, stood and stared. The Jokeman had discarded the motley of his calling; his jerkin gleamed with thread of gold, while his shanks were clad in richly coloured silk.

'Now Scatha take all misbelievers,' said Maia. 'For if as I hear the King sees wonders, no less do we all. Is this some new jest, Jokeman? For Usk turned courtier is the greatest wonder yet.'

But the Jokeman merely regarded her disdainfully. 'The King has put away his books,' he said, 'I my foolishness, and thou thy greasy cap. But an ill grace, it seems, is not so ready hid.' He brushed past, his head held high, and left the woman staring.

Messengers rode again; for the lands of the Crab were wide, extending east to the Black Rock villages, west to the borders of the wild lands where the Sea Kings have their halls, paying no taxes and owing allegiance to none. Marck's summons was handsomely couched; and headmen and priests from all the vassalage, together with their families, began to converge on the Tower by the Gate. All brought gifts; oxen and sheep, beer by the barrel and the tun, horses to make good the bridefee. Though none existed in all the Southguard to match the animals that had been lost. Or so at least claimed the stablemaster, who added hard words on the bargain struck by Thoma for his lord. But the stablemaster was a simple soul, whose fat wife boiled his broth and clothed his children, and who looked for nothing more.

At last all things were in readiness; and a great day came when outriders, who had scoured the Heath since dawn, flew back to Marck's Tower with news of a procession that wound its cautious way among the green bogs of the coastland. A fine procession it was too that finally drew in sight of the Gate. First came priests and spaewives, blowing on gold-bound horns and waving green branches of peace; then a troupe of acrobats and jugglers, dressed in the motley Usk so recently disdained; then a cart drawn by lumbering oxen with the going-gifts of Miri, Princess of the Plain, her silks and dresses, the draperies and Sealand tapestry that had been her mother's pride. Lastly came soldiers from the household of Odann, footmen and helmeted cavalry, their breastplates winking back the morning sun; and a closed carriage drawn by further oxen, its sides wreathed with sprays of flowers and leaves. Its appearance threw Marck, if possible, into greater confusion than before. His hair and beard, once carefully combed, he had scrabbled to disarray; he danced on the roof of the Tower, staring beneath his hand, before turning to shout for his aides.

'Thoma,' he said, 'to the gate, to welcome her. No, to horse; take a troop, go welcome her from me. Take her this ring.'

'My Lord,' said Thoma, 'my place is at the gate.'

'Yes, yes to be sure. Thoma, is it she? Where are my Captains, where is Briand?'

'Here, my Lord,' said Briand. He too had profited from the transactions at Odann's Tower. His tunic and leggings were of richest cloth; his yellow hair and sweeping moustaches gleamed like silk.

'Good Briand, go to her,' said his master. 'And Usk, where is Usk? Let him also ride.'

'My Lord,' said Thoma, shocked. 'To send a Jokeman . . .'

'He sends no Jokeman,' said a sour voice at his side.

The seneschal turned, staring; for Usk was no less resplendent than the rest. His tunic was of green silk, well stitched with precious thread, his cloak lined with red and trimmed with snow-white fur. Rings glittered on his fingers, a jewelled dagger hung at his hip. 'See to your offices about the Tower, friend,' he said loftily. 'I, with my lord's permission, will bear his greetings.' He took the ring, bowing, and skipped for the stairs, calling for soldiers to attend him; and Thoma favoured his retreating back with a glance that was both foreboding and dire.

'Now,' said King Marck, all unaware. 'The bride-price, Thoma; is the balance prepared?'

'It is, my Lord,' said the seneschal heavily, and turned to follow his King.

Every window of the Tower shone with light. The noise of the feast, the shouting and laughter, rang across the baileys; so that the gate guards turned from eyeing the

183

crawling mists to stare up with longing and resentment. Pigs and oxen, roasting whole, dripped and sizzled over blazing courtyard fires while in the Great Hall every available inch was taken up by trestles and the diners. Serving men and girls threaded their way between as best they might, bearing aloft steaming dishes; in the winestores cask after cask was broached, bowl after bowl filled sparkling to the brim.

On the Royal dais, set high above the heads of the commoners, gleamed the greatest wonder of all; candles of priceless beeswax, filling the air with a golden scent. At one end of the long table was placed the painted chair of Marck. Flanking the King, in strictest order, sat the officers of his household; Thoma and Briand, the Captains of Infantry and Horse, the Serjeants with their wives. At the far end of the board, between two women of the Plain, sat Miri. Her black hair glittered with dustings of gold; her eyes in the candlelight looked dark and huge, her face and faultlessly modelled arms seemed brown and warm as the honey wax. She wore a simple dress of green, embroidered at the throat with golden thread; and on her breast, glinting, hung the great Gift of Atha. She sat unsmiling, eating little, drinking occasionally from the cup at her side; and Marck, his head spinning with the heat and wine, gripped the seneschal's elbow urgently.

'It is she,' he whispered. 'The Fairy-girl of the hills. Thoma, *it is she* . . .'

But Thoma, sweating heavily and hampered by an unaccustomed fork and knife, answered with little more than a grunt.

The moon was sinking to the rim of hills, and the mists floating high amid the trees that lined the brook, before the last of the feasters sought his bed. The bride had long since retired to her chamber; below in the Great Hall, yawning kitchen staff scraped up the last of the leavings, extinguished the rushlights that had burned in profusion along the walls, squabbled at the High Table for the drippings of scented wax. In the courtyard the remnants of the fires pulsed sullenly, sending up columns of smoke that mingled with the mist. Between them, close to the great inner wall, stood the Jokeman. The collar of his fine tunic was soiled with food, and he had been a little sick; but he stared up fixedly at the massive pale face of the Tower, the light that glowed softly from its upper chamber into the dark.

In the chamber, Marck stood at the foot of the Royal bed. On it, heaped in profusion, lay creamy fleeces and the skins of spotted cats the Midsea traders brought. Above it hung a drape of yellow silk; and among the skins nestled the Lady. The eyepaint she still wore made her look fierce as some forest creature; and her face was set like stone. Round her neck she wore a delicately worked gold torque, and below it a shift of fine green silk, through which her breasts showed with their firm, high buds.

The King rumpled the linen at his hips, helplessly. The vision had uplifted him; faced with its reality, he was all but dumb. It seemed her very stare drained his strength from him; the room spun a little, and he attempted to smile. 'But my dear,' he said meekly, 'I am your husband now. You are bound to obey.'

Her nostrils widened. 'You are my purchaser, King Marck,' she said, 'and that is all. Obedience may not be bought, as you yourself should know. Like love, it must be earned.'

Marck took a half-step, shuffling his feet. He said, 'Then tell me . . . what may I . . .'

Her eyes with their heavy lashes drifted closed. She said tiredly, 'Restore me to my home, and King Odann. Is this within your power?'

He twined his fingers. 'My child, the gifts are given . . .'

She snapped at him. *'Then leave me . . .'* She rolled her head miserably against the furs. 'Oh why did I come here, why did I let him persuade me . . . No!' That to Marck, who had once more moved toward the bed. He stopped, mouth working; her eyes blazed at him, then softened. She

185

smiled, and patted the skins. 'My Lord,' she said, 'do not alarm yourself. Here, come sit with me. For a little while.'

He scotched, hesitantly, on the side of the bed. A scent came from her that set his pulses racing; yet it seemed he dare not raise his eyes. A silence; then she spoke again more kindly. 'This you must understand,' she said. 'My father sold me, for fifty horses; like a . . . chattel, or a dog. I cannot so quickly . . . give myself afresh.'

He gripped her hand impulsively, and kissed. She stiffened, for an instant it seemed she might pull away; then she relaxed once more. Her fingers were brown and slender, the nails flat like the nails of a boy. He marvelled at her, feeling a great surge of joy; and she squeezed his hand, as if protectively. 'Of course,' she said, 'since as I say you own me, my will is yours. And you will find me dutiful. If you . . . force me I will not resist, for my father's sake with whom I still keep faith. But my Lord, to force would be a dreadful thing, with Athlinn's green knot still about my waist. For the first night belongs to the Gods who made us all. Also, and this you surely know, women who are tired, as I am tired, cannot love well, or truly.'

'I . . .' he said. 'I . . .'

'My Lord,' she said. She squeezed his hand again, and drew away. She wriggled, where she lay among the fleeces. 'How welcome you have made me,' she said. 'And what a fine bed you prepared, I never saw a finer. Or slept therein.' She lay with her great eyes fixed on him, solemnly. 'King Marck,' she said, 'grant me one wish. And make me truly happy.'

'My dear,' he said, moved. 'Anything. Anything . . .'

She gave him a tiny smile, that barely curved the corners of her lips. Her eyes searched his face, moving in little shifts and changes of direction. 'Give me . . . a little time,' she said. 'Just a little. And I will come to love you truly, as a friend.'

She saw the shadow that crossed his face. He wrestled, it seemed, with some compulsion; then he nodded, inarticulate. He said, 'It will be . . . as you say.'

She sighed. 'Oh,' she said, 'how I regret my sharp words now. For I can see in your face, that you would never bring me harm. Now, this is what we will do. Are you listening?'

'Yes,' he said. 'Yes, my dear.'

'You will come to me,' she said, 'each day. And we will talk. Perhaps many times each day. You shall instruct me; for on the Plain they say you are the greatest scholar in the land. Also I wish to see your realm of Southguard; for my father told me many wonderful things. Then when I know your country, and know its people, and truly feel it to be my home . . .' She let the sentence hang delicately in air, and smiled once more.

The heart of King Marck was lightened by the words; and he rose. 'My dear,' he said, 'all this will be done. Now you must rest, for I see you are very tired.'

'Yes,' she said. 'Thank you.' Then as he turned, 'My Lord . . .'

'Kiss me good night,' she said.

He stooped to her. She raised her hands modestly, covering her breasts. His lips brushed, lightly, her hot, dry brow; he smelled the perfume of her hair, and rose. 'My dear,' he said, 'if you should need . . . the housepeople . . .'

She shook her head, eyes sleepy and warm. 'Nothing, King Marck,' she said. 'Good night. And . . . the Gods attend your sleep.' The smile curved her lips once more; it stayed fixed there long after he had taken the lamp, and the chamber was dark.

Toward dawn the Jokeman hemmed in his sleep, and coughed. Thoma groaned, champing his lips like a dog; and Briand turned, and dreamed a certain dream. While in the highest chamber, lit by its marsh-sprite lamp, a strange sound might have been heard; dry and repetitive, like an old shoe scuffed endlessly against a plank. It came from the Royal couch; where Marck of the Gate, greatvassal of Atha the Good, wept in expiation for an uncommited sin.

187

Spring deepened to summer. Once more the martens nested under the high eaves of the Tower, raising their broods of squeaking young; skies gleamed blue and faultless, while white dust rose behind the waggons that toiled down to the great gap in the chalk. They came from Long Creek, and the sea-haunted lands of the west; from Great Grange and the Hundred Lakes and Morwenton itself, the sprawling metropolis where Atha had his Hall. Silks they brought and linen of marvellous fineness, jet and amber from the north, mirrors of burnished bronze; and once a tub of honey from the Misty Isles, brown and rich and smelling of the heather from which it had been won. Nothing it seemed was too much, no expense too great, for the Lady of the Gate; and the Queen fulfilled her bargain faithfully, delighting her lord in many different ways. From him she learned the great tales of his people, their sieges and battles and wanderings; and the King never found a more willing audience. Also she rode the length and breadth of the Southguard, by litter or on horseback, speaking to all not as great lady or Queen but as an equal. For this and for her beauty, she was much beloved; so that children would run to bring her flowers, or field-gifts of cider and beer.

Marck for his part showed her his kingdom with joy; the swaying, rolling uplands of the chalk, dotted by gravemounds old when Time began; the tree-lined coombes, drowsy with bee-sound, each with its nestling village and chuckling stream; the Great Heath, empty and vast, rhododendrons blazing beneath dark-topped clumps of pine. He showed her fishing villages, clinging limpet-like between sky and sea; headlands that strode each beyond the next, hazed with sunlight against the brilliant blue; ragged saw-edges of cliff, where the mist whirls up in summer and the wind comes in. He showed her the Ledges, where stone groins slope into the water and the sea sucks down and up, and no boat can live; and there she swam, for her Lord's delight, in a great rock pool among green and dark-red fern.

At length it seemed he saw, reflected in her eyes, a dream that had been his own. He spoke of this, one morning in high summer. She heard him through, not frowning; but when he had finished she shook her head. 'My Lord,' she said, 'half of what you have said I admit I have not understood; but it seems you do me too much honour. Lord, women are not Goddesses. This you must know. We eat like you, and sleep like you, we have needs of the body and . . . functions; in truth, no Goddess lives in me. I would not see you so sorely disappointed.'

'But you do not understand,' said Marck. 'You have not listened. I knew you, you see, so many years ago.'

'As a baby, yes,' she said. 'My father told me.'

'No,' he said. 'No, no, no . . .'

She knelt, and took his hands. She was wearing a new white dress, and her hair smelled of summer grass. 'My Lord,' she said, 'you have been kinder to me than I would have believed. Kinder than my own father, who once was all I had; and I am your Queen, so I can speak frankly. Do not make me a Goddess, King Marck, or think in such terms again. Goddesses are for worshipping; and I . . . am not worthy.'

He touched her hair. 'You do not understand,' he said. 'But why should you? Miri, if a Goddess is in you, she may not choose to reveal herself. But . . . listen, Miri,' he said earnestly. 'You have brought me great joy. My dear, have you heard the people? Have you heard what they say? They say, "King Marck laughs. King Marck is happy." And Miri, this is true. Listen to me now.'

She sat beside him, hands in her lap, and smiled.

'This was my dream,' he said. 'But words are not enough. Have you seen . . . the grass, the greenness of it? Green, and soft . . . And the grain, standing against the sky? And the sea mist, how it stripes the hills? And with the sun behind it, *gold* . . .'

She said, puzzled, 'My Lord?'

He flexed his hands, stammering in his eagerness. 'This was my dream,' he said. 'That I *was* the grain, and earth, and creeping things upon it. And mist and sky, the stones the Giants placed between the hills. I was the land, Miri, and the land was me. In the dream I found a woman, who was also the land; and we made children who would . . . know the land, and live out golden times. And . . . this too was the dream. That we died, returning to earth; but we *were* our children, and their children's children, and the golden grain again. It seemed a . . . Mystery, a worthy thing.'

She stared at him, with troubled eyes; then took his hand, and laid her head against his shoulder. 'I cannot say,' she said. 'But . . . perhaps, some day, these things will be.'

Nothing further passed between them at that time; but it seemed the notion of the Mystery remained with the Queen. She spoke of it some weeks later, to a serving-maid. Autumn was on the land; a calm, mild autumn of gold and blue. In the Tower rooms the first fires had been lit, crackling with sweet-scented cones. Before one such hearth Miri lay, amid piles of fleeces. She wore a skirt of pleated green linen, held closely to her hips by a splendid belt broidered with gold. Between her breasts hung the Gift of Atha; but she was otherwise bare. The girl, a daughter of a Sea King's thrall, knelt beside her. Something of the sea seemed to have marked her wide-spaced eyes, which were blue as Miri's were brown; they sparkled now with amusement as she laughed. She took up a little vial of scented oil, poured a few spots between the shoulders of the Queen and began to massage gently.

'Why do you laugh?' asked Miri. 'This I have on no less a word than that of my lord the King, who is the wisest man in Southguard. And probably the world.'

The girl giggled again. She said, 'Yes, my Lady.'

'Then may it not be true?' demanded the Queen. 'I have the parts of a Goddess, Atta, as you may perhaps have noticed. It follows I have something of her power.' She sighed. 'Lower, Atta, lower,' she said. 'Just there I'm *very* sore . . .'

The girl poured more oil.

'What would you have me do, in earnest of my power?' asked Miri. 'Shall I call up a demon?' She propped her chin in her hands, eyes vague. 'Perhaps I shall raise a tempest,' she said. 'Like the ghost-wizards did in our fathers' time. Do you not tremble?'

Atta grinned, but made no answer.

Miri pouted. 'I have it,' she said after a while. 'Since I am not believed, and would have you worship me, I shall bring the lightning. Will you love me then, Atta? When you see the hilltops smoking, and every Tower split?'

For the first time a trace of uneasiness showed in the outlander's face. 'My Lady,' she said in an unsure voice, 'these things should not be mocked.'

The Queen rolled over into her lap and seized her wrist, watching up with glowing eyes. She said, *'I do not mock.'* A little pause; then she lowered her lids sleepily, and smiled. 'Kiss me, Atta,' she said. She pulled the other's head down, slowly; then took the sea girl's lip between her teeth, biting until she pulled back with a gasp. She laughed then, composedly; sprinkled oil, and guided the other's hand. 'I shall do as I choose,' she said. 'And you will serve me; for a Goddess can do no wrong.'

II

The weather worsened toward the end of the year. First came gales from the south; winter gales, hissing and filled with sleet. They turned the sea to a smoking plain of grey, flung great waves crashing at the battered cliffs. Boats drawn high on the foreshore were smashed or swept away, thatch and tiles torn from cottage roofs. Later came torrential rain. It beat the last leaves from the trees, mashing them to brown pulp. The brook that flowed below the Mound became a racing flood while night after night Marck's housepeople lay awake, feeling their beds shift under them and creak, hearing the boom and roar as the wind fought with the Tower. Shutters burst and the fastenings of doors, the oiled silk panes from the windows of the

Great Hall. Torches streamed beards of flame, till they were extinguished in fear. Then the wind died away. It left the Tower dripping, silent, and fearful still. For a rumour had run, from the Serjeants to the gateporters, the porters to the grooms, the grooms to the mews servants and their wives. None knew how it began; but all took to walking carefully, and speaking in low tones. No fear, however, sustains itself for long; so that when nothing further chanced the bolder or less reverent members of the household began to do a much worse thing than huddle and talk. They began to laugh.

Of all these happenings, one man seemed unaware; and that man was King Marck. Through the wild weeks of storm, and through the dark, calm days that followed, he worked incessantly, copying out sheet after sheet in his angular, precise hand. At last, after so much heartsearching, his mind was calm again; and a new subject had come to him. He was writing, for his Queen, the tale of all the Sealand Gods; Athlinn and Devu Spearwielder, Gelt who forges the lightning and Scatha who sends the Runners of the Night.

It was on one such gloomy afternoon, soon after the turn of the year, that the royal scribe heard above him a familiar cough. He stared up, amazed; and on the beam, his thin legs swinging as of old, sat Usk. Rich living had fattened him so that his tunic stretched tight across his belly; but he wore his cap and bells, and had twisted his face into his most unpleasant leer. 'Now, King,' he said, 'I see a well-accustomed sight. What occupies thy royal wits now?'

'Nothing,' said Marck, troubled. 'Nothing that concerns you, friend. Usk, why have you done this? You know it was my wish that, having no need of Jokemen, you should not humble yourself for me.'

Usk ignored the question. 'Nothing?' he said. He flung his heels up, cackling. *'Nothing concerns the King,'* he mocked. 'Well hast thou spoken, Lord; with Nothing hast thou concerned thyself, this many a day. And Nothing will be thy reward . . .'

'Come down from there,' said Marck with some asperity. 'Also, explain this nonsense. Or take it somewhere else; already I have heard enough.'

'Come down from there,' said the Jokeman. 'Kings may come down from thrones, Gods from the sky; scholars may take leave of truth, and wise men of their wits. But Usk, in all this jangling, holds his place.'

Marck flushed. 'I said come down . . .'

'Would that I might,' said the other mournfully. 'But I am bound here, Lord. Within the shadow of a greater, the Jokeman's folly goes unseen . . .' He craned his head. 'What writest thou?'

'You know very well,' said his master angrily. 'I finish my book; with the tale of Devu, and the singing bird of Midgard.'

'Singing birds,' said Usk. 'Lord, of thy goodness, tell me another tale.'

'What tale is that?' snapped Marck.

'Of Athlinn and the nymph Goieda,' said the Jokeman. 'That is a better story.'

'You know it as well as I,' said the King shortly. 'The jongleur from Morwenton sang it, not two months since in Hall.'

'Yet would I hear it from thy lips,' said Usk winningly. 'A favour, Lord . . .'

'Hmmph,' said Marck. He turned the pages before him, grumpily, casting suspicious glances at the other. 'Athlinn, who was lord of Heaven, wooed the nymph,' he said. 'But Goieda refused him in her pride, cherishing the love of Basta, a Midgard King.' Then it seemed that despite his annoyance the scholar in him gained the upper hand. 'This is the version I have written,' he said. 'So it is set down in the Saga of Ennys, who was Arco's bard. But in the Usgeard Goieda becomes a mortal girl and daughter of King Renlac, my great-kinsman. Which makes me wonder if . . .'

Usk coughed. 'My Lord,' he said, 'the tale . . .'

'Be still,' snapped Marck. 'Is there no pleasing you?' But the thread of his discourse was lost; he frowned, scratched his head and resumed the story. 'Athlinn carried the nymph to his great Hall,' he said, 'and there plied her with gifts. But Goieda mocked him, putting scorn on him, calling him greybeard and old man . . .'

He stopped abruptly, as if realising for the first time the Jokeman's drift. He scowled; then his face cleared, and he shook his head. 'This tale was told in Sealand in the times of Rand the Wise,' he said. 'Those days are done.'

'Till on a day,' said Usk, 'the patience of the High One was exhausted. Those are thy words, my King. So Athlinn took a spear butt, and with it beat the nymph. Then when he wearied of the sport, he knew her. Then her blood flowed, even to Middle Earth; then the crops sprang; summer came, and the tribes of men rejoiced.'

'Peace,' said Marck wearily. 'Peace, my friend. You do not understand.'

'Then was Athlinn stricken in his heart,' said Usk remorselessly. 'Then for a year and a day the sun was hid; and the doors of Heaven gaped, for Goieda to go or stay as she might choose . . .'

'At the end of which time,' said Marck, 'Athlinn returned. And Goieda washed his hands and brought him bread, repentant. And on her Athlinn fathered all the Gods . . .' He raised his hands, half-laughing. 'Usk,' he said, 'I am not King of Heaven, nor desire to be higher than I am. Under Atha I hold this country, between the hills and sea, and rule as justly as I may. What Gods might do is not in question.'

'No,' said the Jokeman bitterly, 'but honour is. If thou put on thy cap and bells, King Marck, can Usk do less?'

The King's eyes flashed. His colour rose; but his voice remained calm. 'Enough,' he said. 'Usk, I have heard you for the love I know you bear me. Now say no more, but listen. I saw a Goddess, surely, in the hills; and she as surely spoke to me. But perhaps I did not hear her words aright. Later, when I thought I saw her in my Hall . . . but she is a child, my friend. A child who hourly brings me joy. One day she will hold this place and all it owns, my daughter under the Gods. As for this other; before you talk of honour, think on this. Rather men had stayed in darkness; rather the Earth itself remained unformed, than that one drop of innocent blood be spilled.'

'To that I bow,' said Usk. 'For it is rightly said of Gods and men, to spill the blood of the innocent is a crime.'

His tone, and the look that accompanied the words, arrested Marck. He turned slowly, his eyes blue and bright. 'What do you mean?' he said.

'Nay, remember,' said Usk. 'A Jokeman can have no meaning. And such as attach great import to his words are needs more witless than he.' He lolled composedly on the beam; took off his cap, spun it and whistled a tune.

The King rose, frowning. 'None the less you will speak,' he said. 'You have said too much, or not enough.'

'I will *say* nothing,' returned the other. 'But for a token, I will jest with thee.' He caught the coin Marck flung him, bit it as was his custom and stowed it away. 'Gold it was that brought King Altred down,' he said, 'more than the blow that joined his brother to the Gods. Life is an evil thing.' He shook his head mournfully. 'For that love I bear thee,' he said, 'I will tell another tale; of Scatha One-eye, Lord of Night, and Sceola, and the Horseman of Devu.'

Marck's frown deepened. He said, 'I have not heard of this.'

'Then do thou compose thyself, Lord,' said Usk. 'And a Fool shall increase the tally of thy wisdom.' He cocked his head, gravely. 'Sceola, you must know, walked ever on her master's right,' he said. 'This being the side that Scatha King was blind. Till one day Methleu came, who was Athlinn's dwarf and the Jokeman of the Gods. "Scatha", said he, "tell me the tale of how you lost your eye." So Scatha told of the winning of the Sword, by whose power the Night Hounds are held in check, or made to run at bidding. "That is a good tale," said Methleu when he had done. "Yet I say this, Lord; that glory and defeat are like death and life, the two sides of one coin. The Hounds give thee safety in the night, and power over giants and shadows; yet on thy right side thou art blind. Who guards thee there?''

'Then Scatha said, ''The Horsemen given by my Lord Devu; and their Captain, whom I greatly honour.'' Then he remembered how his wife walked to his right. Then he remembered . . .'

He said no more; for an alarming change had come over Marck. He raised his hands, the fingers crooked; then his eyes, glaring round, lighted on a heavy knife that lay before him on the trestle. He snatched it up, and threw. A thud; and Usk stared down in turn, face paling. Then he reached with shaking fingers to free the slack of his sleeve, where the blade held it pinned fast to the beam. He waited for nothing further; but scuttled to the floor, and ran. Nothing more was heard from the King's high chamber all that day. The folk of the household moved about their affairs, casting troubled glances upwards to the Tower, the slitted windows set beneath the eaves. But they remained dark; and the food that was sent, by a trembling serving-woman, was left untouched. But long after the last lamps were extinguished, and the Tower got to its uneasy rest, a listener at Marck's door would have heard, mixed with his groans, one endlessly repeated word.

'Briand . . .'

The dawn light lay grey across the Heath when the King rode to the outer gate. He returned no answer to the muttered greetings of the guards but sat hunched and still, his pale face shadowed by a heavy cloak. The hooves of the horse clattered on the bridge, drummed on the turf beyond; and he was gone. An hour later a second rider passed beneath the towering gantries of the gatehouse. Like his lord, he was muffled in a cloak; and he too set his horse at the Heath, not looking back. The guards exchanged glances, but spoke no word. Nor were many to be found bold enough to voice their thoughts. The day passed gloomily; and by nightfall Marck had not returned.

The fire roared brightly, fed by fresh billets; and round it a ribald company had assembled. Two stablehands, in the grubby green and yellow of the House, seemed somewhat the worse for beer; beside them a porter fondled the youngest and least prepossessing of the kitchenmaids. But the most drunken of the group, by far, was Maia. As ever, her hair straggled from beneath her cap; she stood swaying and giggling, her plump legs spread, her feet bare on the flags. Her bodice was unlaced; and over her ample breasts she gripped two cups. 'Why, thus it would be,' she said, 'were I a Goddess, and thou a noble Captain.'

The stable boy thus addressed guffawed with pleasure; the kitchenmaid shrieked.

'Marry no, good Captain,' said Maia. 'Not till my will permits. For as thou knowest, I am a Goddess. Not till my will permits.' She attempted a curtsey, and all but overtoppled. 'For if thou *force* me, Captain,' she said, 'thy fingers will drop from thy hands. Or some other part . . .!' She screamed with merriment; then became aware, by degrees, of the appalled stares directed past her. She turned, slowly, her own face blenching; and the cups fell and shattered. She put her hands before her, and began to whimper.

In the doorway stood the master of the Gate. He wore a robe of dull homespun; such a garment as his people had once grown used to when he rode abroad. His face was white; his eyes glared, it seemed with all the wildness of his Sealand forbears. His tongue-tip ran across his lips before he spoke. He said, *'You mocked her . . .'*

Somebody whispered, 'My Lord . . .' But the words were cut short by the scream of Marck. The hand he jerked into sight held a knotted flail. He raised it, struck; and the screaming was redoubled. The first blow fell across the woman's forehead, the second on her upflung arms. She scuttled, wetting herself in terror, for the shelter of a table; but Marck laid his hand to it, and the table was flung aside.

It was Thoma, dragged to the place by the incoherent porter, who took the weapon from his master, Thoma who gripped him till the thin shoulders ceased their jerking.

The seneschal stared down then, unbelieving. 'My Lord,' he said heavily, 'what have you done?'

The King also stared. Spittle flecked his beard; but the blindness, that had made him a red man striking shadows, was gone. He saw the maimed eye, the blood that brightened the grubby dress, the fingers from which the torn flesh stood in spikes. The woman crouched, quivering; and he turned, hands to his skull, and blundered from the kitchen. They heard his long cry fall and rise as he climbed the Tower stairs.

The Queen was waiting for him in a dress of blue, decorated with silver thread. Her hands were clenched at her sides, and her voice when she spoke was low. 'I heard . . . cries,' she said. 'What has happened, my Lord?'

Marck stared at her. 'I have been riding,' he said. 'I rode to the beach. But it was empty. The hills were empty, and the sea. You emptied them.'

She said, 'My Lord . . .' But he cut her off.

'In all my life,' he said, 'I lived here at the Gate as a King should live. When the poor cried, I heeded them. Where other hands fell heavy, mine was stayed. Now I face the Gods with a sin of blood. An evil has come to us. You brought it.'

'*I?*' she said. 'My Lord, I . . . do not understand . . .'

'I waited,' he said. 'Waited, and watched. Then I returned, to punish. But he had gone . . .'

'King Marck,' she said, 'hear me . . .'

He shouted at her. *'Why did you not ask?'*

'What?' she said. *'What?'*

'I would have given,' said Marck. 'Anything. Do you not understand? Him, anything . . . To keep you here, and happy . . .'

She stared a shocked instant; then a change came over her face. She said, 'So it has come to this.' She walked forward, eyes blazing. 'All my life,' she said, 'I have been plagued by men. Old men, and fat men, and men who bought and sold. For *these*, and *this* . . . Can I help them?'

'Why?' he said. *'Why?'*

'I asked nothing,' she said. 'Nothing of anybody. To . . . smell the air, and see the summers come, and lie in peace. But no. No, no, no . . . By the Gods, I could be sick. Yes, throw up all the mess and filth men brought me . . .'

She faced him, fists clenched; and he moaned, pressing his hands to his head. He said, 'I brought you love . . .'

'And I gave it,' she shouted. 'All there was to give . . .' She caught her breath; then her expression altered once more. 'What else did you expect?' she hissed. 'Caging me here like a Midsea bird, with none but loutish girls for company, in a room that stinks of old men's piss . . . *What did you expect?'*

He lowered his hands, slowly.

'And now he's gone,' she said. 'You drove him away. So you can lie in peace again. It's over.'

But Marck shook his head. He said, 'It will never be over.'

She tried then to dart past him to the door. He caught her, flinging her back. She fought with him; and he struck her. She fell across the bed; and he leaped upon her, gripping with his knees. First he tore away the gift of Atha King, then her belt and dress, raking her shoulders with his nails. He crushed her to the fleeces, but she kicked and cried; so he beat her again. After which he took her, with the vigour of his rage. She lay quiet when he had finished, trembling a little and with her eyes tightly closed. And so he left her, reeling to his chamber. He closed the door behind him, dropping the heavy bar, and sank to the floor.

Through the Tower and all its rooms, silence prevailed. Torches burned, lighting empty corridors; but no man stirred. Across the baileys, moon-whitened, stretched ragged shadows of gatehouse and wall; and the gates themselves stood open to the empty Heath. An enemy could have crept in from the misty trees; but no enemy came.

It was dawn before one stirred. There came the click of the stable gate, the creak of harness. A horse snorted, stamping. The hooves sounded again, by the gate and on the trackway beyond; then the noise was swallowed up. The morning was silent once more.

From the shadows by the outer gate, one man kept vigil. Spindly he was of shank; and the furs with which his body was swathed accentuated its curious bulkiness. For a time he watched the empty Heath to the north, lips parted; then he turned away, staring up at the high face of the Tower. 'Now I have thee, King, and all thy tribe,' he muttered. 'For this is no minstrel's tale . . .'

Dendra lounged on the high chair of King Odann. His long legs sprawled indolently across the dais; his hair, braided and greased with butter, hung to his shoulders; and he gripped a heavy winecup in a hand that gleamed with rings. Round him clustered his fighting men; and below him on the littered floor of the Hall stood Miri. The cloak she wore hung open; her dress was splashed with mud to the hips, and the pallor of her face accentuated the great bruise that had spread across her cheek.

'I have left him,' she said in a low voice, 'and that is enough. Now I seek shelter of a kinsman, as all our laws demand.'

Dendra swilled the wine in his cup. 'Your kinsman is dead,' he said at length. 'I mean, your father.'

A shout of laughter greeted the words. She swayed, closing her eyes. 'Then justice and mercy are likewise dead,' she said. 'I see that now.' She swallowed, and moistened her lips. 'What is your will,' she said, 'King Dendra?'

Another smothered laugh; and Dendra scowled, raising a hand for quiet. 'Not my will,' he said, 'but the Gods.' You come here, to my Hall, asking for justice. Perhaps you will receive it.' He drained the cup, and set it aside. 'Why did you leave the Tower of the Gate?'

She stared round, in the torchlit gloom; then drew herself erect. She said, 'Its lord put shame on me.'

'Shame?' said Dendra. 'Shame?' He raised himself on the throne, gripping its arms, and peered about him.

'Friends,' he said, 'hear a wonder. The daughter of King Odann talks of shame . . .'

When the noise was done he leaned toward her. 'Here is the justice you came so far to seek,' he said. 'Your crime we will not name; but you will be taken from this place, and heavy stones laid on you. Also, here is my mercy. Your veins will be cut, so that life will run out quickly.'

She shrank at that, as though struck afresh; but when the priests moved forward she rallied. 'Does my uncle,' she said above the rising clamour, 'pass sentence for the Gods, or for himself? My uncle who came to me, a child, the very night my mother died?' She flung away the hands that were laid on her. 'Ever after that,' she said, 'I slept beside the King. And ever after that you raged and wondered. But you will never know . . .'

Uproar, in the Hall. Dendra leaped forward, his face suffused; and she shouted him down again. 'Nor may you take my life,' she said. 'The life I carry is not yours to claim.'

The King had halted, fist raised; now he scowled. 'What?' he said. 'What is this? What life?'

She stared back, mocking. She said, 'The Heir of the Gate.'

He stared in turn; at her heaving breasts, the faces of his followers. Then, slowly, he remounted the steps of the throne. He snapped his fingers, and the winecup was recharged. He drank; and when he put the thing aside none there could read his eyes. He said, 'What say my priests?'

A hurried muttering; and a withered, grey-robed man piped up. 'This is true, by all our Sealand laws,' he said falteringly. 'You may not harm her.'

The King sat back, still with the unfathomable stare. 'Then to these laws I bow,' he said. 'Ruling justly, and mindful of the Gods. No man of the Plain shall injure her.'

Miri pulled the cloak about her throat. She said, 'And the child?'

Dendra put his head back then and laughed. 'The child will be born,' he said. 'My subjects will wish to meet him.' He sighed, impatiently, to the men about her; and she was hustled from the Hall.

The winter that followed was bad, as bad as any in memory. For weeks the sun stayed hidden, while bitter winds scythed across the Plain and through the great gap in the chalk. The lengthening days brought no relief; instead snow fell, great silent shining hills that clogged the narrow ways a spearshaft deep. Wolves came down, howling night after night round the scattered villages of the Southguard. Horses stamped and snorted in their quarters, children wailed; men peered from gatehouses and walls, pulling their beards and frowning into the dark. The Towers were cheerless; but none more so than the Tower of the Gate.

The King was now seldom seen. Servants carried food to the door of his high chamber; but as often as not the platters were left untouched. From the courtyards Marck might sometimes be descried, a vague, hunched shape staring out across the speckled waste to the north; but what the thoughts were that possessed him no man could say.

The summer was cold, with gale after gale sweeping in from the sea. Grain rotted in the square fields clustering round the village walls; what little grew was flattened by the wind. Only autumn brought relief. Then, curiously, the land smiled once more. Flowers bloomed, on the banks of the little brook; reeds were cut for winter flooring, what remained of the harvest gathered under cloudless skies. Days were warm, nights misty and mild. The storm-battered Hall was repaired and patched; but the gloom that had gripped the household remained. For a rumour had come, brought first by a travelling tinker; that round the Tower of Odann were many crows.

The sun was setting in long banners of red when a stranger rode to the Tower. The gate guards marked him far off on the Heath; a Serjeant was summoned and the walls fresh-manned, so that when he came within hail many curious heads regarded him. He turned his horse casually, in the dusty road beyond the outer bridge. His hair, which was fair and long, blew round his face. He wore greaves and a cuirass of Midsea workmanship; heavy gold bangles circled his arms, a long cutting-sword hung at his hip. But what attracted the onlookers' eyes was none of these things. Round his waist, and hanging to the knee, was knotted a thick scarlet sash. It glowed in the sunset light; the war-lanyard of the Sealand Kings, unseen now for a generation.

The warrior was hailed from the gate, and bidden enter; but he shook his head arrogantly, setting his long hair flying. 'Here I remain, chalkdwellers,' he said. 'I bear a message for your master.'

The Serjeant flushed at that, fingering his beard. 'Our King receives no strangers,' he said finally. 'Neither are messages welcome, save from the Gods. Tell it to me.'

The stranger spat. 'The first is this,' he said. 'A son was born to Marck, Lord of the Gate. The rest is for his ears.'

If the consternation caused by the words reached him he gave no sign. He sat the horse calmly, staring past the Tower at the brilliant light, while men ran back across the turf of the outer bailey. A further wait, a stirring by the inner court; and Marck himself appeared, with Thoma in attendance.

All were shocked by the gauntness of the King. His eyes gleamed bird-bright in his sunken face; a soiled robe flapped round his calves and he walked as if with difficulty, clinging to the seneschal's arm. He climbed the steps to the gate parapet hesitantly; but when he spoke his voice, though thin, was clear. 'What is this news you bring?' he asked. 'Say what you must; then come inside, and we will find refreshment.'

The other shook his head again. He stared up, eyes pale. 'These are the words of Dendra of the Plain,' he said. 'Hear, and mark him well. That shame was put on him by the Gate, blood of his House being bartered for unworthy gold. That he will have a window on the sea, as fits his Line; that he will seat him in your Chair, as penance for his shame; and that his arm is strong. For the horses of chalkdwellers breed faster than their Kings.'

A hubbub rose at once from the watching men. More than one soldier dropped a hand to his side, nocked an arrow to his bowstring; while round Marck Tower and gatehouse seemed suddenly to spin. Thoma gripped him; but he shook his head, pushing the other away. He raised his arms; and by degrees the noise was stilled. 'All this is strange to me,' he said, when he could once more make himself heard. 'I seek no war with Dendra; nor with any man in all the world, having given my life to penitence for great crimes. But tell me of my son, if this was the message you brought. Tell me and I will pay you well, with gold.'

The other turned his horse contemptuously. 'No Chalk King pays a Plainman save with blood,' he said. 'As for your son, this also my master bade me say. The child was born high, according to his station; *and there were many midwives.*' He waited for nothing further but drove his heels at the horse, with a long yell.

The watchers saw the Gate King reel; but next instant his hand was up. They heard his voice rise cracked and high.

'Take that man . . .'

Arrows flew, hissing. It seemed the messenger swayed in the saddle; but he collected himself, spurring the horse and bending low. Feet pounded on the gantries and wooden steps, the gates squealed back; and a stream of cavalry thundered in pursuit, fanned out across the Heath.

It was midnight before they returned. They brought back a man blinded and two others ashen and groaning, their limbs wrapped with makeshift dressings; for the Plainman, though wounded, had fought well. The messenger, or what remained of him, they dragged behind a horse. They hauled him to the gatehouse; and from its wall they hung him, by the heels.

A Sealand war-drum is a vast affair, big as two wine barrels and with a skin of tight-stretched hide. Its throbbing in still weather carries many miles; and it was such a drum that spoke, all night and all next day, from King Marck's Tower. Everywhere throughout the Southguard the beat was taken up; till the weary drummers, resting beside their great instrument, heard the answers thudding back like echoes in the hills. The Sea Kings heard them far to the west, and turned uneasy in their beds; the lands beyond the Black Rock heard them, and the Marsh Folk to the north. But fast as the summons spread, the news spread faster; that the Queen was dead, the Heir of the Gate given to the crows. Cressets blazed, on walls and watchtowers, till it seemed the Southguard was aflame. Men marched and rode, armed and grim-faced, converging on Marck's Tower. Two days passed, and a third; then from the hills an army poured, like wasps from a shaken hive.

The winter that followed lived long in minstrels' stories. The Plain was wasted, from south to north; for what the hill folk happened on, they slew. Everywhere across the land, from Long Creek to the marshes of the west, went the red lanyard; behind it followed terror, fire and death. Atha's messengers rode in vain; Towers were sacked, whole vassalages destroyed. Dendra's wild horsemen fought like devils; but the men of the hills fought better. The Plainmen were forced back, raging; and every step was a life. Till there came a day, in an unwanted spring, when King Marck once more entered Odann's Hall.

A great time he stood, in his armour that was battered and stained. He saw the light that flooded the place, pouring through shattered walls. He saw the piled dead, the blood that marked the flags, the women who wailed and crouched. He smelled the fresh, raw stink, perhaps smelled the fear. He spoke then, to his followers. His words were few; but those that heard them grew paler than before.

It was Thoma who, in an upper chamber of the place, came on the Jokeman. In his arms, still stained from the morn-

205

ing's work, Usk gripped a great bundle of spoil. His tongue-tip ran across his lips; and his eyes flickered nervously, past Thoma to the stairhead. For a time neither spoke; then the seneschal latched the door closed behind him, and set down the basket he carried. 'Now, friend Jokeman,' he said, 'we have a reckoning to make, you and I.'

'Reckoning?' said Usk. 'Art thou mad?' He licked his mouth again; then with a return to something like his former manner, 'Thoma, thou bladder, warm work and a very little exercise have cooked thy remaining wits. Let me pass . . .'

But the other caught him, hurling him back. The bundle dropped and spilled; Usk groaned, and the stout wall shook. Silence fell; a silence in which both heard, mixed with the crackle of flames from the outer court, the wails of the condemned.

'Old friend,' said Usk, 'for that I used thee haughtily, I confess my fault . . .'

'Used me, turd?' snarled Thoma. 'What care I for the bearing of a Jokeman, good or ill? It is not for that you answer.'

'Thoma,' said the other, 'by all the Gods . . .' But the seneschal raised an arm, striking backhanded. 'Who,' he said, 'against all use, prompted our King to wooing? Turning his wits with rubbish, and talk of Gods?' He struck again, and Usk fell and grovelled. 'Who brought to the Gate, of all he might have wed, a Great Plain whore?' said Thoma. 'For Crab and Wolf were ever enemies, as well you knew. And who then brought the tale all others kept from him? *Answer . . .*'

'What I told, I told in love,' whimpered Usk. 'Desiring that no shame come to his House. And see how I was requited. Banned from his sight . . .'

'No shame?' said Thoma. 'But for you we might be sitting at the Gate this hour, and King Marck with us. And all this work undone.' Then as the Jokeman gripped his knees, 'Off me, I say . . .'

But the other clung with the strength of desperation. 'Thoma, hear me,' he said. 'I ever loved the King. And thee . . .'

The seneschal flung him away. 'Stop your mouth,' he said disgustedly. 'Your foolishness will not avail you now.'

'Foolishness?' said Usk. He glared up, panting. 'The Towers of the Plain were few,' he said. 'Now they are fewer. Who burned them? A God, with his thunderbolts; or Usk, the Jokeman? Now the Long Creek Kings will come, they who were bound by treaty to Odann. And Morwenton, great Atha . . . now these Kings of ours will waste themselves. And you, a Horseman, wish a tithe undone . . .'

Thoma said, frowning. 'You are mad.'

'Aye,' said Usk. 'Mad to serve a Sealander; I, whose fathers owned this country. And you are mad, we are all mad. But now the wild pigs fight, now we will live on bacon . . .'

Thoma heard no more but closed with him, gripping his jerkin front. 'But my last jest was the greatest,' shouted Usk. 'Who made the rumours fly? Who wound his skein, for a Sealand Queen? Perhaps she was unfaithful, perhaps a certain Captain went to her by night. Perhaps the King was just to take revenge. *Even as I* . . .' His hand flashed up, gripping the jewelled dagger. He drove the blade with all his force at the seneschal's side, into the crack where breastplate and backplate met.

A silence, that lengthened. Thoma stared down, amazed; then he put his fingers to his side; and then he smiled. He took the other's wrist, squeezing; a crack, and Usk once more began to shriek. Then Thoma raised his mailed fist, striking down; then stamped, once and again, with his booted feet. He raised the sagging body to the sill of the one tall window, heaved, leaned out to see it fall. He saw the arms flail, heard the great thud as it struck the courtyard flags. Dizziness came then, and flickerings across his sight. He leaned against the chamber wall, hand to his side, and groaned. He said between his teeth, 'Now he will never know . . .'

He took up the basket he had carried, heavily. On the stairs, he staggered; and a flicker of movement shot past his feet. He closed his eyes, breathing harshly; then he shook his head. 'A vow is a vow,' he said. 'That we should come to this . . .' He moved forward painfully, gripping the basket. 'Kitty,' he called. 'Name of the Gods . . . here, kitty. Kitty-kit-kit . . .'

The heights of the Plain rose vague and sweeping in the early light; and the endless wind blew, shivering the manes of horses, stirring the many flags. The Tower of Odann, and the stockades that surrounded it, stood silhouetted and stark. Round about, from where the army had encamped, rose the smoke of many cooking fires. Oxen grumbled in the baggage lines; but from the great dim flock of men who stood with upturned faces came no sound at all.

From point after point on the Tower projected the massive arms of gallows. Now a signal was given; and on the nearest, ropes and pulleys creaked to tautness. An animal bellowed, in fear and pain; then the carcass, huge and misshapen, swayed swiftly up the Tower wall, hung black and twisting. Another followed it, and another. First they hung the stockade cattle, then what horses remained; then the remnants of the garrison, then every living creature within the walls. And of them all, the tiny furry things on their gibbets of twigs took longest to die.

Later, when all was still, fire was brought. The flames ran swiftly, small at first but spreading and brightening, till the whole great place roared like a furnace, a beacon visible for twenty miles. The fire burned for two days, fed by sweating men who tumbled into the glowing embers all that remained of gatehouse and gantries, bridges and palisades. At the end of that time the hillock stood bare, and the Tower and all it had contained were gone; but Marck's vengeance was not ended. Waggons were drawn forward and back over the still-hot ash while others toiled in long lines across the Plain, each with a glistening load. Only when their cargoes had been spread, and the hill and its surroundings coated ankle-deep with salt, did the King retire, to his Tower in the pass.

In the spring of the following year, a small party of horsemen rode swiftly along a lane bordered with hawthorn and elder. The day was bright and warm, puffy clouds chasing each other across a sky of deepest blue. Birds sang from the bushes fringing the rutted path; once a magpie started up and winged away, in dipping flashes of white and black.

The leader of the little group seemed by no means unaware of the sweetness of the morning. He glanced round him as he rode, at the Heath that stretched shimmering in the distance, the pines lifting their dark heads above the rhododendron thickets. Once he sniffed, appreciatively, the rich scent of the may; but at a bend of the track he reined.

Ahead, in its chalk gap, stood the Tower. Even from a distance, its aspect was unwelcoming. He saw the stained walls, weatherworn and grim; marked the shuttered face of the keep with its strapwork of timbering, the heavy outer works that fronted it, the village that straggled at the foot of the Mound. He glanced back to his escort, but gave no further sign; instead he touched heels to his horse, rode jingling down the narrow way between the dusty houses. Children ran from their scrabblings in the dirt, women stared up open-mouthed at the party and the devices it bore; the pennants with their white horses and the gilded staves, each topped by a four-spoked wheel.

The Tower gates stood open; the traveller had half expected them barred. He rode beneath the portal with its massive wooden groins, nodded curtly to the men within. A page ran to take his reins; he dismounted stiffly, walked forward. To the stout knight who confronted him he said, 'The lord of this place, the greatvassal Marck of the Gate; has he been informed?'

'My Lord,' said the other, fidgeting under his keen

stare, 'your message was passed.'

'Good. Then bring me to him.'

'My Lord,' said the knight uncomfortably, 'I am Thoma, seneschal of the Gate. Will you take wine?'

The Great Hall, airy and cool, belied to some extent the grim exterior of the place. Cups and a mixing bowl were set out on a low table; a serving maid in green and yellow hurried forward, but the newcomer waved her aside. 'Present me to King Marck, I pray you,' he said. 'And make no delay. I have journeyed far, and have many miles to travel before nightfall.'

Thoma wiped his face. He said, 'It is not possible.'

The other's voice rang sharply. 'What? Am I denied?'

'You are not denied,' said the seneschal. 'He . . . sees no one.'

The herald drew a sealed packet from his riding tunic. 'Then,' he said, 'I will see *him*. I am charged by Atha King to deliver this into his hands. His, and no other. Where is his chamber?'

He turned for the curtained stairway; and Thoma stepped before him, arms spread. He said pleadingly, 'My Lord . . .' Then he stopped; for the other had raised his knuckles level with his eyes. On the middle finger, carved in a dull-green stone, he saw the prancing horse.

'Yes,' said the herald sharply. 'His great Seal. Who denies me, denies him. Now, take me to your lord.'

Thoma turned with a gesture of despair, tramped before him up the broad wooden steps.

At the head of the third flight an open door gave a glimpse of a sparsely furnished chamber; but the seneschal did not check. The other followed, frowning. A further climb, and Thoma stooped to fiddle with a catch. A trap swung back, letting in a flood of air and light. The messenger stepped through, and stared.

They had emerged on the roof of the Tower. Below him huddled the village. To either side the flanking hills rose clear in the bright air, crossed by their sheeptracks, dotted with clumps of scrub; while from the great height the sea

210

was visible, an endless plain of cobalt stretching to the south. These things he saw at a glance; then his attention was concentrated on the sunlit space before him.

Everywhere, pinned to the steeply pitched central gable, on poles set above the breast-high parapets, meat lures swung and rotted in the wind. To one side, their feathers stirring idly, were heaped the fresh carcasses of a dozen crows, while in the far corner of the place stood a hide of weatherbeaten canvas. Slits in its sides provided loopholes; from one he saw the tip of a slim arrow withdrawn. 'What is it?' asked a thin voice querulously. 'What is it now? You have spoiled my sport . . .'

Thoma stepped heavily to the door of the hide, and raised the flap. He said, 'My lord, King Marck of the Gate.'

For days before the arrival of the army, the hill folk knew of its progress. By night its campfires glowed for many miles; by day the dust rose towering in its wake, a cloud visible from far off across the Plain. The foragers it sent before it scoured the country, paying good gold for grain; and the noise of its passing shook the ground. Here were infantry in rank on rank, bright-cuirassed with their pikes and spears; here cavalry in gaudy cloaks, each troop with its banners and pennants. Here were war engines of every shape and size; catapults and trebuchets, their great arms lashed, ballistas with their massive hempen skeins; mantlets and scaling towers, the Cat and the Tortoise, the Mouse and the Ram. And here too were Midsea weapons, the legendary firetubes no White Islander had ever seen, the tubes that spit out thunder and bring the lightning down. They rumbled past on their squat, iron-bound wheels, each drawn by a dozen plodding oxen, each with its contingent of turbanned, white-robed engineers. Behind them came slingers and archers; and behind again rode Sealand chiefs with their war bands, massive men in bright-checked cloaks and leggings. At the head of each troop jolted the sign of the Wheel; and over all, cracking and rippling, reared the White Horse of Morwenton, the Mark of Atha's house.

The Gate heard of his coming, on a grey morning when the clouds rolled low over the seaward-facing hills and spatters of rain drove like slingshots across the empty Heath. Then was the faith of Thoma sorely tried; but after half a day the drums began their pounding, and once more the lines of men and horses crept out blackly from the fortress in the pass. A mile from the Tower the seneschal deployed, in a crescent straddling the road; and here the Royal vanguard found him. To his right, bogland stretched to saltings where the sea birds wheeled; to his left, half-seen behind veils of rain, were the hills.

From his position near the centre of the line, Thoma watched the King's outriders fall back. The main body rolled on, to halt two hundred paces from his men. The cavalry checked, swinging to either flank; then the ranks of infantry parted. Between them lumbered the firetubes. The teams, unyoked, were herded to one side, and the pieces trained. Some were shaped like monstrous fish; others, the greatest, took the form of dragons. But all opened black mouths to gape at the opposing force; and beside each stood a dark-skinned man, a torch smoking in his hand. A silence fell, in which the sough and hiss of the rain could be clearly heard; and the seneschal glanced grim-lipped at the man beside him. 'Flagbearer,' he said briefly. 'I will speak with them.'

A page rode forward with the Mark of the House, the red crab on a field of yellow silk. Thoma nodded to his Captains of infantry and horse, and cantered forward. Halfway to the King's ranks he halted, bareheaded in the rain. A stirring, among the infantry; and a man moved out alone. A gasp from beside the seneschal, a swift uncovering; and the other reined, sitting his horse coldly. Like Thoma, he wore no helmet. His mane of hair, once yellow, was badger-grey, and the years had marked his face with weariness; but he held himself stiffly in the heavy war saddle, and he was armoured from neck to feet. 'This is a sorry thing to see,' he said at length. 'My subjects come to war with me, breaking the fealty they owe.'

The seneschal swallowed. 'We break no oaths, Lord Atha,' he said. 'Nor do we war, save with those who war on us. My Lord, why do you come? If it is to punish, then we must resist. For the word of each man here is given to the Gate.'

Atha nodded grimly. 'Loyalty I respect,' he said, 'though I see little enough of it. But loyalty is not in question.' He raised an arm, pointing. 'One word from me,' he said, 'and you are swept away. You and your army, like chaff before a wind. Now answer me, will you hold the path? Will you speak, for all these peoples' lives?'

A voice behind them said, 'He has no need.'

Thoma turned, slowly. Marck wore his battered armour, and a sword. A hillboy led his horse, a shock-haired lad of maybe some ten summers. The eyes of the King shone brightly, tears mingling with the rain that soaked his cheeks, plastered the thinning hair close to his scalp. 'They are all my people,' he said. 'My good people, whom I lead . . .' He halted some six feet from the King, regarded the ranks behind him and shook his head. 'This is Thoma, seneschal of the Gate,' he said, 'and my true and faithful man. Deal justly with him . . .' He peered again, shortsightedly. 'Why do you come before me with such array?' he asked. 'We were not prepared, we would have prepared. It is not knightly, not done like a King. You sent no word . . .'

'I sent you word,' said Atha grimly. 'But none returned. Who spurns my messenger, sent under my Seal, spurns me.'

Marck shook his head again. 'I saw no messenger,' he said. 'The castle folk . . . but they are good people. I have been . . . much engaged. It has not been . . . easy, keeping your peace in the west.'

'Of that,' said Atha dryly, 'I was made aware.' He leaned forward. 'King Marck,' he said, 'it is not good to sit here, in the rain. And my patience is an old boar's patience; short. Will you fight with me, or no?'

The wandering attention of the King was riveted. 'Fight?' he said. 'Who spoke of fighting? Was it Thoma? He was most remiss . . .' He scrambled from the saddle; and the boy hastened to take his arm. 'We came to do you honour, as your subjects . . .' He was on his knees, gripping the hem of the King's rich saddlecloth; and Atha stooping from the horse, endeavouring to raise him. 'My Lord,' said Marck, sobbing, 'great evil came. I was its author. And now, at night, I cannot rest, there is no rest. But you, with your great army . . . deal justly with them. And you will sit in judgement on me; I am content . . .'

Atha signed to the column; and priests ran forward, dark-habited, each with the wheel-sign topping a golden staff.

'I am well content,' said Marck. 'But, Lord, this child, born of a forester. His father died, his mother cannot support him. I commend him to you, take him to your care. I did great wrong . . .'

'Old friend,' said Atha gently, 'go with these Brothers. And be calm. All is well; later, I will speak with you.' He waved again, and an officer spurred forward. 'Tell the firetube masters to stand down,' he said. 'And send my Captains to me.' Then to Thoma, 'Lead the way, good seneschal. This . . . greeting does you honour. Ride with me, and tell me of your lord; for I sup with you tonight.'

The dawn had not yet broken over the Heath. Above the tall trees that fringed the Mound the sky showed a broadening smudge of silver; but the brook with its tangled banks still lay in velvet dark. The Tower reared its brooding height against the scarcely paler west; and all round, twinkling and dim, gleamed the campfires of the waking army.

Atha paused in the lower bailey, sniffing the ancient chill of the brook air. Then he turned to the man at his side. 'Some say I leave a madman in my path,' he said quietly, 'and some a traitor. Who do I leave, King Marck?'

Marck chafed his thin hands together. 'A loyal subject,' he said in his tired voice, 'who would fain ride with you to this war.'

But the other shook his head. 'No,' he said. 'No, Marck, I have another need of you. Sit here, and be strong for me; hold the Gate till I return, and I shall be well satisfied.' He gestured to where, a pace or so away, two priests stood like shadows in the night. 'For the rest,' he said, 'I leave you these good Brothers, who are men of God and strong in wisdom. They will bring you comfort.'

Marck said dully, 'There are no Gods. This much wisdom has taught.'

'No Gods,' said Atha vibrantly. 'But one God, merciful and just. Who came to us, a man among men, in Sealand; who was broken on the Wheel and yet raised up, to bring eternal life. This was taught me by his priests; and this I believe.' He circled his hand, forefinger raised. 'See this Sign,' he said. 'By it I have sworn to make these islands one; to raise up the weak and lowly, bringing mercy to every man. For this, I ride west. The north we have subdued, to the shore that fronts the Misty Isles. Six Long Creek Towers burn; foes to the Crab, on whom I put my heel.' He made the Sign again. 'One people,' he said. 'Worshipping one God, and walking without fear. They will be a proud people, and a great. In this, as in all things, I need your skills.'

But Marck shook his head. 'I have been through a long valley,' he said. 'Even now its darkness calls me. And she calls me, at night from all the hills. She who was so little.'

Atha's hand was on his shoulder; he felt the trembling start, and tightened his grip. 'No,' he said gently, 'you have not understood. You have played with madness, King Marck. But play is for children; and you are not a child. It is over.'

Marck bowed his head. 'I am not worthy, Lord,' he said. 'Take the Tower from me. Give it to another, and let me end my days.'

He felt the other's answer in his silence. Finally Atha shook his head. 'No,' he said. 'Neither may you escape in death. It is not his will, whom I serve.'

Marck said in a muffled voice, 'But what remains . . .'

'Remains?' said Atha vaguely. He stared round him, at the dark expanse of the Heath. 'The stars,' he said, 'the empty hills. We are all alone; it is a Mystery the Brothers will explain.' He shook the gaunt man gently. 'I, to bring wisdom to the Scholar of the Gate,' he said. 'You sought to own her, buying her with gold. Old friend, *you own her now* . . .'

He turned to gaze up at the Tower with its looming face. 'Another thing you will do,' he said. 'Get out your books, and find the way. Build me a Hall of stone, such as the Giants knew. Strong founded, gripped to rock, proof against arrows and the firetube darts. Build it to Heaven; and let it stand for her, if not for me.'

Marck licked his mouth. He said, 'I cannot.'

Atha shook his head once more. 'You have still not understood,' he said. 'The Brothers teach, and I believe, that death is a beginning, not an end. That on a certain day we all shall rise, in glory before the Lord. Then she will see it, if her bones have now no place. Will she not know, it was made for her?'

He turned away, pulling on his steel-banded gloves. 'Other men will come, from other parts,' he said. 'To marvel, and to learn. So Towers of stone will guard the realm, and its folk will be free from fear. Fine Towers they will be, King Marck; but none finer than yours, the first.'

A horse was led forward, with a stamp and jingle. He mounted, and turned. 'Build the Tower,' he said. 'Keep this place for me; and may the great God guard you.' His hoofbeats thudded on the sloping turf; they heard his voice at the outer gate and the quick laugh of a guard, surprised as if by some jest.

Marck had made no answer. He stood now staring up; and it was as if he saw, sketched against the night, the walls of a mighty Hall. His mind, despite itself, was busied afresh. It saw already patterns of joists and stairs; the slings they would use to hoist the blocks, the scaffoldings on which masons would work. He saw, finally, the sun burn on the cliff of new white stone; and the flags that topped it, proud against the blue. The Crab of Sealand, the Horse of Atha and the Wheel of God. It seemed his heart was lightened; so that he called to the priests, ran to the gatehouse steps. He saw the looming figure of the King pass into dawn dusk; he saw the clustered roofs and moving mists. Then it seemed the new God entered him so that he saw other things, too many for remembrance or the telling. Flowers broke free and sailed the sky, clouds sailed like flowers; and a great Deer rose and shook his smoky head, down there below Corfe Gate.